Additional Acclaim for *How It Was for Me*

"With wit, compassion, and remarkable dexterity, Andrew Sean Greer's collection explores the eruption of buried truths.... Greer has an ear for dialogue, a surrealist's eye for the telling detail and the ironic epiphany, and a stable of seductive misfits.... Greer is a master storyteller."
—Abby Pollak, *San Francisco Chronicle Book Review*

"Greer reveals characters in direct but subtle prose.... Each story is polished and assured."
—*Publishers Weekly*

"This collection is a miracle of eloquence, strange as a dream, yet bright and inevitable as daybreak—days after you've read it, you'll be desperately pawing the pages, praying there's one you missed. Clean your eyeglasses and clear shelf space for Andrew Sean Greer, because you're going to be reading him for a long time."
—J. Robert Lennon, author of *The Light of Falling Stars*

"The world of letters became a richer place with the debut this year of Andrew Sean Greer. *How It Was for Me* collects eleven elegant and luminous stories that are as unpredictable as they are wise.... I'm looking for Greer's next book."
—Peter Gadol, *LA Weekly*

"These stories by what seems to be an unforgivably young author are so good, so finely written and polished, that one is tempted to paraphrase Sinatra's remark about Sarah Vaughn: 'Every time I hear her sing, I want to cut my throat.'...Be assured that Greer's style, as perfectly realized as it is, is his own. Moreover, it's polished in a remarkably old-fashioned way."
—*Frontiers Weekly* (San Francisco Bay Area)

"Greer writes like a dream. Literally. You tumble into his stories and enter worlds at once familiar and strange...and when the light's just right, you think, Fitzgerald. The writing reaches those kind of heights. Greer is a true talent and *How It Was for Me* is a wonderful beginning."
—David Gilbert, author of *Remote Feed*

D0188467

How It Was for Me

How It Was for Me

∾

ANDREW SEAN GREER

Picador · New York

Seven of the stories in this collection originally appeared in the following publications: *Story*: "How It Was for Me" and "Titipu"; *Esquire*: "The Future of the Flynns"; *Ploughshares*, edited by Richard Ford: "Come Live with Me and Be My Love"; *The Paris Review*: "Life Is Over There"; *Glimmer Train*: "Four Bites"; *Boulevard*: "Cannibal Kings."

Picador® is a U.S. registered trademark and is used by St. Martin's Press under license from Pan Books Limited.

For information on Picador Reading Group Guides, as well as ordering, please contact the Trade Marketing department at St. Martin's Press.
Phone: 1-800-221-7945 extension 763
Fax: 212-677-7456
E-mail: trademarketing@stmartins.com

Design by Nancy Resnick

Library of Congress Cataloging-in-Publication Data

Greer, Andrew Sean.
    How it was for me : stories / Andrew Sean Greer
       p. cm.
    ISBN 0-312-24105-4 (hc)
    ISBN 0-312-24126-7 (pbk)
    1. Seattle (Wash.)—Social life and customs—Fiction.
I. Title.
PS3557.R3987 H69   2000
813'.54—dc21
                                           99-056643

P1

Acknowledgments

MANY THANKS TO those who helped with my work over the years: Kelli Auerbach, Skip Barton, Alexa Brandenberg, Mai-Lin Cheng, Eve and Carla Cohen, Kate Gadbow, Daniel Gaetán-Beltrán, Mark Girouard, Alaraby Johnson, Jeff Odefey, Mary Park, Scott Renschler, Robert Riger, Angela Robinson, Laura Rose, Ryan Shiraki, Lizzie Scott, Amanda Ward, and my patient professors Robert Coover, William Kittredge, Deirdre McNamer, Meredith Steinbach, and Ed White. I am indebted, as well, to Richard Ford, and to Denise and Mel Cohen for their award support.

Thanks also to those who labored with me over these stories: Will Allyson, Brian Bouldrey, David Gilbert, Allyson Goldin, Rhian Ellis, Daniel Lee, J. Robert Lennon, Erika Mansourian, Jill Marquis, Andy and Alicia Paulson, Lois Rosenthal, and Ed Skoog.

Great thanks to George Witte, Josh Kendall, and everyone at Picador USA. Also to Kathy Robbins, Cory Halaby, Dorianne Steele, and the entire amazing Robbins Office. Greatest thanks of all goes to Bill Clegg, my agent, who always stood up for me, inspired me, and did everything but write these stories for me. Thanks, Bill.

Most of all, I am grateful for the support of all my parents, my grandparents, my twin brother, Mike, and, of course, David Ross.

Contents

Cannibal Kings

༅

THE SKY IS a crowded attic. Clouds at different heights look like old chairs and cushions, stuffed heads of animals, wheels, instruments, a claw-foot tub. Davis stands below, chilled on a street corner, having stepped from his bus into Seattle's Chinatown. He is sniffing the air and wondering if the patrons in that restaurant will turn and look at him, notice him, hands in pockets, on the sidewalk, sniffing. He waits for a look, but the eaters keep on eating. Most people in windows never turn.

He will, within days, be in a well-furnished room on the edge of a school campus, staring at a boy who picks his scabs and eats them, and soon enough he'll find it too much to take, somehow, the draped and fringed plaid curtains, the lacrosse sticks nailed to the walls, the framed painting of snow in a schoolyard, after these long days of snow, and soon enough he'll think of each memory in terms of scent, the way a cougar mind might function, drifting back on the wet odor of light in spring. Davis will remember this smell of *humbow*, catfish hot-pot grease, green onion in the moist gray air, which seems to carry scents on platters toward him, the invisible waiters of the air, the carts of soft wind.

He must be hungry, but do not misunderstand him. Do not mistake his poverty for vanity, because it seems so in the circumstances: well-off parents, decent schooling, and a familiarity with drinks and ties and the small precious food rich people eat. He has an idea of himself so strong now that he's quit his job—such an idea has not come often in Davis's life. He has a sense that a thing his stepmother told him as a teenager might be true—that he might "have an eye for things." For what things? He doesn't know. Better things, delicate or broad, maybe for buildings or fractal design. Who knows? The purpose of joblessness is to train his eye or, rather, to trick it into seeing its own talent. His only talent, you see. It has only just occurred to him that he might have one—and how lucky if it were true!

He has no ready cash, though, for tricking his eye, and he doesn't know how long that will take, so he's been working in his apartment this whole January, turning the heat down by degrees until he realized, just the other day, that a vase of daisies left unattended had frozen—or that's the story he tells. This job he's heading to now is a piece of luck, then, a coin found in the street. His friend (more an acquaintance) Margaret has been tutoring young Vietnamese boys for prep school exams, teaching them the tricks to getting in, the kinds of words prep schoolers should know, the importance of metaphor—"tornado is to wind as maelstrom is to . . ." Usually she also accompanies these boys on their interviews, sitting in plush rooms and convincing stern directors of the brilliance of this young mind, the quiet, amazing things the blinking boy might do. But this time, with this young boy Trung, Margaret can't be with him. Someone else has to lead him into rooms with overlapping rugs and grinningly read his soft palm aloud. A stand-in tutor. A fraud.

So that is the job, you see. Davis is to pose as Trung's close friend, his mentor and instructor, and paint him like a hero to the committee, the principal, the dean or whomever. Three days of driving to schools and this intense lie, but Davis is at an age when lying is a common thing, something tied together intricately with all the interviewing he has done, for jobs, for grants, for college, and even for prep schools. Don't judge him—could he really say, "I'm an aimless young man who is just looking forward to lunch"? Thus his only experience for the job at hand is not a degree in English, but his acquaintance with brick towers, carillons, hazing rituals, small-brimmed cricket hats, and how to sing in a quartet.

The interview goes well, you should know—the one with the parents. A small apartment of stiff green colonial furniture, Vietnamese health calendars tacked to the walls, a stunted, tinkling chandelier. The parents ask him few questions, and Davis asks only the ones that he prepared to seem professional. As if this were a profession of some sort, to pose as something else, to fake your way through another job. The mother is thin, smiling, her forehead creased with worry, turning always to the hidden kitchen, which makes her black ponytail flip against the wall. The father is stout and tired, wearing a red apron. He has only taken a moment off from his grocery store downstairs. Surely they are thinking this is taking too long—why is he talking so much, this young blond man? This droop-eyed young man touching pink hands to his even pinker face, babbling through his thick chapped lips? Isn't this already settled?

Davis is not even listening to himself, however. He is looking at the head now peeking from the kitchen steam, a small boy in an oversized red college T-shirt, chewing on his palm. The skin of that palm seems soft, unathletic, unused to helping at the grocery store. There is the smudge of a birthmark on his cheek, and Trung (for it must be Trung) is staring, the kind of stare you make when you think no one else can see you, but Davis can see him. Davis waves to no response, just the gnawing mouth on the hand, the birthmark bobbing on the ripples of motion. Davis smells the raw steam and thinks of his long January.

Cabbage, chili oil, sweet lemongrass, and chicken fat.

✐

What follows are a series of long waits in rental-car agencies, long pauses in conversation, as if breath were being conserved, long, blinkless stares into the sky, seeing the impossible flakes of snow first appearing, the snow that rarely comes to Seattle at this point in winter, sending instead the mere cold dampness of wind or sudden sighs of rain. But we never remember pauses or silences, in the way we never notice all the bare sheets round a sleeping body. Davis has been trying on this car ride south to Centralia, to St. George's Boys' School on a plot of old farmland, trying to puzzle together some sense of this young Vietnamese boy quietly breathing from the red hood of his thick coat. The coat is too large for him, too new-looking to be a hand-me-down, too long to have been meant for his growth spurt—instead, the kind of coat that might make a child think you didn't know him, or meant it for some future him, some teenager too far off to recognize yet. Davis teases Trung with jokes, tries to learn his favorite music, his secret habits, his talents, but Trung is hopeless.

"How about food? What's your favorite food? Mine's hamburger."

"Human brains."

"That's not food, Trung. How about spaghetti? Or, oh . . . *nim chow*? Is that Vietnamese?"

Just a glance of wide, fascinated eyes from beneath the hood, a murmur too thin to make out in the heaving sound of the rental car's heater. Despite his reticence, it's clear he likes Davis. The sign is this barrage of unnerving answers to everything.

"TV shows? Sports?"

"My favorite sport is human brains."

"That's becoming clear, Trung."

"My name is not Trung. It is Davis."

"But that's my name."

"Now it is mine."

On and on in this way, the snow soundlessly filling the air like summer light. Davis does not notice this, brightness on a day whose sky is taut with clouds, although summer comes to him on its own, in memory, the chalky smell of tomato vines, the scent of their warm skin pressed to his nose, the feeling of tiny hairs on the fruit, and cigarette smoke pushing through summer like an obligation. A girl comes into Davis's mind along with summer. An actress in town for a Shakespeare festival, her hair always in a braid, her voice choppy and rough, corn being husked, happy to hold hands with him, or sneak down to the lake at night to swim, or kayak into the salt water; almost anything he wanted to do, she did, without judging, giving her few spare hours of time to him, usually sunset hours, letting Davis lead her. He has been penning a letter on the surface of his brain, a letter to her, something to let her know how close to him she really got.

At lunchtime, Davis begins to talk to Trung. About art, and how like Davis the boy is, with generous parents, a future at a boarding school, a future bright with learning and prospects and amber light and those things. Davis is filling the space between them with words, as his stepmother always does at dinner. Trung listens more intently than he should, his coat off, picking at a Salisbury steak and smiling now. He believes in Davis now, somehow, and tries to remember these important words. He is so young still.

Corned beef salted, damp cooked greens, warm sausage gravy on potatoes.

✑

The first interview is fine, easier than Davis thought it would be, nothing more than a visit with Trung in the office of a kindly dean of students, tropical plants potted everywhere, great cabbage roses blooming on the wallpaper, a soft pink rug. The snow outside has stopped and there is sunlight for a moment—Davis has been concerned for some time about the tires on his car, and now it looks like there is no storm coming after all, just a light film he can see covering the broad green, not even enough for the snowballing boys careening past the window. The questions are simple, broad, all about Trung's goals and favorite subjects. Whenever Trung pauses, Davis fills in the details with something he's learned on the car trip, something Margaret has taught him—for instance, the comment that Trung is excellent at art, which is half made up, but which goes over so well with the dean that Davis will always use it in the interviews.

"He has an eye," Davis adds with a peaceful smile, and the dean shares his smile, tangling her fingers. Trung sits and says something about a superhero he admires, and this seems charming also. Davis is then asked to leave, and as he waits in the grand hall, a two-storied library ringed with balconies surely no student ever uses, he thinks how used to lying he has become. This is a pleasant thought. He sits back in the thick leather chair, not noticing the light fall of snow again, and he is relieved that he can be a fraud. So much in his life he is expected to have done; now it is nice simply to pretend.

His school wasn't like this one. He has to admit his was even nicer. Even the most cramped first-term lodgings were of wood, with all kinds of surprising doors and cabinets, bookshelves with unreadable turn-of-the-century boys' books in them. Davis remembers his school vaguely and therefore fondly, and one reason memories have not stuck firmly is that he wasn't much of a superstar there. There were plenty of boys, rich or funny or handsome, who demanded cults, but

Davis wasn't any of these things, and as time went on, he became less rich, less funny, and his looks were never boyish again except for the ruddiness of his rough skin. The friendships he made turned out to be frail things, fading outside the greenhouse of school years, so Davis is left with forced nostalgia, droll anecdotes of lonely nights and boyhood cruelties he says he "had to have" to continue into adulthood. It was all for a purpose.

There is another drive, to a nearby rural boarding school, this one more severe, and though this time Davis finds himself having to perform without Trung there as a prop, alone with a counselor in a high attic room of the administration building, dark and woody, with a brooding man who bends over his desk, looks over his silver glasses, Davis does fine. He is riskier this time—he makes up stories about Trung, about the time the two of them went sea kayaking together on Lake Union, tossing back and forth small poems in English they had memorized. The next time he tells this story, he will smile as if it were real memory, and the time after that, when the snow has fallen so deep that drifts can hide a young boy, it will feel just like memory. Davis will barely be able to tell the difference.

That night, in a motel recommended by the secretary, they order room service on the parents' money, an extra order of sweet-potato fries, two hamburgers oozing blood jeweled with fat. Trung eats only a third of his and watches, chewing on the fleshy mound of his palm, speaking now and then about how Davis eats too much. He even eats Trung's leftovers.

"Tell me about your friends," Davis says between bitefuls. It has not occurred to him yet to ask about this subject, which might be crucial for interviews.

Trung, in blue satiny pajama bottoms, raises his eyebrows and spreads his words out from a jutting lower lip: "I've got two friends, Sang and Randy. We are always at Sang's house."

"What do you do?"

"Draw pictures." He grins at his false tutor. "Of car accidents."

"So you like art? You like drawing, then? See, I tricked you."

But Trung is still grinning, his birthmark bounced up near his eye: "Cracked bones, split skulls, oozing brains!"

"Stop it, Trung," says Davis, putting down his hamburger.

"Once we had a party and one boy cut his fingertip off!" A rally of guffawing as Davis sits unprepared to react, cracking half a smile to seem game, wondering if this joke is meant to draw him close or frighten him.

Davis's friends were nothing like this, prep school losers who dipped tobacco so as not to get caught smoking, one boy still wetting his bed, another full of dirty jokes and a disturbing wandering eye, all of them terribly frightened of the boys who seemed capable, athletic and sure, talented and awarded by the faculty. Davis's friends lingered, clearing their throats, in the halls after basketball games, smelling the success they would never really get, all later tripping over their own doubts into careers in disparate fields, all similar in their vague duties to help the salesmen, partners, vice presidents who really made the deals. In their youth, though, one of their favorite games was to all dress up in black, paint their faces dark, and stand in the shadow of the bell tower, seeing if people would notice the glow of their white eyes in the darkness. Few people did, and this was success for Davis and his friends. Their sorry purpose was to disappear voluntarily.

Trung calls his parents for the first time of the trip and leans tense-mouthed against the window as he talks, turned away from Davis. He talks in a language probably no one in the building understands, but the tone is all too familiar—bored, tired answers. Long pauses, then something meaning, Okay, okay, I will. He carefully hangs up the phone and climbs into his bed. From under the wool blanket, he calls out good night in English.

Davis thinks about himself at this age, not as mysterious at all. Bright and talkative, impressive to adults in a way Trung has not proved himself to be—but the son of academics has to be this way, has to grow up able to perform at cocktail parties, play a piano, recite a verse, show early signs of mastery. Davis thinks often about his family. His mother left before he knew her, and his father left when he was fifteen, not long after Trung's age. Just a stepmother to bring him up from there, all wooden beads and velvet hats, a woman thrilled by so much because of her deep sadnesses, a hardworking woman who once wanted to be a potter, taking up a new job to tend to him. There was no one else to watch, so she did it; she watched his different selves as they emerged— the invisible boy, the vain teenager, the opinionated young man, the graduate moving from job to job like a donkey stumbling into gopher holes. Davis thinks back on himself, not clearly—when did this "eye" of his first appear? So much of him is gone, replaced.

The fries grow colder as Trung falls asleep, buttering his hair with their sweet smell.

∽

Today, the sky is clenched in a fist. Overnight, snow has conquered everything, and as Davis rises to the window, he breathes twice quickly to see how everything has changed. Travel will be tough today. Despite the trouble, despite the slow pace and skidding wheels, the sight of cars abandoned in the meadows, which yesterday were green, the interviews go well indeed. Davis and Trung have to take a ferry to an island out in Puget Sound, then drive a long way to a quaint town on a peninsula, a town attached to an old abandoned fort. The houses are clapboard, pink and yellow. Snow piles in the flower boxes. Things look a bit abandoned, the people kind but desperate.

The interviewers are impressed that Trung and Davis would survive the snow, as if it were a question of survival. In fact, the halls of both schools are packed with muffin tables and silver urns of hot chocolate, and it is clear that even faculty have been trapped here by the snow, staying the night out on this peninsula. The schoolboys look wild and excited, throwing snow everywhere, and their eyes catch Trung as if to bring him with them, make him wild again with them. Trung's head follows them as he passes into the warm offices of admissions. The interview rooms are soft and bright with light, although the sunlight has left by the time of the second interview. Both deans are in thick sweaters, rubber boots, their faces red and blazing with the thrill of imminent disaster. Both are distracted from the interview, from such a distant thing as a future student; they are instead dreaming of tomorrow, the snow three feet above the grass, the chapel bells tolling, offices locked, the cafeteria loud with impromptu talent shows, a Latin chorus, a scene from the school play. And time. Time at last.

Davis doesn't notice. He tells his story about the kayaks and poems, about Trung's "eye," about the wonderful staring boy in the too-big red coat. Trung refuses to remove the coat, and clicking sounds keep emanating from underneath the hood, bizarre little sounds that Davis tries to cover with the tone of his voice. Yet they are there, *click crack, click crack.* Who is this boy? Davis rambles on about a Shakespeare festival they attended. The deans lean back, smiling, flushed with pleasure, tapping their pens softly on their blotters. Davis's voice is a lullaby to deans.

Cafeteria noodles, glutinous, unsalted butter on hot rolls, wet wool and bleach.

There is another ferry today, the second. The clouds shift overhead in their intricate designs, a high net for the screaming gulls, and the wind on the upper deck is incredible. Trung presses against Davis, asking to go below, but Davis pats him and says, "Another minute, just a minute." The Olympic Mountains are out in spiny glory, glowing with ice, and the Sound stretches endlessly between the banks of pure snow, snow broken by nothing, not even by docks, a landscape utterly content with itself, and there is no way to think of this as familiar anymore, as civilized. The area seems remote, as far from things as Davis could ever hope to be. Nothing is traveling along the mountain roads. No yacht sways by with Christmas lights. No seaplane leaves no growling trail.

Around a curve, when the ferry finally docks on Whidbey Island, he and Trung run into someone Davis knows. A young woman, a friend of the girl from the Shakespeare festival. She is small and thin, her head shaved, with just the shadow of hair, everything on her striped or brightly colored: her scarves, buttons, eyes. "Davy Boy!" she calls him, and he is delighted to see how much she remembers him. He takes it as a sign that her friend, the girl he thinks now he might love, talks of him. "Davy Boy, what are you doing here? Who is this?" she asks, and then he has to explain the situation, and somehow it sounds even more ridiculous than ever, as if the job itself were the lie, a subterfuge for getting Trung across the Canadian border. Even the shaved-head girl seems doubtful. She offers no information about the girl Davis loves, says only, "You know her, into everything, like a cat!" and then the whistle sounds and she must run off to catch her boat. They wave good-bye, and Trung asks, "Is that your girlfriend?"

"No," Davis says. "She's my girlfriend's best friend, though."

Trung looks back and chews on his hand, his childish habit. "She is my girlfriend," he says quietly.

"Sounds good."

Their next hotel, their last one on this trip, is far fancier than Davis imagined when he made the reservations. Columns, a fireplace in the lobby, and the clatter of a formal dining room just closing up. It is dark outside, the air cold and curtained with snow, but inside all is warm at the Lawrence Inn. Their room sits cozily under two dormer windows, shades pulled, and everything is prim and neatly matched, woolen blankets and green-pink-striped chairs, satin curtains, bright Dutch plates hanging on the walls. They are high above the nearby boys school, in this richly furnished room, and it all seems to Davis like they are unexpected travelers from the snowbound world, shown into the attic room of a manor house while the ogre-master is off hunting.

Trung has already unpacked his clothes into the bedside dresser. He sits on the bedsheet, smoothing the quilt, staring at the fabric. Surely he has never known a room like this, not coming from that close, steamy apartment over the grocery store, not with his poor parents saving pennies from the till for his new life in prep school. How will he explain it to his friends? The taste of it?

Davis opens the shade. They look out on the campus, ghostly white squares. A fire is burning somewhere, and he can almost smell the smoke of it. Snow is still falling; there is no end. He turns back to Trung's fearful expression, the ever-look of adolescence.

"I remember a snow like this, actually," Davis says matter-of-factly, filling the air again. He's been talking like this for days now, telling Trung these kinds of reminiscences. This time he stands by the window with one hand on the slick green drape, the slight smile on his pink face warping his thick lips, the soft light catching the unshaven hairs of his face, so pale that only now are they visible. He has the kind of light eyebrows that you can only assume are there when he lifts them to speak: "It was the winter of the cougar. That's what we called it, because a cougar'd been trapped down in the city by the snow." Trung giggles and puts his hand over his mouth. Arm by arm, he is finally removing his red coat. "No, really!" Davis insists, leaning his head gently and letting his mouth lines wrinkle in cloth folds. "No, it came down from the mountains somehow, before Seattle was as big as now. It still happens. But this cougar got caught in the snow with all of us, and you'd hear about it from time to time—somebody's cat got eaten, or a pair of rabbits. Usually that, pets. It was hungry, you know, out of the mountains. What I remember is that the children had to stay indoors. Because—can you believe this? The cougar had eaten a child. It had a taste for our children. Maybe it was a rumor, but we were all told we could be eaten out there. We had to stay inside, we couldn't even play in the snow! Can you believe it? My one memory of a snowstorm." Trung smiles tentatively, eyes gleaming.

Davis chuckles, clicks his tongue, and turns back to the still scene of Lawrence School huddled in itself, remembering less laughingly now the time when he was too young, the right size for a cougar in winter. He thinks about what he has known for hours now, since the ferry ride, that the girl in braids from last summer doesn't think about him at all, doesn't miss him, that to her in California he is as distant as a meal that she once ordered. A form, a remembered odor. And that this is no surprise, that he has already known this. Love was just a story he told himself in bed.

He can taste the glass when he touches his tongue to it, cold butter.

∽

The last interview is at the Lawrence School. They are snow-bound. There is no light in the air that does not seem to come from the snow, and no movement except its sandy drifting. Davis and Trung trudge down the hill from their hotel room, their good shoes covered in plastic bags, making their way toward the pointed chapel roof, echoes bringing the sifting noise of their steps. The world smells of nothing. After a while, Trung walks behind Davis's footprints to make his work easier. Davis does not talk much, does not prepare Trung for the interview ahead, remind him of his talents, his "eye," his fluency in English, or his hidden brilliances, which will never show up on tests. Instead, just the rasp of breath and step through snow.

At the interview room, at the door of this room bright as a greenhouse, Davis is stopped and only Trung is allowed to enter. The dean will talk to the tutor second, says the secretary as she smiles. Davis sees Trung's glance over the shoulder of his enormous red coat, frightened, picking at the scab that has formed on his left hand. Davis makes a grinning salute and sits down himself in the waiting room. The windows are draped and fringed with plaid curtains, and lacrosse sticks are nailed opposite him. There is a gleaming urn of cider, the tower of Styrofoam coffee cups stacked, a white segmented thing. The air is all cinnamon.

The snow entraps the room. It rises to the level of the windows. How could one sit and read a magazine with snow nosed up against the windowpane like that?

Davis sits, hands folded, in a plastic chair as the secretary types at her low desk. He thinks of his stepmother brooding over burnt pottery projects in her cold flat. He thinks of the girl with braids ranging over San Francisco, sunlit and forgetful, eating a mango or a pear flown from the summer hemisphere. He thinks of the small boy in the red coat sitting past that wall from him, chewing his fingernails or fingers, the boy who seems so unformed to Davis, his fearful looks clashing with his unnerving comments. Who is he becoming? What was he like even a year before? Odder? More like a child? Davis thinks of the haphazard crew of people he's ended up with, how ill-matched they all are for one another, hoping it is part of some plan, these random influences, and not necessarily a grand scheme. A little plan, with tiny gears. Someone's plan for him.

Davis is soon called in by the dean, and he enters a hallway covered with sport photographs in gilt frames, athletes and club presidents from a century of Lawrence School. He passes Trung at the doorway with a pat on his black head. Trung looks up with an open mouth, a sudden smile as he grabs for Davis, maybe for his hair, but then they've passed and Trung is off into the waiting room, dragging his coat, and Davis is suddenly sitting in a polished black chair, grinning nervously at the dean.

"You're the boy's tutor?"

"Yes."

Davis shifts and looks at the man, trim and middle-aged, his hair and glasses a decade out of style, his hands large and rough as they sort papers. Half of a tongue sandwich sits damp on his desk, sloughing its wax-paper skin.

The dean looks up again. "I should tell you that Trung just told me all about it."

"What's that?"

The dean smiles. "He told me you're being paid by his parents to pretend to be his tutor."

Davis laughs, leaning his long roseate face back into the window's glare. What else could he do? "That's a funny way of putting it," he says. "But I guess that's true."

"So you're not his tutor?"

"Well," Davis says, still smiling, eyeing the sandwich. "Let's just say that he's not my student."

And the young man goes on explaining, in a clear way, how he is still qualified to talk on Trung's behalf, all the time allowing his mind to sit stunned, speechless. Why has Trung said this? Has he been doing this all along, allowing Davis to spin out his stories of kayaks and poetry and art while the boy waits to whisper secretly in the deans' ears, his birthmark bobbing happily, telling them what nonsense it all is?

"There's more he told me," the dean says, tensing his face.

"Such as?"

"Oh, silly things. Did you two prepare for this interview? He said his name was Davis, and that he'd been in a battle with a cougar. Clearly, this isn't true. Do you have any insight into this?"

There is much more to tell: all the extravagant stories Trung apparently just gave the dean about his life, his white mother, his youth in a nice house in the suburbs, how it burned down, his interest in pottery, a girlfriend out in Port Townsend who shaves her head. Davis tries to picture the young boy's face. Would he be gleefully reporting his false life? Or would it be serious, the lies he never wanted to tell? How fully, though, the dean seems to enjoy this retelling, and Davis recognizes the desperation of a man trapped in a winter room. So often the boys who come in here must report the dullness of their carefully conceived young lives. How often would this man come into contact with madness?

But as the dean, obviously a cocktail-party raconteur, goes into a giddy telling of Trung's false vacation story in Yellowstone, Davis finds that he can easily imagine someone talking in this way about him, laughing about his theory of his "eye," which he now cringingly realizes he has told too many people about, his job-hopping, his own brand of random opinion, which he yells at gatherings to get attention, the constant adoration of new women, all bad guesses, all obvious avoidances of reality, and, of course, the one woman last summer in braids. Davis even fooled himself that time.

The fragrant smell of sandwich bread, mustard's yellow acid, tongue smelling like tongue would taste on tongue.

The dean and Davis share a handshake and a loud laugh as the interview ends, and Davis walks out knowing that soon in the mail Trung's mother will find a white envelope, more than one surely, a thin one with a note politely stating how little room there is in their school, how well suited crazy, truthful Trung would be for some other place. Yes, this will

happen soon enough. Around the corner he comes, down the
hall of sepia boys in their pyramids of athleticism, grand and
smiling, all with their gleaming futures bright in their eyes.
What boys never made it into the gilt frames of this hallway?
What boys came and went without anyone noticing at all?

Davis enters the waiting room silently. The dean has left
him with a feeling of caution, and the first thing he sees in
the cinnamon-scented room is Trung, reading a magazine on
outdoor sports. The boy wears his thick gray sweater, striped
with red, and he looks overheated against the frosty windows.
His left hand is propped awkwardly against his lips. It is the
palm with the scab, and Trung is chewing it, picking flakes
of blood between his teeth, touching them with his tongue,
bringing them into his mouth and savoring them.

Davis thinks, We eat ourselves alive. He remembers his
friends in school, ugly or weak, chewing their nails, picking
their noses, sucking at the blood of dormitory accidents, looking up with eyes that dared him to ask why, what they were
doing, eating of themselves. The insect sound at night of nib-
bling, sleepless boys comforting themselves under the
stamped sheets of their school, amid their sleeping rivals, taking these scraps for their hunger, grabbing this brief chance
to tear at their awful shells, perhaps with dreams of rising like
djinns from the sealed lamps of their bodies. Davis can feel
even now the itch and hunger. He recognizes his own narrow
indecisions and remakings, the new Davises his stepmother
has patiently witnessed all these years, each failing to accom-
plish whatever was promised, doomed to be replaced. The
product of this dull hope—as if each year that passes, he is
less one being surviving than a series of rogue cannibal kings
seizing a throne. Is this what everybody knows? he wonders.

Davis takes Trung's hand from his mouth. The boy's palm
is bleeding in little gems of blood, and he looks up, not happy,
not grinning in his lies, but solemn and staring, with both

eyes and that still birthmark, staring in the same way as the first afternoon they met, in the steam of lemongrass and chicken fat, and the memory makes Davis salivate.

"Let's go," he says, and Trung moves, unquestioning, out into the snow. The secretary asks something, but they're gone, plastic bags left behind, their good leather shoes crunching in the damp ice, and Davis sees the boy in his red hood staring again, meaning, What happens now?

And what does happen? Do they climb the long way, one by one, up to the hotel to prepare for a sad phone call to the parents? Do they wait for the bright golden snowplows to appear and save them from their dangling firelit cage on the hill? What does a young man do with his ward, trapped and hungry in a snowstorm? Does he lift him in his arms and run with him?

There they are, smaller from your viewpoint, hand in hand in the wilderness of the ice glare, their false selves clattering on their chests, the faint wind passing by them, through black tangled branches and tufts of rusty weeds, bringing the smell of smoke and mittens, of whiteness melting into whiteness, into their translucent room. And if you shook this room with giant hands, what would remain?

How It Was for Me

∽

IT WAS A shock to realize, as Percy spread the facts before us in the insecticide-smelling toolshed, that our piano teachers were witches. Not real witches—we knew that, even at ten years old—but practicers of some subtle treachery against us. Their curled gray hair from another era, their fake eyelashes, bosoms scented with violets, their orange muumuus and carpet-covered bags—what else could we make of these women? Their scrolls of eerie writing seemed more potent than normal adult nonsense, and their sharp commands showed such control over a world we thought was beyond controlling. We even guessed there was a diabolical purpose behind their monotonous exercises, as if they were training us for some ominous task—a horde of little boys with nimble fingers descending on the world, eyes hard as marbles, tapping out "Chopsticks" on some unimaginable weapon.

But more than that, it was a relief to know there was a plot behind our lives after all. You could hear the sighs coming from our little chests. You could make out smiles in the darkness of the toolshed. And I was the most relieved, to realize I was merely under a spell, under a curse of sharps and flats, because I'd begun to think I was a little crazier than a boy of ten should be.

This relief in the hot shed bound us together that day. We hadn't much in common except our lesser status in the world, and now this sad fantasy. It was always the four of us: me; my best friend, the genius Max; rich Raja Din; and Percy. The shed was Percy's and, uncharacteristically, so was the revelation of the witches.

"We have to watch them carefully," he told us, eyes wide as bulbs in sockets. He was a white-haired goblin of a boy, hyper and difficult, born with a terrible name that had Roman numerals after it. Nothing was expected of the males in his family except that they bear this awful name, so Percy's parents didn't care much about his grades or how late he stayed out by the creek while they sat at dinner. His parents never bothered us back in the toolshed, so we were always there, borrowing a piece of Percy's freedom.

"I've been taking notes on Mrs. Runkle, and I think she keeps voodoo dolls in a case in her living room," he said. "I saw them." Even in the dark, his face was white and unreal.

Raja tapped on the dirt floor with a stick. "You're right!" he said, glancing around, his overgrown curls shining in the slats of light. "You're right!" He was always repeating himself; I don't think he had much of interest to say, but we liked him because his life was so weird. He seemed unable to cope with the wealth he was born to, earning twenty dollars for every B he made, then spending the money on us to make sure we remained his friends. "Take each of you ten dollars," he'd say at his sleepovers, and, of course, we would. The frightened look in his eyes never changed, though, as if he weren't sure how much would make us stay.

So I ignored Raja, and looked to Max. If Max didn't doubt it, then it must be true. But Max was making funny little noises in his throat, an asthma panic; I knew it scared him. Max, with the plastic glasses, with the soccer shirts and bubble-gum decals, with the cocker spaniel we trained to run into the girls' room at the pool. Max, with the happy, skeptical, bickering parents from Boston, with the sulky older brother who was rebuilding his car to look "more dangerous." Max believed it. The boy who had to finish three math problems before he got his breakfast, he believed our piano teachers were witches. So I did, too.

∽

Unlike the others, however, I didn't have an old-lady piano teacher with suspicious bags of Coffee Nips to offer me, a bust of some Satanic composer on her Baldwin, a silver glint to her eye. My father never used the normal routes, so when I told him everyone else was taking piano, he just waved the neighbor's son over for a beer and asked if he'd teach me. I was horrified, but what could I do? They laughed over the beer, and I sat there with a Nehi, trying to keep my father happy. Mark Mancusi was the son's name, a man thirty or so, with a wide black mustache, soft eyes, a faint smell of oaky cologne, and an unorthodox way of teaching piano. I'd never learned "Chopsticks" or "Heart and Soul" or "Für Elise" like the other boys. Mark Mancusi never even taught me how to read the left hand. Instead, he had me learn chord systems, learn the methods of improvising a boogie-woogie to the *Star Wars* theme, steps toward the freestyle improvisation I saw through the window of his house at night. He would be at his piano, eyes closed, mustache in the air, with his hands moving over the keys in lazy dips. I remember the purple color of his eyelids, and how his head swayed back and forth.

And there was something about me at that age. I was afraid not to agree with my friends, because I thought they might begin to notice. But who could notice? It was just that at times, in school mostly, I'd go a little crazy. It would come on me like a secret being whispered in my ear, and then all the noises in the room would sharpen, begin to grate on me, until the sound of page turning became insufferable. Then it would fade away, and I'd force myself to forget, which I have. That piece of childhood is mostly gone.

∽

"Are you in?" Percy asked me. What could I say? I knew Mark Mancusi wasn't evil; in fact, he hardly seemed to notice I was there when he was caught up in showing me a ragtime.
"Duh! I'm in! Course I'm in!"
And we laid our hands on the dirt together. I could hear the shouts of parents through the neighborhood, calling kids in for dinner. None of the shouts were for us, and they darted inside my head like dragonflies.

∽

My father wasn't really interested in my piano lessons; he was always thinking about "the grand scheme of life." He never got to see much of that scheme from his office downtown, a business that sold "executive gifts," which were engraved Lucite clocks and things. The life he meant was outside that, and that spring the grand scheme had brought a new '78 Mercedes to our carport. When I climbed inside for the first time, it had the warmth and lush smell of a sultan's litter. It was deep red, the color of an all-day sucker, and if you secretly licked it when your father wasn't looking, you could imagine it tasted sweet beneath the fuzz of pollen. My father drove me through the neighborhood, pouring music from a thousand speakers, letting me turn the dials and switches, blast the air conditioning, as the cherry blossoms gathered in the crevices of the windshield, pink confetti, so numerous, we could never quite scrape them out. They were there, shriveled, for the life of the car—not a long life, because in a month I'd awake and the car would be gone, and Father would smooth his brilliant tie, lean down, and whisper the new great things he'd found for me: a talking robot head, a hot-air-balloon ride for my birthday, a plan for replacing the staircase with a slide. And a wonderful woman for me to meet, someone he might marry, a sculptor who had a talent for baking pies. "How about that, champ?" he'd ask with the smile that couldn't help but thrill me, his wide-spaced eyes focused so directly on me for once. "Eh? Lucky ducks, us two!" And what about the car? "A lodestone," he'd say with a dismissive wave. He'd smooth the last remnants of his blond hair. "Things are things, champ. Don't confuse them with life."

I tried not to. I tried not to bring up school too often, or problems with my friends—"Phantom worries," my father said, grinning. He wanted me to draw him pictures of the castle we were going to build; he wanted me to play a game to *The Bob Newhart Show* where I had to drink Coke when someone said, "Hi, Bob"; he wanted me to cultivate a foreign accent to fascinate the women he brought home. Sometimes at the grocery store, he would begin to talk loudly, waving his hands in fake sign language, and I'd play along as the deaf child, nodding my head, fluttering my fingers, pounding my chest. "Wonderful kid," he'd say to the lady who had stopped her cart to admire me. He'd turn back, sideburns glistening with sweat from our game, and shout, signing away, "WANT SOME RICE CAKES, SON?"

But why motherless? I don't know, not even now; my father never talked about it. He couldn't have been easy to live with, but all I remember of my mother is her sitting in a brown car, pressing her thumb to her forehead. Maybe she was a little crazy, too. But her main talent was for disappearing, which she did, for always.

Max said once he'd like to train a honeybee to fly away and find my mother, but I'm not sure my life would have been better with her. Say what you will, but childhood was good for me, even if I never knew when my father would lock himself in his room, when toys would arrive for no reason, when I would feel my craziness coming on. It was good. I was afraid, almost, that genius Max would train his bee, and the little golden speck would be off to bring me what I hadn't really wished for.

∞

We compared notes on our piano teachers a week later at Raja's sleepover. It was a mansion, really, nothing like my own ranch home on a cul-de-sac. It was one of the new houses built to carry the boomtown influx. We all lay on the living room floor in sleeping bags, our flashlights under our chins, and if you tried hard, you could smell the newness of the room, the sap in the ceiling beams, the dusty scent of the shaggy wool carpet. A metal sculpture hung from the ceiling and dinged occasionally. Raja was telling about Mrs. Yee, his teacher, but all I could think of was how when Raja was little, his parents walked around with him on a nylon leash tied at the waist, to keep him safe. He never liked to talk about it. I wondered if the leash lay in his closet, catching his eye when he reached for clothes, warning him of what life once had been.

"She's got this little thing, this box in the living room, you know? Right near the piano," Raja told us. "She kept opening it and sort of looking in. I think maybe there's like . . . kids she taught in there, all shrunk."

"Not likely," Max said, sounding like his physicist father.

Raja looked a little afraid of Max. "I think so," he said, staring at me. "I think so."

Percy agreed: "I bet it's true! 'Cause, like, who you know ever took Mrs. Yee? Who escaped her"—and then he added on words from a movie we'd all seen—"*poison clutches?*"

Overhead, the sculpture dinged, dinged again. Something in the other room sounded almost like a conversation we could not quite hear, but it was nothing. The dogs moving and sighing.

Max clicked his tongue. "Okay, I'm not saying there isn't

something *weird.*" He said the word slowly, his glasses catching the light, two box kites in the darkness. "Like Miss Vakerteen, she's my teacher, and you know what? She said she can't sit in the sun. I heard from somewhere she's a dwarf, like not to look at, but *officially.* I think her arms are too short for her body, and that's how you know someone's officially a dwarf. And her limp—I'm guessing she has no toes."

"Really?" I said. "A dwarf?"

But Max didn't get to answer, because Percy decided to launch into Mrs. Runkle again, the giantess, giving her fangs in this telling: "She flosses them! Right there, like she's saying, I'm hungry, like she's saying, Look at my fangs! Can you believe it? And she uses those words, you know what I mean. . . ."

Raja and Max groaned.

"*Andante,*" Percy whispered, looking at me now with his gnomish eyes. "*Fortissimo, legato.*"

Max: "That coda thing creeps me out. . . ."

I stopped listening to him because the sound of the sculpture above us was becoming too sharp in my ears, and I knew it was one of those moods of mine that would pass. The other boys were laughing now, babbling about their teachers, and I tried to smile, but I was in a kind of panic, feeling as if I'd left something somewhere. Perhaps I could even hear the faintest whispers. I tried to steady my breathing—the whole scene felt underwater, and their voices were beginning to anger me. After a few minutes, I could hear more normally, and the anger and panic passed. They were all looking at me.

"Yeah," Percy said. "What about your teacher? That faggot."

They hadn't noticed. I know now that it was hard to notice, since I was so quiet anyway. They were certain I'd been silent because I was saving a truly weird detail, like the glowing irises of Mark Mancusi, or the hairs covering his palms.

The three were resting their heads on the floor, looking at

me as if we would always be friends. I started quietly. "Sometimes I can see him in his house, like at the window, and he's playing piano without looking at it . . . like he's possessed." They all smiled.

But we wouldn't always be friends. In high school, Max and I would end up in different classes from the others, and I'd never talk to Percy again after I turned fourteen. He'd simply evaporate from my world. Raja would find a way to bribe the popular kids in class, and we'd see him once in a while at parties, wearing a striped tie, laughing. There's no predicting things—I would always know Max's life, his years in school, his bad period, his wife the historian, his baby daughter, Amanta. I would be there the year his brother blew himself up in the garage experimenting with explosives. I would see the burnt side of their house, and Max standing on the curb, his eyes clouded by this single unexplainable thing. I would be there, long after we'd left the others behind, holding him and not caring that he cried. But in the darkness, three heads in a row, who could have guessed?

Later that night, armed with Max's genius, we planned the machine.

෴

It was around this time that my new pedal car vanished, and I searched in the carport, moving shovels and rakes in case I'd missed the obvious. I squatted near the woodpile, grinding my teeth, and began to wonder about these toys that came and went so often. I didn't think about my father. Instead, I pictured those witches my friends had described, fanged and dwarfish and bouffanted, gesturing their piano fingers and spiriting my pedal car away. Maybe they were touching my life, too; maybe it had always been them. I became suspicious; lessons with Mark Mancusi took on a nasty edge, with me pounding away a rotten boogie-woogie just to prove I hadn't practiced. I remember his worried look, his words trying to soothe me into relaxing for the music, hippie words: "You're trying too hard. Let it flow. Let your left hand just make it up." Witchy words, as well. Late at night, I would make fun of him for my dad. I'd stand in front of the television, and there Dad would be with a highball on the couch. I'd droop my eyes, play a lazy piano in the air—*Let it flow!*—and the two of us would crack up on the floor. We always did that to each other.

The next week, Dad planned a special dinner for me to meet his blond lady friend. He went to a lot of trouble over it, marinating and chopping and sending me over to the neighbors' for a fondue pot and then again for a set of forks. "Half-assed is no good at all, champ," he said, stirring a steaming pot and then grinning from the clouds: "Isn't life wonderful?" I spent much of my youth waiting for these spurts of enthusiasm, the bright afternoons he'd drag me out of school to head to the beach or a sickening roller coaster, the evenings when he'd have matching suits for us laid out on the couch, outfits for a play he was taking me to. The new cars. The toys.

I liked her, too. Her name was Shelly and she wore a big flowing dress that had roses all over it, and a hummingbird pin right in her hair. She disappointed my dad because she wouldn't eat the steak, but she loved the fondue, and with the cheese dripping from her fork, she told me what she believed in—things I'd never heard of: auras and messages written in stars and how we hadn't really landed on the moon.

"And I'm not saying," she clarified, "that we *never* landed, you know what I mean? Just that we didn't land in 1969 like they say."

"Do you think there's witches?" I asked.

She swallowed, smiled at my father, who was looking uncomfortable. "Oh, I don't think so. Not like in the movies. But there are powerful people who are really in touch with the universe, you know what I mean?" Her eyes, shadowed in bright blue, blinked at me. She kept asking that the whole evening, "You know what I mean?" and I nodded, although I hadn't the slightest.

Dad kept his hand on Shelly's shoulder while she talked, and he wore his quirky-upset smile. I think he would have preferred me in one of my disguises—as the little boy he'd brought over from Belgium, or his son by a temperamental opera singer, or the petulant math whiz—anything except the kind of kid who made him feel ridiculous. But I liked her, although I'd never see her again. I really did like her.

∽

The machine was a wonder. It involved two boxes of plastic building sets, Max's old transistor (which could be both telegraph and radio, depending on how you bent the wires), his father's antique (to us) chemistry set, wood from Percy's basement, and various glittering wires Raja stole from his mother. It was Max who found ways of connecting all the different parts, of putting the bubbling test tubes of baking soda beneath the paper fans so they turned like parakeets on their wires, of setting up a circuit of electricity to coil through the whole elaborate device, making it seem like all the activity was to light one small red bulb held in a thimble at the top. It was my idea to run the motor from a paddle wheel on the creek. So the machine was built on planks beside the creek, and we stood with jeans rolled up, our toes getting cold, as the apparatus grew in glass orbs and sparkling wires.

"You think it'll work?" Raja whispered.

Percy nodded. And that's how we felt—of course it would. How could anything this complex not work? It seemed the perfect antidote to this adult world we were combating, to the careful sabotage being performed on our lives, not just by the piano teachers but by every adult whimsy, all of which seemed just as randomly elaborate as a device of glass beakers and nests of filament buzzing over a creek. Maybe, looking back, we should have made the machine out of the totems from our lives—Raja's nylon leash, the crayon drawings on Percy's wallpaper that no one cared to wash away, the sheets of math problems left for Max each morning, the expensive toys that came and went with the fortunes of my father. We listened seriously to the zap of electricity across a metal arc Max had created. The scent of ozone jabbed into the air, a smell that always reminds me of that childish pride we felt. Later that afternoon, after we'd left the machine, Max and I walked back home. We kicked clods of dirt from the bases of apple trees along the street, and the cars rushed by us in the hot air; it was the hour for fathers to come home.

"I think Blanca takes piano from Miss Vakerteen, too," Max said. He meant the Venezuelan girl in our class, who sat in the back of the room with earphones on.

"Uh-huh?"

He was playing with an oak tassel, taking it apart bit by bit. "She's always getting in her mom's car right before my lesson," he said.

"She doesn't even speak English."

"Yeah."

"I heard she asked Bo Holsten to go with her, the other girls taught her to say it, she didn't even know what she was saying."

He said, "Her mom wears those big gold sunglasses."

"We helped Blanca out," I said. "No more piano teachers, right?" I looked around for a twig or a leaf to fiddle with, but it was all concrete and grass, and the apple branches were too high over my head. We walked along quietly for a little while.

"I feel really sorry for her," he said.

"What'll we do about the machine?"

Max looked up at me then as he pulled the tassel apart and I felt my mind coming to pieces like the thing he held, breaking off into tufts and floating out as the panic started to take hold. I stared at Max and clenched my teeth, trying to push it down. I could hear bits of the world in crisp detail: his feet scratching the concrete, a glass bottle somebody was kicking around the corner, the crackling tires of a slow-moving car. I hated feeling that way in front of him. I wanted Max to ask me why I looked so angry, because I hoped he'd help, because Max always knew everything. He might know why a boy could feel things rasping at his brain once in a while. He might know about crazy people, or he might say what I really wanted to hear, which was that things like this happened to every-body, always, just no one ever talked about it.

But what Max said was: "Isn't that your dad's car?"

It was the new Mercedes, the all-day sucker, sitting in the shade of an old maple. There were two men I didn't know climbing inside, two men in T-shirts and work boots, smok-ing cigarettes and starting the car to a roar of loud music. It was the music I remember, and I breathed heavily so it wouldn't panic me with its loudness. I almost couldn't take it. Max and I watched them rev the engine and drive away, and he started to say, "They're stealing your car! They're stealing it!" but I knew they weren't. It wasn't the first car I'd seen disappear from our lives. It was just that I'd always understood their absence in the way kids do—half knowing, half trying not to know. About how father couldn't pay, about how the people took them back, and now I simply saw where those beautiful cars went, and the kinds of men who took them. I turned away and felt my heart pounding.

I tried to make the world soft again. I tried to imagine what was happening across our neighborhood that afternoon in spring, with the hot air blowing up and a boy going slowly crazy and an anti-piano-teacher machine churning away be-side the creek.

Maybe Mrs. Yee was lying in a chair at the pool, her bouf-fant hair covered in a swimming cap, her little mouth curling in discomfort, like a fern when you touch it, and the tingling sensation of her fingers beginning to ache. And maybe Mrs.

Runkle was blowing a whistle at the goal line of a girls' soccer match, feeling a tightening across her breast, like a spiderweb drying there, and she drops the whistle, grasps for a bench, and falls, breathless, onto the newly painted lines. Or Miss Vakerteen at her deadly piano, fingers stuck to the keys for an instant in the middle of "The Hungarian Rhapsody" as she feels herself shrinking another inch on the piano seat. A little yelp of pain, and the spell's undone. A little something of what I felt.

And, of course, poor Mark Mancusi making a tuna fish sandwich in his mother's kitchen. I thought of him as my own heartbeat began to irritate me. A man I was too young to understand—weird, lonely, probably gay. Of course nothing happened, of course he didn't grip his skull and feel his eye-balls burning, but it was enough that I made a machine to break his influence over me. When I look back, though, wasn't Mark Mancusi one of the few influences that saved me? From being just like Percy or Raja? Surely he was no witch; he'd never planned any special destiny for me.

I imagined all the adults, reading books or lying asleep in hammocks or sipping beer in front of the television, not won-dering what would bring us to build this ridiculous machine. And my father seemed so different from all the adults I was hexing in my state. I imagined him on the couch, a cold wash-cloth over his eyes. He had probably forgotten about the car, dreaming up a trip for the weekend we couldn't take, or even better . . . the two of us lying on an island beach, eating hot dogs and the meat out of fallen coconuts. I knew he always put me in his foolish thoughts.

Childhood is so fuzzy when you look back; I don't know, for instance, when these episodes stopped coming. Certainly I started to breathe again that afternoon, and the air receded and left me calm with the thought of coconuts. It could be my craziness grew fainter as I grew older. I only know I stopped believing I'd ever been that way, ever grown angry

at a housefly because of its racket. Even now, those moments
seem not quite mine to remember, the way dreams beg to be
forgotten. I've let that time leap from me, a great dark cat.

Max ran to the spot where the car had been, in the shade
of the maple, his sneaker in a spot of grease as he pointed
down the road, where there was nothing. Then he yelled, a
clear, loud yell that parted the air. I stared down the road
where Max pointed and didn't say a word. He hadn't a notion
of what might come for him. Max kept yelling because he
thought this small a loss was tragedy.

Lost Causes

∽

THIS WAS WHEN I was beautiful. My beauty had a window of about four months, from May to August of my twenty-first year, then disappeared, so I can talk about it honestly here. It was so quick—zap!—like the green light flashing over an ocean as the sun sets. You gasp at the sight; then it's gone. That was me. Previously ordinary, suddenly beautiful, ordinary forever again. I have friends who only keep pictures of me as that young man from that brief time. Maybe they hope it will come again.

The only other thing you have to know is that I wasn't aware of this beauty. In fact, I thought I was a gangly towheaded creature who had to stoop under doorways, who wore his clothes all wrong, who never could master the art of catching someone's eye without blushing. And I blushed all the time. My skin was as pale as rice paper. People used to say dirty words around me just to watch my blood rise.

It was in Lisbon, Portugal. I'd gone there as an accident, almost, after graduating from college. I had no idea what I was doing, had been a failure at most things. I was nursing a ridiculously broken heart over a man I hardly knew, and carried around with me the outline for a novel I would never write. But why Portugal? I knew a man who was moving back there, an acquaintance really, a man in his thirties who threw parties in town for all the young college boys and had always been kind to me. So there, you know so many things about me now: beautiful, self-conscious, gay, pale, naïve.

At first I loved Lisbon. This friend of mine, whose name was Sergio, had nothing but good intentions toward me, and he arranged everything for us, even though I was only a friend and not a lover. I was, above all, a stranger to everything we met: the curving brick streets, the hot air rising with pigeons, the house phones metered by the minute, the voices coming invisibly around corners. He led me through this. We looked for jobs together, dressed in our white shirts and ties, and sat by sunny phone booths with a roll of quarters and the phone book, the *Páginas amerelas*, calling English-teaching schools. We lost a couple of jobs at places we visited before realizing that, with my blond hair and short sleeves, we looked like proselytizing Mormons.

The job I did get was because the British man who ran the language school thought I was handsome. That's how it began, on one of the first days, when I had already sunburned and peeled and, underneath, some other, fiery creature began to appear. Again, remember, I never knew. I knew only that Desmond (my British employer) smiled and gave me the job, and that he had me up at his house in Cascais many times that summer, taking me to the ballet with his lover, serving cold poached salmon and mayonnaise, teaching me to eat on the back of a fork, having me swim naked in their pool.

The Portuguese men, too, paid attention to me, mostly because I was as tall and blond as a cornstalk. Those qualities were rare in Portugal and, apparently, highly valued in a young man. When I ran squawking into the water on the nude beach at Caparica, sunglasses were lowered to watch my (I suppose) wax-white bottom. Even looking back on photographs, I can't find anything particularly striking about myself then. Long Scottish face, burnable ears, Roman nose. Ordinary. I have only the evidence of my face's effect: men fixing my computer for free, paying for my bus fare, arguing over me in bars. I thought it was all a cultural subtlety I didn't understand.

∽

But I want to talk about my last week in Lisbon. By then, Sergio and I had our second apartment of the summer. We had shared the first one with an overweight Bostonian who marked his decanters with a grease pencil to be sure we didn't steal from him. Arnold was his name, I think. He had a face like a pockmarked melon. We lasted only a few weeks before piling our suitcases into a cab without telling him. My new room had a sliding glass door, which I covered in red wrapping paper from the *Arabian Nights*, and the privacy this afforded me was my one great luxury in Lisbon. I looked out on a grass and cement courtyard. A rusted child's toy sat in the center: a seal perched on a spring.

I was coming in from a trip downtown, trying to take my last pictures of the Castelo de São Jorge and the vertical cable cars. I had taken the subway and walked a long way to our apartment, and it was terribly hot. I had a loaf of bread and some milk, which was sold in bags. Picture sweaty, exhausted me climbing the stairs and plunging through the door. In the background, turn on a soccer game from the nearby arena.

The apartment was filled with light. There was the faint smell of grease, not unpleasant, and Sergio's work tie was still hanging from the back of a chair. Our two roommates seemed to be napping in their room: a hairdresser and a pharmacy student from Pôrto. There were two messages on the machine.

One was from Sergio's most recent Portuguese boyfriend, a boy named Miguel, who was, if I am not mistaken, somewhere around the fifteen-year mark. But the phone call wasn't for Sergio. It was for me, asking me if I'd like to have coffee. This was in broken English, which itself was surprising, since the last I'd heard, Miguel knew not one word.

The second message was from Sergio himself. We were not getting along well. Sergio demanded perfect cleanliness from me, including washing all our clothes daily and hanging them up in the "drying room," and I ridiculed the boys he brought home by catching Sergio's eye. I knew he wanted me to approve, but I wouldn't, and so we lived not understanding each other and not trying. I half-listened to the message:

> *David. You have to pick up Roman Patterson at the Rato station. It's incredibly important.*

Who was this? Some new friend of Sergio's I was supposed to pick up at the train station? There was no time, no date, no reason given. The Rato was where we'd lived previously with Arnold, and I was certainly not going to travel all the way back downtown. Besides, I had no car. Pick up? What was this supposed to mean?

I called his friend Fernanda and left the same message on her machine, then promptly forgot all about it. One more person staying in the apartment certainly couldn't change the situation much, but I was not about to facilitate things.

I forgot to mention that I had a headache. Add to this a dizziness after hearing the crackling voices on the answering machine. Diagnosis? The first shy entrance of a streptococcus, its bacterial toe tentatively dipped into my weakened pool. But I didn't know that yet. I assumed it was the heat and poured myself a glass of water. I fell asleep on the couch for hours.

∾

A knock on the door. I awoke to find myself walking to open it, and my first thought was how deep in the afternoon we all were, how the tiny window in the upper corner of the living room had been opened by wind and this orange light was coming through, fringed by the tips of flowers. The knocking was slow, polite. I opened the door.

It was little Miguel, the fifteen-year-old boyfriend. He was quite tan, with large, slightly bloodshot eyes. He wore an African-patterned shirt and each arm dangled from its stiff sleeve. He smiled at me—how is it I can think back on him with fondness? He must be much older now, deep into his twenties. Those thin arms are probably braided with sinew and the black hair sun-streaked with red from nude beaches. He's had so many lovers by now. But back then, when he was Sergio's innocent, I found something terrifying about him. In the doorway, saying things in Portuguese to me and holding out what looked like a calculator, he had a snide crook to his mouth—a child's selfishness and plotting, and, naturally, the inability to hide it.

I did not understand his Portuguese. I tried to explain that Sergio wasn't around, that he should go home and have dinner with his mother. He held out the calculator again. That orange light from the small window above us cut him across one eye and down his neck, a Catholic light. I took the device from his hand. In a moment I saw it was a translating machine. On the crystal display, it read:

LOVE YOU

I stared at that for a moment without looking at him. I typed in "NO UNDERSTAND" and translated it back into Portuguese. Then, when I handed it back, I saw the smirk was gone. He was alight with expectation, one eye in orange light, the other shadowed blue, both blinking hope at me. He read the message. He typed and handed back the device.

LOVE YOU

This time, I didn't type again. I shook my head and said, "Sergio." There was a moment, I could see, when he had to think, when he had to realize that I did understand. His mouth opened a little. Then he mimed picking up a phone and talking. He sent me another message, this one less amorous:

SERGIO BAR

I was reading that strange phrase, trying not to catch his eye, when the phone rang, and it was Fernanda. She was using a raspy stage whisper, and claimed, "I cannot speak over the phone." This was a good excuse to get rid of little Miguel, which I did. I think I might have (in my pantomime) promised to talk to him later, possibly agreeing to meet him. In any case, he did not seem as disheartened as he should have, standing waving at the door, his left earring jingling with scattered sunlight. He looked clean, hopeful. I carried the phone between my ear and shoulder and squinted at him, hunchbacked, wondering (as I foot-closed the door) what it would be like to be so young, to misunderstand a rejection, to think you were in love with someone such as me: pale, unbeautiful, and mute.

⸎

That night I took a cab to a condo on the outskirts of Lisbon, one that overlooked a hill of olive trees, oily leaves metallic at night. It was Fernanda's place, where she lived with her teenage son. She was a nervous woman. I remember she was unable to answer the doorbell because her pasta water was boiling, and I entered, to see her in a pink cocktail dress, patting her hands desperately into the steam.

All of Sergio's friends were there that night: Fernanda, her son, Alexandro (who shyly disappeared for rugby practice), fat and happy Luis (the Orchid King of Lisbon), Victor Serrano (the longhaired psychologist), Fernanda's recent boyfriend (more later), and myself. We were all seated in her white-couched living room. The balcony door was closed due to an extravagant wind. It was an emergency meeting of Sergio's friends, a meeting called by Fernanda to discuss what had happened to Sergio.

"Yes, you know he is in jail," she began, speaking in English for my benefit. In fact, the whole conversation seemed to be for my benefit, as if it were crucial I understand. Yet I was barely older than Fernanda's boyfriend, who lounged idiot-style on the couch, playing with the flaps of his leather jacket. So I lied about knowing: "Yes. What for?"

Fernanda pursed her lips. "You know what for, David." She said my name as if I were Portuguese: "Dah-*veed*." It sounded exotic coming from her. She explained: "Those credit cards he paid for everything with. You know."

I knew perfectly well. Sergio had somehow thought Visa would never find him if he didn't give them his new Portuguese address. This was before the credit-check machine; shops and restaurants had only those sliding carbon-makers, which worked completely on faith. All of us had benefited from this ruse, accepting from Sergio unpaid-for meals of prawns in garlic, electronic devices (such as little Miguel's translator), gifts of train rides to spas where we stood with mud drying on us, then cracking off, revealing our red, purified nudity. Perhaps we'd all pretended not to know, or believed if Sergio thought it would work, it would. Or that, stupidly, the universe would always let us live this way, this ridiculous way.

"Jesus," I said, looking over at Victor, who was expressionless. "Did the Visa police come along or something?"

Victor, a handsome man with shoulder-length sun-streaked hair, told me, and he pronounced my name like an American: "David, the bar, Ninety-six. They got back his bar bill and caught him when he was there with Miguel."

I put my hands up. "Oh! Oh, Miguel stopped by just today! He said something about the bar!"

Victor shrugged. No one cared very much about Miguel, not even Sergio. I pictured my friend Sergio in his tight jeans and white shirt, his potbelly hidden, bringing over drinks to young Miguel in the epileptic lights of the 96 club. Boys all around, dancing in their desperate glances and clothes. Sergio's hands raised above the nodding crowd, in each a fizzing gin and tonic with its glowing lime. Perhaps that was all Miguel could see of his older boyfriend—the two icy drinks floating about the crowd, the two limes—that is, if he was even paying attention, if he was not thinking, for instance, of me. But if he was watching, he surely saw the drinks fall into the crowd and then, minutes later, Sergio being taken up the red-lit stairs, his shirt untucked and his face turned away.

What did the boy do then? Decide he could either care a great deal or not care at all? Decide to fall in love with someone else?

"What about the phone call?" I demanded, and they looked at me in my petulance. My fingers wiggled with impatience for the story, played my thighs like a keyboard. "What about this Roman Patterson? You sure he was with Miguel?" But as I said it, I was also sure, because Miguel had said so. I looked around at nervous Fernanda, smirking Victor, and the rest of the men. I asked again, "Anyone know a Roman Patterson? At the Rato station?"

Fernanda suggested it was the Rato police station, but this made no sense, because Sergio was being held in a prison across town. Perhaps his lawyer? It was too late to call, we decided. "If we don't understand it," Victor said sternly, "then it is not ours to understand," a statement that, in general, I rather strongly disagreed with, but which that night I had no interest in pursuing. I had tried to fight with Victor before, in a restaurant while sharing Alentejan stew. We fought over modern psychology, which I thought I knew something about, and I swore I hated him and the way he would sweep his hair behind his ear before speaking, but, in contrast to this feeling, our heated words led us (obviously and unfortunately) to his bed.

I glanced over at Victor, who was jutting out his lower lip and rearranging his saucer. Behind him, Fernanda's young boyfriend became mildly animated and turned on the television. Apparently, the conversation was over. Little seemed resolved.

I began again. "What's the plan?"

Fernanda got up to take our plates and said, "We should meet, yes? Let's meet tomorrow afternoon at the prison. We should speak with him."

The chubby Orchid King leaned forward, frowning. He wore a black T-shirt and a shiny lavender jacket, and I suspected he was inconceivably wealthy. He kept a boy at his home, I'd heard, a rather prominent soccer player. He said, "I am not buying an advocate, a lawyer."

Fernanda patted his hand. *"No te preocupas."*

He added what we were all really thinking: "None of this surprises me."

∝

Victor and the Orchid King went to the windy balcony to smoke cigarettes while Fernanda and I did the dishes. It surprised me, since I knew Victor experienced vertigo, had been discharged from the army for this (being unable, for instance, even to look out from the tower of a former mosque). He'd told me this one night after we had slept together, when I visited his house and he left me there on the street, under a blinking streetlight, while he got his laundry. He told me this as if it explained something—for instance, why he had no real interest in me—and then mumbled into his cigarette that he was sorry. That night at Fernanda's, I saw he took to the balcony because it was the place for men, despite his vertigo, and that I did not belong there. I was uncomfortable that this was assumed, because I knew the gendered duties in Portugal.

I knew the importance of these roles. I carried pots of spaghetti into the kitchen and wondered if I had not helped make the sauce, would I have been granted the role of the male and smoked outside? What if I had not slept with Victor? What had made this pose—me balancing dishes beside jittery Fernanda—seem so inevitable?

Her arms were deep into the suds. We were washing the dishes before putting them in the dishwasher, which barely worked (and worked on coins). Her skin was dark from tanning, not from her genes, and years of this had made her face tough and furrowed. As I clinked my load down beside her, she leaned over and spoke.

"Can I tell you something?"

I picked up a dish towel. I was beginning to notice a sparseness to this room, an absence of necessities like flour and sugar, personal magnets, herb plants dying by the window. There were none of those. There was nothing but cool Mexican tile in beige. "Sure," I said. Recall, I hardly knew her.

She stopped washing and blinked seriously. "I'm in love."

"With who?"

She shook her head and smiled as if I were teasing her. "With Francisco! You are no good!" She was referring to the boy in the other room, leather-jacketed, sullen, and three years older than her son.

I played along as if I were a wit, pinching her cheek and making her glance back and forth from the hot water in embarrassment. Really, I was stalling for time. What does one say? Only this: "That's wonderful."

I expected an elaboration of her emotion—statement of intent, detraction, even defense—but she only giggled. Her whole manner spoke to me that she had been wanting this for a long time, to return to the naïveté of youth. I admit that standing there, seeing the grin she couldn't force from her mouth, it didn't seem impossible at all.

"I'm in love, too," I told her, but she had switched on the noisy dishwasher by then and turned to me, questioning, perhaps having half-heard. Perhaps, though, she simply did not want to respond, but wanted to be alone in this giddy state. Perhaps love was so crisp in her mind that she could not bear to share it with me, which was only her right.

∽

I showed up at the *delegacia de polícia* the next day at our appointed hour: four o'clock. Back then I was insistent on time, so I had rushed all the way. The others were all thoroughly Portuguese about time, however, and I should have remembered that. Victor was unusually lax about this, and as I walked toward the prison, really only a sandy stuccoed police station with a bell tower and a rock-garden courtyard, I wondered if he would really come at all. He'd given me a ride home from Fernanda's the night before, and in the car, he pried (with surprising delicacy) into my emotions. He asked me why I was angry with him. I remember the landscape outside was utterly black, and I had no idea where I was or in what direction we were pointed. Once in a while, we would cross a bridge with marble muscled statuary, and every time, Victor's head would revolve. I think he was one of those men who reacted chemically to the male body, in any form, like a teenage straight boy getting an erection while looking at the Venus de Milo.

I said I wasn't angry, then said I was surprised we'd never talked after sleeping together that night. I was surprised he'd never called me. I stressed the rudeness of it, all the while tapping my head against the window. I look back and wonder if the blue and yellow lights striping my face could have made me prettier than I was. But remember, this was the time when almost anything could do that.

We wrangled over this point, but I didn't want to argue.

It wasn't important. I laid the topic to rest because I knew I didn't have a chance here. I saw he was concerned, and not mildly, but it wasn't for me. It was an anger at himself for not solving this sooner, not seeing I would be a complication. But I wasn't going to be a complication. I had already decided that. I let him go. And when a little later he quietly asked if I wanted to sleep at his house, I demurred and pointed out another statue: a young man battling a serpent. As Victor turned, and as we came alongside the statue, I knew this was best for him: sitting between two objects of haughty stone.

I went inside the prison gates to see if I could visit Sergio. Again, there was a courtyard of dwarf junipers and stones— some warden's pet project?—and two dark archways on either side of it. I chose the left, and came upon a guard post with two quite amiable men in round hats who were willing not to understand me in English, Portuguese, French, and pantomime. The last consisted of me imitating a prisoner: grabbing invisible bars and shaking them Cagney-style, running my tin cup across the metal, pickaxing in a rock quarry with a ball chained to my ankle. It reached this level of ridiculousness because, recall, my streptococci were reproducing in my throat and what I thought was sadness and desperation was (or was possibly) merely a high fever. Even at four o'clock, the sun was out and blasting us, so I couldn't feel my own heat. After my feverish show, the guards folded their arms, tipped back their hats, shook their shining faces, and stroked their mustaches. They pointed to the other archway, where I saw Fernanda already waiting, hand to her eyes.

"Have you seen Sergio?" she shouted. This seemed inappropriate, calling out in a prison as if it were a high school hallway. I ran over.

"No," I said, waving my hands. "I can't find the holding cells."

She squinted, as if this were a side issue, and hugged me.

She took my hand and led me past the courtyard, listening to me and nodding, a patience I had long been seeking.

The next archway, we found, was much more promising. Not only did it contain all the expected bulletproof glass and wire-mesh booths but Fernanda could speak to the guards in their own language. It turned out that only relatives could visit prisoners. Fernanda tried to coax them, and before I tell you whether it was successful, I should describe what she was wearing: a short brown leather sundress with sharp rivets where the straps attached, high-heeled sandals, and a fevered lipstick. Perhaps I say "fevered" because of my own circumstances. In any case, the sundress (astoundingly hot, I assume) showed her tough, freckled cleavage, and one advantage of being a short woman is, I suppose, the fact that tall guards can glance down into your dress and, wide-eyed, wave you past the metal detector.

She smiled and waved back at me. "Watch out for Francisco," she said.

"What?"

She shook a finger as she clicked down the prison hall: "You are no good!"

I realized she had brought the eighteen-year-old. The Portuguese John Travolta. He was waiting outside, surely, and I hoped someone else had shown up. Perhaps Victor, or Luis, so I could pass the time. When I got outside, however, I saw Francisco slicking back his hair outside the gate. I am amazed at my snobbery, sometimes, and my utter blindness of myself. Because the way I viewed sexy, dumb Francisco—certainly that is how the Portuguese saw me: self-absorbed, silent, and attractively young.

I was left alone with Francisco for a full hour. During that time, he bought me two beers (I was trying to calm myself, but only worsened my fever) and tried to talk with me. He knew a few words of English, things like *walk*, *must*, and *best*, and I knew as many of his language. We leaned across the bar and exchanged these words. I began to see what Fernanda could love in him: small jet eyes and unshaven chin, a kind of naïve arrogance in the quick way he raised his glass to drink, the torn T-shirt, the generous sunlight behind him, floating in angles across the wall as the glass doors swung open and closed. Perhaps I looked the same to him. Perhaps these words—*walk, must, best*—were the only ones we needed. When he smiled at my Portuguese and nodded, pretended I had communicated something real about myself or him or this place, I knew we were only reflecting each other.

After a while, he made us leave the bar and walk out in front of the prison. This took much sullen pantomiming on his part, because we were not only supposed to walk but walk in a specific way. Walk *this* way, I could imagine him saying in Portuguese, an old joke, but there he was, motioning for me to roll my shoulders and shuffle my feet in feigned disinterest, pacing the prison block like a pair of hustlers waiting for a john. This went on for some time. It was easy but pointless, and as embarrassing as being forced to play a game you hate (football, for me) and forced to play it well. I rolled and shuffled, looked up at the hazed blue sky and peaked bell tower, and I followed him turn after turn. It was hot and miserable, and who knows why I did it? After a while, though, I realized Francisco didn't know I was gay. Unlike the night when I did dishes, here I was, like him, performing teenage machismo before the police as if this were something I was born to do, as if I claimed this long-lost phrase of movement as my inheritance. He looked back at me with his greased head and nodded as if to say, Brother, this is how men walk.

We stopped when Fernanda reappeared, her sandals sticking to her heels at each step, her fingers frantic with a small purse I hadn't noticed before. She held up a hand and bent her head wearily.

"He is in there," she told me, then said something to Francisco, who patted my shoulder and ran across the street to the bar. We followed him slowly.

"So what's the story? What's up?" I asked.

But she wanted to tell this as a narrative, and didn't answer me. "When I first got in there, I met him in a room and he looked awful. Unshaved. Dressed in some uniform. He said they'd given him cold coffee in the morning because they were afraid he'd burn himself to death!"

"Over Visa fraud?"

She shrugged. "He told me about Roman Patterson." It was lipstick she was putting back in her purse, I saw. Perhaps reapplied for the guards' benefit. I could hear the leather dress sticking and unsticking to her sweating skin as she walked. It was a sexy sound, hearing her body shift in its slick skin. It alluded to a nakedness. She continued: "Roman Patterson is him, is Sergio."

"What is he, some Interpol agent?"

"No," she answered impatiently as I held the door of the bar for her, "he lied about his name. He lied and was taken to Rato, where you were supposed to pick him up and they would not be able to trace him back."

I asked, "So this is my fault? How was I supposed to know all this?"

Francisco already had three Cokes out for us on the Formica counter, but he had disappeared into the bathroom. Fernanda and I were in the window now, in the direct sun behind the greenish glass, a mirror beside us. Waves of reflections snaked our faces.

She put her hand on my wrist. I forgot she was my mother's age, and had my mother's stern eyes. "David, David. I am worried," she said. "I think Francisco's doing drugs. What do I do?"

"Drugs?" This was out of nowhere. I glanced at the swinging bathroom door.

Her face was falling now, sun-wrinkled and dark with makeup. "What do I do? He sits there saying nothing, with his hot jacket on. He's run away from home. He had no money." She held my wrist tightly, waiting for the answer.

I told her, "If he hasn't got any money, then he'll run out of stuff. And then either he'll quit or he won't, but you can't help him. He's not dangerous?"

"No."

I could only smile, because Francisco was back, glassy-eyed, with a faint mustache of sweat on his upper lip. Indeed, he wore a black leather jacket zipped to his neck. For some reason, it made me sad to think our walk together had not been his misrecognition of me as a straight man, but just another brand of quiet raving, like my own.

Fernanda continued talking as if nothing had happened: "Of course it's not your fault, David. Sergio's stupid. They forced his real name out of him finally and moved him here. He spent the night and got cold coffee. That is all."

I sat back, appalled. "*Forced* his real name? What does that mean?"

She sipped her Coke. "Sergio's not a strong man, David."

"They beat him?"

She shook her head but didn't answer. Francisco put his arm around her and she handed him a five-hundred-escudo bill. She started talking to him in Portuguese, leaning up slightly to see his eyes. They were both in profile to me then, and could have been behind a one-way mirror, or projected on a screen, for how distant I felt from their world. Not just this Portuguese one of prisons and bell towers and dwarf pines and sun. This romance silhouetted against the green glass. This thing they both believed in, despite the common sense that it would fail (and it *would* fail), despite their accumulated experience with lovers. I was so distant from that stupid hope.

cѕо

Later on, the others came to join us. Not just the men from the night before, from the council at Fernanda's, but also Sergio's boyfriend, little Miguel, who had changed into a white starched shirt and shorts, making him look all the more young and prematurely sensual, and my roommates, the hairdresser and the pharmacy student. The last two were whispering with Miguel, who was not saying anything, just looking at me. I wondered if he had been to the apartment again today to find me, and had befriended these two oafs: one with a slick Caesar cut and a blue tooth, the second bald, thick-lipped, and vacant. Small but intense, little Miguel achieved, in that company, the air of a leader.

Victor was also there. He had come from work, he said, and this was obvious from his tan linen suit and white shirt. It seemed such colonial attire for a psychologist, as if it were part of his therapy to produce a languid demeanor for his patients. I watched him sit down across from me, brush back the shoulder-length hair, and imagined such an office: louvered blinds striping the walls with amber light, a wicker ceiling fan, palm fronds blowing in a hot wind, perhaps a fake insect smear on the wall, all to create this soothing, equatorial atmosphere. The therapist Victor in his wrinkled linen, swabbing his tan forehead with a handkerchief, intoning, "Picture yourself floating on a green salt sea. . . ."

Fernanda explained the situation: "Sergio's tried to be tricky, and now he's paying for it."

Because I could not speak Portuguese, I had Victor ask little Miguel some questions about that night: what had happened in the bar, if he knew Sergio was using a false name. I heard their quick accents, the difference in their voices, noticed how Miguel kept glancing at me, flickering the whites of his eyes toward me. Victor seemed almost bored with the boy, unflirtatious. Perhaps he was tired, or knew boundaries. At one point, the fifteen-year-old shook his head and instead asked Victor a question, which seemed to take the older man by surprise. Victor looked at me and answered quickly. Everyone at the table seemed to shift while I listened, and Miguel smiled, sharing this smile with the roommates.

Victor explained that Sergio had merely abandoned his boyfriend there. He'd been silent with the police the whole time in the bar, and ignored Miguel. That seemed fine with Miguel, who (like Sergio) had other things on his mind.

The Orchid King said again, "This does not surprise me."

We all acted as if I had not understood what the boy asked Victor. Perhaps they thought because I couldn't speak it, I didn't know a word of Portuguese. But I did, and I know the boy asked if I was a good lay. Victor told him to be quiet.

I, too, pretended not to have heard, saying sharply, "Well, I have to say, I mean, this *does* surprise me. He's my friend and . . . I knew he was defrauding with credit cards, but I thought he was *smart*. Who'd lie about their name to police? Doesn't this seem desperate? Did he seem okay, Fernanda?"

Fernanda looked at Victor, though, as if he knew. I saw Victor taking control of the talking now, having overcome Miguel's bad taste. He said, "David, he's done this before."

"Really? Why didn't this come up last night?" I glanced around.

The Orchid King waved the waiter over and said, "Let us not talk this way. Let us have a beer and decide what to do."

I tilted my head, annoyed. "Well, this is my friend. . . ."

He ordered beers anyway, but Victor leaned over toward me. I could see his brow was sunburnt today, perhaps would become redder as dusk came on. I thought of him heading to the beach, taking the roofless metal train across the dunes, careless with the sun and happy to see all those naked men. Victor said, "This was years ago, the last time he was in Lis-

bon. David, we were all going on a trip to Brazil. Brazil?" he
asked no one in particular, then decided to settle on it. I remember I liked the way he kept repeating my name, as if this
were a story told only for me. I like to think it was. He went
on: "And he sold us tickets because they were cheap, David.
It didn't matter to us, but it was a good price. At the gate,
we found out they were under different names, maybe stolen.
Who knows where he got them. Fernanda."

Fernanda looked down at the table, rearranging her purse,
and said, "It was very embarrassing. To be in a public place,
and turned away." She stared firmly at me and contradicted
Victor: "They weren't stolen."

The Orchid King called Sergio an asshole in his language,
crossing his arms. Our drinks arrived. I was getting dizzier
and dizzier, high on beer, the sunlight, and my body's own
debilitating chemicals. The next day, the pharmacy student
would take me to the British embassy, to their clinic, and
there illegally prescribe me penicillin. But that afternoon at
the hot glass-topped table, I was woozy, heat-struck, some-
what happy with this bacterial spin.

"I have an idea," I said quite out of nowhere. Someone
must have been talking, but he or she stopped and everyone
looked at me with interest. What made them do that? Was it
my bloodshot eyes? I am willing to bet—and this is not ego-
tism, since it was long ago—but I will bet it was my face, and
how lovely I was then. It was the last time I would ever be
beautiful, but I could stop a table.

I repeated it, woozy: "I have an idea. Let's find a Catholic
church, one with statues of saints. Maybe go out in groups.
Go out and find a church and find Saint Jude, the patron saint
of lost causes. We can buy a candle for him and pray for
Sergio. Sergio is a lost cause. I can't think of anything else to
do but wait. Isn't that what one does? We should go out and
buy a candle."

I can't tell you even now where that came from. I had no contact with the Catholic church, but I looked at Fernanda and she began to nod her head.

"Yes. That's what we should do."

She touched the table and nodded some more, facing the rest, who were quiet and unsurprised by all this. Fernanda told them, "Don't you think? Victor, you and I will look together." She twisted around, holding Francisco's hand, and spoke to him in Portuguese. Meanwhile, all around the table, people began to talk and form groups, plan trajectories, remember churches they had seen around here. Some remembered churches in other places with Saint Jude, ones from their childhood in other parts of Portugal, one in France, in Spain. Some talked about their own names and the saints they could pray to also, for whom they had not lit a candle in years. They were so relieved. They all looked at me and I felt this look was admiration.

The owner opened the French doors beside us, bringing in the scent of the garbage and mud gathered in the street. He also drove away a harem of blue-white butterflies drinking in the mud, sent them spreading like a ripple in the air.

∽

I was left with Francisco again, plus the pharmacy student. As much as he annoyed me, I was glad to have the pharmacy student along, because this time he had to do "the walk" with me. Francisco insisted on it. Perhaps whatever drugs he'd taken were wearing off, because Francisco took off his jacket and rolled and shuffled with it slung over his shoulder, his white T-shirt dark with sweat and tight on his muscles. The pharmacy student stared at the young man's chest, and I think this was why the student agreed so readily to our ridiculous strut. We looked like an old-fashioned gang: the Jets, ready to rumble.

The pharmacy student found that he couldn't get much talk from Francisco. And as much as Francisco wanted to take the lead (triangulating us like migrating swallows), it was obvious he was not headed particularly toward a church. We would, possibly, saunteringly, happen upon one if it suited him. We, the followers, decided not to argue, and the student began to talk to me. He knew more English than I expected.

"You worried to Sergio?" he asked me. He was, again, stylishly bald, with an enthusiastic way of swinging his thin arms.

I said, "A little. He is probably okay. We should not worry." I had learned to speak clear and easy English after one of my fellow teachers, suspicious that I was hired for my looks alone, complained that my vocabulary was too large. I was told to store it away for a while. My roommate seemed to understand.

"He does not love Miguel, yes? You know."

I said, "I know." This was true. Sergio, I knew, could have loved him, but he hadn't seen Miguel as something worth the trouble.

The young man patted his shaved head. "So you could love Miguel."

I smirked. "Not a good idea." A vendor was selling greasy orange *bifadas* from a rickety aluminum stand, and the smell of onions and meat came pleasantly toward us.

"Yes, yes," my roommate stated. He had a long face and dark eyebrows, and this made him always seem sad, wistful. "Why not?" he asked.

"Miguel is . . . too young."

He laughed and pointed at me. He said, "You like him. If you say he is too ugly, then no. Too young, then you like him but are feared."

In front of us, Francisco turned around. Perhaps all this talking did not fit "the walk" as he envisaged it. I admired this vision of his, so strong for someone who otherwise did not seem to care about much.

I kept my voice down and explained: "No. I do not know him. Miguel, he does not know me. So, you see?"

"Miguel know you," the pharmacy student said, peeking up at me slyly. "He sees you naked."

I said, "What? When? He's never seen me naked." I was prudish at home. Maybe he'd seen me in a towel. Perhaps that's what he meant. Some schoolgirls walked by, adults, really, but dressed in dark skirts and hair ribbons and giggling, so that they hung on, tethered themselves to a former age.

The roommate laid out the scenario for me: "After your baths, you close your doors. We can see between the paper. We stand on the couch and watched you . . . push-ups. Miguel, too. That is why he loves you."

The doors, those were the sliding glass doors of my room, and picture again how I had covered the glass with red wrapping paper, golden *djinns* whirling in a crimson sky. The job was imperfect: If one moved close, one could see between the gaps, especially the young men who had turned off the living room light, knelt on the couch near my glass "wall," and squinted an eye. Put your eye to the rip below a *djinn*'s head, and watch me coming in hot from a bath. I wipe back the water dripping from my hair, lift my arms over my head to do this, so the slender muscles connecting my arms to my chest are revealed, and recall that I am unexplainably gorgeous at this age, at twenty-one. Sunburn marks my neck and arms, my upper chest, but it is hardly distinguishable from the general pink of my skin from the hot bath. I am blushed all over as I drop and fold the towel, as I start the push-ups I am convinced will never build over my boniness. Tall, thin, and blooming.

The ugly pharmacy student built this image for me. He, the snaggletoothed hairdresser, and childish Miguel all squatting and watching me. There were crowds of pigeons around the student and me now, and Francisco scared them into the air in silvered sprays, as if they were an ash heap we kicked through. My bald voyeur had a grin on his face as we neared the church, but not only couldn't I communicate my horror to him in words he could understand, I did not know what to say—how was the horror mixed with pleasure? We crossed the soot-stained steps beside a woman selling mint. Three young men had debased me without my knowing, had shamed us all *just to glimpse my skin*. Just to look at *me*. I studied a bright mosaic of a rampant cherub, thought of someone watching me like this, a paper-framed nude. Three men fixated on my image—when in my life would this ever come again?

∽

My companions separated from me once we were inside the cathedral, the pharmacy student sneaking west down to the choir gate, Francisco waiting outside to swagger in front of the steps, kicking the swells of birds. I walked slowly down the dark nave with the two or three other visitors, our shoes tapping loudly in the silence, and there was something to the air, also, a viscidity, as if whatever smoking incense or seeping catacomb smell there was had slowed the particles of the air and glued us all there, stuck us like insects. I was hot from the smoggy outside and from my strep, and I moped along beside the pews, staring at the statues and trying to discover who they were. There were little clues to each one—molded snakes and arrows and roses—but I didn't have the language to decipher them. I recognized only St. Jude, because standing beneath him, gazing up with a finger on his chin, was little Miguel.

No one was around him except the bronze figures of the canonized—São Jorge, São Francisco, São João Baptista—underlit by rows of iron holders on stands, a few votives guttering, the saints' hands outspread to the boy, as if parting black gauze curtains to approach him. Miguel was sweating, I could see, just on his upper lip, though his all-white shirt and shorts made him seem frosted like a cold glass. I walked up to Miguel and was convinced he didn't see me, couldn't even feel me coming near him. When I was his age, and had my crushes, I was always aware of their presence, because I was always seeking it. But even when I shuffled loudly against a votive holder, he didn't notice. He stared up at his saint. Perhaps he had already lit a candle, or was planning to.

I said softly: "*¿É isto o Saint Jude?*" He turned to look at me and did not change his expression, although it was already one of open surprise. Perhaps it's a quality of age that I've forgotten, the early wish to let things surprise you. Or maybe it is not a wish. Maybe it is inevitable. His face tapered toward the chin, which he still held in the air to look at me (for I was tall to him). His mouth was slightly open, only because he had been caught alone, and I think children close their mouths only around adults because they are trying to control their impulses, learn these limits. Alone or watching a gripping play, they breathe noisily through drooped lips, raise their eyebrows, stretch their necks to see. A child transfixed— this was Miguel's expression, although he was not (I must remind myself) really a child.

Miguel had never heard me speak Portuguese before. I was asking him if this was the patron saint of hopeless cases. He nodded without closing his mouth. I wondered where his partners were, because this church was outside their route, and it occurred to me he had separated from them. Perhaps he left to find me, or perhaps (and this now seems more likely) he left because he didn't care one way or another, for Sergio or for me or for any of us.

He said to me, quite straightforwardly, "*Que bonito és,*" and I could see then that I was quite beautiful. I pictured myself in that votive candlelight, and who wouldn't see himself as a bronze saint? Isn't there something about that thick air and fluttering darkness that makes us want to be worshiped, and can't we imagine a fifteen-year-old boy already lonely with surprise, looking at us as if we were worth seizing? What we never could be: worth adoring? I pictured myself in that light, and though I saw someone separate from me, far more distant even from the nude American doing push-ups behind a paper wall, this teenager peeking through a rip, though I knew Miguel hadn't understood at all, I took the moment. I would not be handsome in a week, even, when I returned to America. I knew that. So is it surprising that I took the boy's cool cheek and kissed him?

Because I don't regret the kiss. The moment was comprised of something complicated and pathetic. That, too, is in all church light, floating in the stained air with the fog of dust. His body was skinny when I held him closer, only two years into puberty at most, nothing like a man's. I felt his ribs like matchsticks, and his too-mature tongue slipping into my mouth. Perhaps he was not even fifteen; I believe he could even have been younger, picked up by some man in a public pool or shower, brought into an adult world of clubs and naked asses and "relationships" like a convert on the preacher's arm. Who am I to say he wasn't ready? All I can say is that I was not. And that I kissed him to prove I was.

At that moment, it did not even seem out of place for a twenty-one-year-old American to kiss a boy near a votive altar. Wasn't this, after all, a cathedral from the Renaissance, from a time of men in love with boys, in a country where such things had happened? I hear that in Morocco, not far from us across the Mediterranean, men and boys walk down the street hand in hand, sneaking kisses like lovers. It did not seem immoral at that moment, or even irreverent. The silence of the church seemed to approve; certainly no one came up to stop us. It made me think that it was all right to kiss little

Miguel, press him to me, give him my fever, pay back the street boy who'd spied on me, my friend's own boyfriend, the friend whom I was trying to save.

I don't regret that kind of self-delusion. I am still deep in it. But I will never be the golden boy again. I know this, and that is why I can look back and excuse almost everything about myself. I know I will never, as I did that day after kissing little Miguel, stride back through a church square and feel each eye on me, order a drink from the gargoyle-shadowed stand with confidence, seeing the girl blush and glance up at me, and I will never stride across a street heavy with traffic because I feel no one could kill me. Never again will I look back to see a Portuguese boy all in white, standing in the church's entrance, beaming because he knows more than I will ever know, and has fooled me with it.

Later, the group of us found ourselves at the prison again, Victor and Fernanda, the roommates, the Orchid King, Miguel, standing outside the black iron gates with the oval inset door, hot in the sinking light, with nothing to say. We stood in silence, sweating and avoiding one another's eyes, because none of us had lit a candle for our friend. When Sergio emerged from the oval, waving at the crowd of us with his wide ring-glinting hands, none of us were thinking of him. Just for the instant of his arrival, each of us failed to hear him call our name. We had all spent the afternoon walking the streets of Lisbon, searching maybe for a church, but also for a bar, a park bench, a jittery bus ride, whatever place we could find to be alone. Our wishes rose, too, like waves of heat from the city, not one of them for our friend. They never are, nor can be. I knew all that in the instant of Sergio's arrival over the iron curve of the doorway, when Fernanda looked nervously into her purse, Victor stared off at a passing boy, Sergio's young boyfriend glanced triumphantly at me, and I fixed on a marriage procession coming from a church, the bride all in black lace on a horse, *Amor* painted in gold on her dispassionate breast. I would not sleep for many nights.

Then I ran forward to unshaven, weary Sergio and, with everyone shouting around me, hugged him suddenly enough to make him gasp, held him rough and close because he was, you know, my very best friend.

Life Is Over There

❦

THE FIELD IS flattened like a book too long left open. There is the newly painted white crease of the spine, there the muddy dog-eared corner. The boys wait in their lines. The shouts are just beginning.

All the parents fill the space around the soccer game, the space between the lines and trees, with their puffs of cigarette smoke, their folded corduroy arms, their red-white coolers and blue-pink baby strollers of silent brothers and sisters wrapped in afghans. The afghans are all gaudy, every one, because a prominent theory holds that children of the seventies should be exposed to mathematical patterns. Tangerine-and-lime geometry. The theory will pass, and the afghans will find themselves on the beds of guest rooms, then in attics, then in church donation bags. But for now the afghans are present, quietly imbuing brazen knowledge, and this puts the parents at peace. These parents are intent on their children's success, on their young boys out on the field this championship game. The boys know this. The boys, in their shiny striped shirts and long bright socks, are still trying to remember the rules to this game. No defense past the center line, one thinks, hoping no one notices his doubt.

The autumn trees are quaking their crisp hands above it all, dropping them in dozens to the field, lurid hands or gloves thrown into a ring.

Off to the side, pushed back by the throng of parents in these first struggles of the game, are the children who are always there, sometimes in greater numbers than those on the field, the brothers and sisters of the champions, the ones not great enough today. Other days, in the future, but not now. They are brought along because no parent could stay home. Every doctor and real estate agent knows the prominent theory of families at the sidelines, so they are all here, missing their appointments, applauding these first hesitant kicks toward the goal, these first stained knees. So the other children are brought along. They fill any gaps left between the parents and the trees, and wander into the trees themselves, toward the little gullies and rotted forts they've built over the years to house them during the shouting. That is, most of them do. A few are out beyond that, by the creek, and the shouting is unheard beside the water.

And in the corner of everybody's eye, as if it were impossible to wish away, even in all the hopeful tussle of cleats on the field, the kicked mud and grass, is Mr. Poppy in his wool army coat out near the goalpost, clapping with his mouth open, urging on the team. In the gasping spirit of the game, all the parents try to forget him.

But the sidelined children see him. Even the ones by the creek can see him. And later, when the last goal has been made and fiery-cheeked boys are shaking hands on the field, they will watch him through the raw fingers of a leaf pile. Waiting for their parents, they will watch his happy applause, his glasses flaring in the chill sun.

It is cold, but only once you step into the navy shadows of the trees. The smell of the air is smoke and oranges, the rusty scent of dirt kicked up by boys, one lone cigar. Otherwise, by the creek, in that cold, there is no odor. Like some violet spell, the jangling creek silences everything. The creek, and around it the mealy dirt strewn with pull tabs from beer cans like silver insects, and around that the meager glade, which to these children seems like a cathedraled forest.

And here they are. Making little boats from pieces of wood, struggling to find a way to fit a mast onto a piece of bark without breaking it, carefully fitting an oak leaf as a sail. Debbie has discovered that a tuna fish can is the best raft, and she proves this in race after race. She is a bony girl, a sixth grader formed like a bird with winglet shoulders and a tense face. In autumn, her lips are always chapped, and her mouth constantly works at them, biting away the skin. Her long brown hair is held back by elastic trimmed with little clear baubles. Debbie is young, and smart, and has read *A Wrinkle in Time* too many times to recall. She often thinks of the heroine, Margaret, in her warm attic bed, combing that mousy hair. She often thinks of the adventures in store for girls with mousy hair. Again she places the tuna fish can in the water. Swiftly, haughtily, again it passes other boats.

From the field, if they could hear it, would come shouts of "Gary! Defense, Gary!" which is a call to her older brother. A call from her father, who demands success.

Another boy there, Martin, is furious with Debbie's boat. It isn't a boat at all, he claims. "You haven't built anything," he tells her. Time after time, he straightens the bark rudder of his own ship, which he has named *Darth Vader* and which is overly complex for this kind of game. The only purpose is the survival of the boats through the metal glitter of small rapids, but Martin is intent on perfection: His has a rudder, and two acorn pontoons. Martin wears glasses strapped to his head with string. His hair is permed (a whim of his mother's) and sticks out frizzily everywhere, but perms are not uncommon for boys at this time. Some of the soccer boys even have perms. As a matter of fact, Martin himself is on the soccer team, and he wears the shimmering uniform of the team in red, the long socks, the black cleats. Martin has been on the bench all season, though, so he has learned how to play in the woods. He has had time to perfect a bark rudder on a pinewood boat. And all this time, he mumbles; it is a poem he is to speak at a school assembly, one his mother picked from Emily Dickinson. It is an inappropriate choice, but she is a brilliant woman caught in this spiral of split-level houses, so she tries. Martin surely doesn't know what it means, but he is memorizing it, and rattles it off constantly and quietly.

The words run together like this: *I cannot live with you it would be life and life* . . .

Debbie's boat is disqualified and she chews rapidly on her lip. She finds another raft, a shelf fungus growing on a tree, pokes a mast in it, and wins again. The triumph of mousy-haired girls. This game wasn't her idea, though. It was Kristin's, and Kristin seems hardly to be trying.

Away from them, Martin's team is loudly winning, and the boys do little dances they've seen on television. Their red shirts shimmer in that sun, and Mr. Poppy applauds. He smiles his happiness everywhere.

Kristin is another matter. Down by the water, she takes off her shoes and steps in. The creek parts around each leg, ruffling at her ankles. It must be icily cold. She has four boats going at once, all the same kind: a moss raft carrying a stone. She has begun to realize how prone to sinking they are, but some of the thrill of boat races is the fragility of the crafts, and there is joy in watching things drown. Down another goes, under a rock. She is younger than the other two, a sister of a soccer player, like Debbie, but really nothing like Debbie in any other way. Thin blond hair in pigtails, tan coveralls rolled up to her knees, a pink vinyl jacket half off her shoulders, the buttercup hood hanging behind her like another head. She's strange to all the other children. She's known to lead groups of boys down this creek to a huge pipe that leads under a road, a superstitious place none of the boys will enter.

She's known for walking in there all alone. Parents warn their children from her, their own kind of superstition. Kristin isn't bright or skillful. She isn't charming or talented at "Für Elise" at the piano like the other girls, doesn't show up at parties in a pink prairie dress, or know a single tap dance, but she is dangerous. Look at her in the water without her shoes, while everyone else breathes clouds into the chill air. Look at how careless her life already is.

In a few years, her brother out there on the soccer team will be hit by a car. The whole neighborhood will be struck with horror, and she will turn to her mother in the kitchen and see that face unveiled for a moment. Her mother will show something so reckless in a parent; she will show her own dislike for her daughter. It will hide itself in her face quickly, and she will run to hold Kristin close. But Kristin will have seen and known it. That's years from now.

Off by the field, at halftime, coolers are being emptied of their Gatorade and the air steams from hot chocolate falling into Styrofoam. Debbie's bully brother, Gary, walks dejectedly toward his thickly mustached father, who is silently smoking a cigar. It is he who smokes the cigar that covers the air. Gary is waiting for the words he knows are coming.

Martin, by the water, rattles off his Dickinson: *I cannot live with you it would be life . . .*

The parents are all curious in their halftime poses: pouring chocolate, lighting another cigarette, chatting up a neighbor, rubbing a boy's red ears to heat them. Martin's parents are here, finally worrying about their son, although he's been gone before, and they find nothing too awful in his being alone. A prominent theory says that children of the seventies need time alone in order to be geniuses. They hope what he is doing is some sign of genius, and they wish that they could see it. She in her brown leather coat, her black oval sunglasses, her ponytail of black hair, casting her glance to people she doesn't really know. He remembering his own youth and lack of skill at this, at sports, remembering, too, how their own son almost did not make it on the team. The other fathers petitioned for Martin to be left off, for the improvement of team skill, for a rowdier sport. Martin's father, also in glasses, also in a leather coat, fought in his nasal voice for his son's admission, but only won because the league rules say it is a public team, meant for all boys in the sixth grade. He hopes that Martin never heard about this. Kristin's parents are also here, talking to their son, and if they knew what was to come, they would hold him tighter, allow him little vices, little tantrums, but no parent can know such a thing.

The parents turn their heads to lock on their children, and those who cannot find their children keep their heads revolving. So many corduroy coats and crocheted scarves. So many leather buttons. They are trying not to notice Mr. Poppy, or think of Mrs. Poppy, who has left him.

And back at the creek, just as the soccer match begins again, the boat races have been abandoned. Tuna fish cans catch on twigs downstream, and Kristin's mossy boats are torn by rapids. Nobody is watching; Kristin has a new game. They are farther down the creek now, near a low rise in the shore, which Kristin calls "Dead Man's Cliff," a name she made up, and she and Martin are drawing a treasure map on notebook paper. It is a fake map, leading from the soccer field to the circle of stones Debbie arranges on the cliffside. There is no treasure, of course; the dirt under the stones hides only dirt, but that is the purpose of the game. Later, Martin will drop the map onto the field for some red-cheeked soccer boy to happen upon. Boys cannot resist a treasure map. The three can see the future so clearly: a boy in cleats finding this map, leading his friends into the woods to this stone circle, scrabbling vainly at the dirt in cold twilight.

No one is watching their furious activities, Martin dirtying the note on its anachronistic lined paper, Kristin hopping up and down Dead Man's Cliff to check all progress, her hood flapping behind her spookily, Debbie wiping mousy hair from her face as she arranges the stone circle with pebbles she's found in the creek. Three are in her pocket: a green one, an orange stripe, a mottled calico. All children collect things. She chose them carefully from the cold stream, but hours from now, when she takes them dry from her pocket, they will all be gray. They will join her collection of other gray stones. At night, sometimes, Debbie dips the stones in tap water and smiles at their hidden colors.

But later, much further in the future, when she has started high school, she won't remember that. She will have waited too long in that attic room, like Margaret, no adventure coming, no wind under the door. A science geek for too long, poisoning frogs in the garden, she will change. One day her brother, Gary, and his friends, popular jocks by then, will come home to the Worch house, to find Debbie in teased hair, lipstick, a neon tube top. She will attempt a gawky seduction of her brother's friends, and the hilarious story will spread throughout the school. There will be no living down a thing like that.

From the field, if they could hear it, would come a call from the coach. He's calling Martin's name, but no one answers. He is just doing it for kindness, anyway, and it doesn't really matter in the end.

And Martin, Martin is thinking of winter coming. It comes to mind because of the last line of the poem, which he does not understand: "And that White Sustenance—/Despair—" He can only picture the snow that will cover all of this, the field, all these woods, the creekside. There will be only the black scurry of the water through the white. He is thinking of the year he was walking home from school in a deep, icy snow and found his friend Jeff running up the hill to tell him all the bullies were down at the corner, waiting for him. Gary Worch, all of them. They were waiting with ice balls. Jeff told him to cut through Mrs. Featherstone's yard, but Martin wouldn't. He'd learned this; he'd read this somewhere, that he would regret running away, that he would later be proud of walking unafraid into this danger. So Martin walked calmly down the hill, and even when he saw the dark coats of the bullies hidden behind trees, he didn't blink. He walked on, and when the ice balls fell upon him, he saw how wrong he'd been. It felt like a stoning, and one of his legs collapsed. He sat in the ice and cried like a baby, before these boys, who were scared suddenly, and did nothing but stare. Martin learned never to be brave again—there was nothing in it. At least, with cowardice, the shame is silent.

And better to hide in the woods during a soccer game than face the fathers who'd voted him out. Better never to be forced to fail.

Out of nowhere, Kristin mentions Mrs. Poppy.

On the field, there has been a reversal of fortune, and our home team seems to be losing. The yellow shirts have taken the day for now and the parents are concerned, yelling out for no reason now, just to have their children hear a voice. The geometric ball flies overhead, and two boys try to hit it with their head like Pelé. Neither of them manages, and instead they knock into each other. The boys stagger off, dazed, about ready to cry. The parents in the crowd try not to titter, and Mr. Worch gives them a glare, munching his cigar.

In a row out east of the field lie the station wagons, paneled and chromed and dusty from the autumn air. Someone has left their lights on, although why anyone would drive with lights on such a sunny day is beyond reason. Someone else is sitting in a Town and Country, scarfed in polka dots, listening to the radio. Mrs. Worch, conducting an opera.

It all was this way a year ago: the sun shifting in clouds like a change of mind, the air as tight as apple skin, these cars, these lines of boys, these shouts. A year ago, Mrs. Poppy was also here in suede boots and a brassy belt, jumping up and down and waving a pennant that had nothing to do with the teams. She was a teacher in the grammar school, and Martin remembers her short skirts, her carefully curled red hair, her glistening skin and deep eyeliner. Every boy remembers how she leaned over during class with one hand to her blouse, covering her cleavage. She was, and still is, not a young woman. In fact, her third child entered college just this September, and that was when she left for Maine, when she caused all the stir, when she brought on in the minds of parents thoughts that could not be told to children. Why did she go? The simple answer seems to be that she loved another man. But look at Mr. Poppy in his plaid hat, yelling to the boys who are recovering their field. Why is he so happy? And see the wives shiver briefly, in an accidental, perfect line, like a chorus: nearest Mr. Poppy, Martin's mother in sunglasses, with a bitter color to her face, out of place as usual, staring at faces like photos on a piano; then Kristin's mother with pale, feathered hair and bits of gold all over her, pausing in her giddy chatter; and Mrs. Worch out in the parking lot, mouthing the opera under a scarf. A tiny shiver passes down the line.

She loved this other man—nothing new, even in 1979. But what chills the wives is that she had always loved him; he was a red-haired love from her youth, calling to her from the snow outside her window as a girl. But for some reason—pregnancy, parental admonition; there are no details to this story—she married Mr. Poppy and moved from Maine to this suburb. They had their children, recarpeted their floors, and somewhere through the years, he learned about her red-haired love, and wanted her to stay, so a deal was struck. She would live with him, teach math, raise their children, attend the soccer games and wave her pennant. She would live that life until their last child left for college, and then she would leave. She would resume her old life with the red-haired boy. After twenty or so years, that hour tolled, the child was off, and then, without a word to anyone, so was Mrs. Poppy.

The wives are all still, holding their scarves, their hair blowing in a sudden gust, and they picture the teacher's bag sitting in its closet, always packed. They see gaunt Mrs. Poppy boarding a train, her suede boots lifting onto the step. They know what she felt, leaning her auburn curls against the cold glass of the window as the train jolted forward. Or rather, they can only remember that rip of joy.

None of them, none of the parents on the sidelines, can remember any sign in her of passion. Her gloves never trembled in her hand at church; her eyes never glazed wistfully in conferences; she never stood dreamily in her daffodils. They had always thought themselves the wild ones, with stories of their protests, their wild marijuana days in college, rumors of swinging couples. And Mrs. Poppy was the square one they happily measured themselves against, picturing how she tatted her lace so friendlessly, tasting just this minute portion of life. How laughable and sad it had been, how comforting. But perhaps Mrs. Poppy knew this much of passion: that to keep it, you mustn't spill a drop.

"Hooray," yells Mr. Poppy. Hooray. Their team is winning now. The red shirts bustle toward the goal in these last seconds of the game. Gary is aiming for a score . . . but who can't turn sideways just a bit and see Mr. Poppy there? The wives frame his form with their thick glasses, sunshades, hands cupped over eyes. They will never understand compassion. Instead, they see his lost wife at a fireside in Maine, under a blanket, watching her man chopping wood out in the snow, his red hair blazing. Martin's mother thinks of some handsome physics major back in college, explaining quantum theory; Kristin's mom remembers boys in high school, frightened boys in letterman jackets; Mrs. Worch recalls a young man who could sing opera. They'd thought that life was fiercest moving forward. Who knew it could have such clauses?

The goalie fails to stop the ball. The boys are leaping. Hooray. Hooray Hooray.

Silenced by shouts of triumph, a mumbling boy comes out of the woods. In his mind, the words all run together, but in his mother's, they are separate, writ in hesitation:

> *I cannot live with You—*
> *It would be Life—*
> *And Life is over there—*
> *Behind the Shelf*

They are all coming now, the three of them. Martin adjusts his glasses, carefully drops their treasure map onto the grass beside the coolers. Who knows who will find it? They are playing a new game now, and it isn't clear who thought of this one, but they step quietly behind the lines of parents who clap in unison and laugh clouds of breath into the air. Silently, the three head for the giant leaf pile near the cars, a crisp stack of air crackling in their fingers. They climb inside, careful, wordless. The world in there is dark; the light blinks through in stars over their heads. They can barely make one another out, smelling the rusty scent of leaves around; they can hear one another's noises. This game is a quiet one. They are hiding as best they can, seeing if when their parents make their way up to the wagons, they will notice them in the leaf pile. But this game is harder than just hiding.

Kristin crunches leaves in her soft hands until they crumble into dust, which she scatters on her lap. She is wishing herself red as an ember, bright and red as a hot piece of iron. Debbie fingers the stones in her pockets and blinks dust from her eyes, thinking on the destiny in her mousy hair, which will not come quickly. And Martin, he is murmuring, buzzing words through the soft leaves, the chant he won't be able to forget now. They all hide, each knowing, knowing with certainty that they can't be hidden. Despite the cover of leaves, they bet their parents will see them as they climb the hill, catch the peeking light in all the shadow, run and correct all wrongs. The three children shiver in the cold, watching Mr. Poppy laugh, seeing his ghostly wife beside him. They all beg for greatness.

Blame It on My Youth

∽

YOUTH IS A tender terror. Even the young will tell you so, improvising on their lives as on parlor pianos, stuttering out a boogie-woogie somewhere in the mess of ivory they've found themselves at. Even at that rooftop party years ago in Seattle, everyone would have nodded, would have turned from their conversation of jobs and pet peeves and new flames and agreed. A fearful guessing game. Then a turn back to the drinks, the chatter, there on the rooftop brilliant with afternoon sunlight, the bright air like a sheet of glass you were pressed against.

It began with a bet. Or, rather, it had taken an hour of conversation and a pitcher of margaritas near the bar to lead this young man and woman to a bet. Margaret, who wore wire glasses and a blue dress in which her thin body moved like the clapper of a bell, had wandered along the edge of the rooftop party, shielding her eyes from the glare of the water, until she'd found Pete and his friend and tangled herself in their conversation. Pete had a wine-bottle body corked with an innocent face, and while one hand held a bouquet of magnolia and clover close to his vest, the other shot out in the air, much like Margaret's often did, pulling at atoms as he talked, plucking and pruning the invisible rosebush of his ideas. He wore glasses, too, rimless and nearly invisible, but flashing as he turned his fidgeting head. He drew Margaret in, told her about his job as a chemist, built with her a theory about the people at the party. She and Pete hit it off because of their drinks and their nervousness in crowds, the way she teased him about his dull chemistry theories, and his shy interest in her life. Eventually, Pete's friend Alberto, who had been silent as they chattered, finally slid off on his own with a silent wave of his hand. From the look in Alberto's eye, Margaret could tell two things: that like so many other men at the party, these two were gay, and that the friend had loved Pete for a long time. Seeing the tall chemist's awkward grin, she knew something else: that Pete would never love him back.

Pete blinked up at the porcelain sky, shading his eyes with a hand. He asked, "You seen the host of this party? The birthday boy?"

She nodded, although she really hadn't noticed. Some muscled boy named Nick.

Pete asked, "You ever wonder what it would be like to be gorgeous? I mean to turn men's heads? Not that you don't already." He looked at her suddenly, aware of his awkward voice again.

"I have a theory about that," Margaret said, sipping her drink.

He grinned, pushed his glasses up his nose. "I knew it. I knew you'd have a theory."

"Handsome men are always less interesting than plain ones, you ever notice?" She leaned against the concrete railing, crossed one arm under her breasts. "I think gorgeous men know they're dull, and they're miserable. I think being beautiful would be like being a British royal. Terrifying. Surreal and terrifying."

She wasn't lovely, and he wasn't handsome. None of the people there were beauties of any kind. Perhaps earlier, before they cared, or even later in their lives when they were changed or fully formed, some did or would shimmer enviously, but not at this time. At this time they were young and fine, nothing more.

He toasted her in the air. "I love theories like that."

They spoke for a little while of bad boyfriends, of their pathetic jobs, of the impossibility of this party, since there was no new man here to attract, or even to excite an interest. There was only the host, who was way out of Pete's league. This chemist had an excited quiet about him, as if he had a secret about you which he longed to tell, and this made Margaret talk even more to impress him. She talked about how she was from the South, from the Carolinas, and that her mother told her "you couldn't get farther away from me" and how true that was. They were in their private corner, and that afternoon sun blazed light from everywhere: broken glass out on the railing, windows from the downtown buildings, earrings and rings and bottles. Margaret would close her eyes as they talked and could see pink and blue figures still crawling across her lids. It made one lose one's depth and sense of things. It was drugged air.

"I have an idea," Pete finally said, leaning on his elbows and lifting his black eyebrows. "I have a bet."

"I'm all for it. As long as there's not too much movement involved. I'm a little tipsy."

"Just your lips. You see those two girls over there?" He leaned over and pointed, and indeed two teenage girls sipped anxiously at their beers. Their clothes were tight, hair overdone. This was a party for a band, so they were probably fans who had sneaked in somehow. Margaret looked over at Pete, at his tall, unlovely frame, the glow of his face, and she saw how excited he became at his own ideas.

"Those girls?" she asked. "Yeah?"

Pete came close with his sideways grin, his dark curls of hair, and she could smell the flowers he had been holding, a present for the host. "I say we bet twenty dollars on who can kiss one of them first."

"I've never kissed a girl."

He stared at her with an open mouth, his lashes blinking prettily. "Well, what do you think *I've* ever done with one?"

And because of the drugged air, the kind of afternoon it was, their exasperation with the moment, they reached out hands and shook on the bet. Each walked forward and tried out just the kind of seduction they were unused to, all odds against them, the gay man and straight girl flirting with the utterly wrong gender and bending their looks, which were not beautiful, into something tempting for a teenage girl, just for one kiss. Margaret found herself butching up to the brunette in the black T-shirt, punching her shoulder humorously as she saw the girl hiding a smile under her palm. Was this working? Was there a gleam there of possibility? It was ludicrous, but Margaret talked on about how lovely the girl was, how refreshing to find youth here at a dull party, and she saw how this flattery altered the girl's eyes. It was terrible—she recognized so much of it. She saw in this young creature so many of her own moments when she took someone at their word.

But when she glanced over at Pete, expecting to catch the same flailing try at seduction, she saw an amazing thing. Pete, tall as a movie star now, was kissing his girl.

He held the back of her blond head as if he'd done this his whole life, the young gay lab assistant with the nervous fingers, pressing his lips to hers and closing his eyes intently, seeming to believe for this moment in what he was doing. Margaret and the brunette were silent as they watched. Had they ever seen a thing so sweet? Weren't the kissers both, in a way, innocent amateurs at this? The kiss passed, and in an instant there was an angry boyfriend clambering through the crowd.

How they got out of that mess, Margaret never really understood. There were swinging arms, accusations, pushing through the party, until she and Pete were outside on the Seattle street with three teenage ruffians from the suburbs. Pete looked shaken with fear, talking quickly and foolishly, picking at the air again, telling them within minutes that he was gay and there was nothing to fear, as if these three would find this information comforting. Margaret saw new hate rising in their faces, saw how this hate felt like pleasure to their dumb blood.

"He's lying," she said, and saw all the faces under their baseball caps turn to her. "He's my boyfriend, and he's drunk, and I'm more pissed than any of you. Lay off him. He's mine."

The original fist-swinger pointed at Pete, who was clutching Margaret's hand. "This fag's not your boyfriend," the boy insisted.

There was no pause before Pete and Margaret took hold of each other and kissed, deeply, feigning a long passion for the brutes, who quickly vanished into the building again, more confused than satisfied. But the kiss went on past the need to convince, until both let go and looked, to see the sidewalk empty. The kiss was a childish move, Margaret knew, like closing your eyes before a high dive. But it had worked, and now she was left buzzing from a human touch she'd not had in a while. Pete looked stricken and sad above her.

"Don't worry," she said, smoothing his wild hair. "They're gone."

"Jesus. Bad idea. My fault, bad idea," he said, still staring around him, his fear still close. They could hear the party bellowing on above them, dropping confettied noise.

"How did you get her to kiss you, anyway?" she asked.

He turned to look at her, the fear still trembling in his temples, a smile working over his thin lips. "I just said she was beautiful. Isn't that what everyone wants to hear . . . when they're that young?"

"Let's get a drink somewhere. Somewhere else, obviously."

"Remember, you owe me twenty bucks," he said, pointing a shaky finger.

That evening they sat smoking cigarettes they weren't used to. It was in his apartment nearby, a place of two tiny rooms, which should have been one, and when Pete leapt up to make omelettes for them, Margaret felt amazed that he could squeeze so much out of such a cramped space, the way Mozart can emerge from the most unlikely violin. They drank all he had in the kitchen, which wasn't much, and Margaret found herself describing the last mountain-climbing boyfriend, who'd stopped calling her, the dull aching feeling when she rang him up and found his phone disconnected. Pete told a story of how his last boyfriend had never slept with him because he was "only attracted to his mind." Then they sat quietly in too much smoke and his bad jazz. He softly asked her what she thought was the loveliest part of her body, and she shyly unrolled her stockings and showed him her long legs, and he took off his shirt and showed her his arms, and they laughed that they had this in common: Neither mentioned their plain faces.

Later they fell asleep in the other room, which was taken up entirely by the bed. Their glasses lay crossed on his bedside table, glittering, the television soundlessly bloomed with light, and they both lay on their backs with their cold feet pressed against each other. Margaret stared up at the ceiling as if it were the surface of a pond. Soon, noiselessly, she turned and touched him awake, his eyes gray and tired, the weird light making his face tremble like the body of a bird. Both of them were dizzy from the evening, blind without their glasses, and the world was a gauze-covered thing. Only once they had begun did both realize they were kissing, taking off each other's clothes, revealing her beautiful legs and his matchless arms, feeling even their own skin so vaguely as she led him through sex. It was not that he didn't mean to—I don't want to give that impression. It was just a very lonely moment in the bed, and she was so warm, and despite his clouded eyes, he knew how to accept a gift. It did not surprise Margaret when, much later, he whispered this was his only time with a woman. She closed her eyes and smiled, falling asleep thinking of her old loves, how they all made her feel as if she'd never been a child.

∞

On into fall, they would meet once in a while, especially when the rains came. It's hard to believe that it would continue, their furtive sport in the down of his bed, but none of it was ever arranged or asked for. They simply ran into each other at parties, or found themselves the only ones available for a gray Sunday movie, and these times turned into opportunities for sex beside the closed curtains of his tiny window. It wasn't love. He wasn't made to love women, and she was no exception. But remember how young they were, not able to make sense of their world yet, not fixed like adult stars on a black sphere, but doubtful and changeable as planets. Touch is still touch, despite your mind, and Pete could sweat and smile with her as if they worked against a common enemy in that bed. Think of the relief knowing this wasn't love. Not to have to touch a body burning with that.

And what a fantastic secret! They had to be so careful around their friends, especially his, because if those men knew what their plain, boyfriendless chemist did some weekends in his small apartment, they would have seen betrayal. His crowd of well-dressed, smart gay men would not have understood. They had accepted him as ugly, as lonely and too shy to be much fun at parties, as the awkward giant with the tense grin who absentmindedly wore two watches on the same wrist; they had seen past all these things because of the one thing he *was*. He was like them. He was an ill-fated lover of men. How could bottle-shouldered Pete have explained his Margaret to them? How can I to you?

So it was kept from everyone, even from Pete's friend Alberto from the party, the one who'd kept his own secrets, which Margaret had glimpsed. It was not a romance, or an affair. It was a time not to think of such things. It was the mindless play of children in the sand; it was the gratitude of sleep.

Did I tell you that she worked on a ferry in Seattle? A bad job, one she would soon leave, but she spent her days motioning the cars onto the ferries from the city out to the islands. She tied her long auburn hair up in a scarf, hid the rest of herself in overalls, and calculated the way to fit those honking cars onto her boat in the right order. It was a mathematical job, Pete pointed out, a job of calculating shapes. It was true; her mind worked steadily until the cars were boarded and she held out her hand to the disappointed latecomers. The gate closed; the horn blew. The ferry moved from the dock, and there she was, free on the deck as they sailed off on the salt water, free to be quiet and alone, and sometimes she thought of Pete in those long gray stretches of the day, wind grazing her ears coldly, the waves below her as multicolored as the rustling leaves of a tree, of a wind-shook tree. She thought of how he didn't really know what a beautiful woman's body should look like. Hers was the only one he knew.

There was another ferryman on the boat with her, but they never talked because of the wind and water roar of the upper deck, and because they both recognized the value of time alone. But she watched him in his overalls. Close blond hair, a constant sniffle, the tattoo of a rose on his left hand, in blue.

He often shyly smiled at her, turned away with his big rose hand to his face. Sometimes, having sex with Pete, she closed her eyes and thought of that ferryman. She held Pete's warm back and thought of rougher skin than this. And was that infidelity? Or was that the same dream he was in?

∽

They never went to her place. Margaret had explained that no one ever went to her apartment, that it wasn't a place she met people, but a place she escaped to, all her own. No one was invited there, not even her mother, had she ever come so far from the Carolinas. But you can look: piles of books in reddish tones, not literature or dictionaries, but odd collections, a long series of Nancy Drew and Girl Scout adventure books, maybe ten or fifteen overdue library books on seafaring vessels, pulp novels with their covers torn off, tossed into old bronze spittoons and hampers of dirty sweatpants, old sneakers. There were three file cabinets of her old correspondences, bank statements from her college account, which she could not bear to close, unused receipts from old tax years. You can see why no one was allowed in here. Often enough in conversation about some mutual event, she found people looking at her oddly, saying, "Really? I can't believe you remember that," so what would they say of her room? Would it seem terrible then to remember so much?

That night, though, she was the victim of etiquette when her weird neighbor, a would-be jazz singer, pounded on her door in tears and somehow worked her way inside, sitting on the plush blue ottoman and watching television, sniffling, letting Margaret bring her tissues and glasses of water as she told some sad story or another. Margaret sat there bewildered—she was a woman who drew lines so taut around herself, she did not know what to do when they were crossed, when this sobbing woman hunched over and crept inside. Only when Pete called did she have a solution.

"Pete! Thank God!" she whispered, glancing over at the neighbor, who was helping herself to a box of ancient maple candies. "You've got to do me a favor."

She heard Pete's interested "Hmm" over the phone. "This is unusual," he said softly.

"I need . . ." she said, and then turned to cup her hand over the phone. The television began the theme song of some long-canceled show risen again. "I need you to come over."

"What is this? Are you okay?" There was a catch in his throat, which said they weren't yet the kind of friends who asked these things, who thought of each other's lives beyond themselves.

"It's hard to explain," she whispered. "You need to come over and pretend like we're having a fight."

A half hour later, there was a loud knocking on the door, and there he was, red-faced and furious, his glasses shimmering, the black-haired giant shouting about some kind of letter he'd found in the glove compartment that needed explaining. The neighbor was frozen with her cup of hot chocolate for a moment, and then mouthed a quick "I'll see you later" to Margaret as she sneaked out the door under Pete's waving flanneled arm. The door closed and Pete stopped his yelling, looking over at Margaret with wide, open eyes and a smile half-hidden in his fake rage.

Margaret was shushing him but laughing. She made him close the door and turn up the television before she'd explain, and then he was grinning, not quite laughing, because he was only the punch line to the joke, but loving it. I tell you about this night because this was how they always were with each other. Just as on the first night at the party, with the bet, they amused themselves pretending, and it was their joke together against an unwitting world. But why? When had love itself turned into a secret prank?

That was also the first night he saw her room. She stayed surprisingly quiet as his eyes ranged over the piles of paper, over the shining covers of the library books, bookmarks sticking out of them like thumbs. Her quiet came because, as he looked around, he told her the story of his evening, and it was the kind of aching story that she knew.

"Sorry, I shouldn't have called," Pete said, smiling still, sideways again and fakely. His brown wool coat was thrown over an armchair and he sat on the edge, not wanting to inhabit her things fully, looking away from her and touching an old newspaper from the date of her birth. "I just wanted to call, and here you have me coming over! So it seems so dramatic. I ran into Nick again the other night, remember?" It was the host of that first party when they'd met, whom Margaret saw as a self-created beauty, all muscles and careful tan hiding his flat face and eyes too far apart, but she knew gay men didn't care about those details. "I asked him on a date. Can you believe it? And he went!" Pete's face was flushed all at once. "We went bowling with Alberto and Bob, not really a date, I guess. . . . I thought it was. And we all got really drunk, especially me and Nick, you know. Well, you know."

"You didn't!" Margaret whispered, excited. "Really? You slept with Nick? But that's great!"

"Yeah," Pete said. He turned the pages of the newspaper with one finger. Then his eyes moved sharply to hers. "Yeah, it was great. I mean, I can brag about this to everyone. And he was really sweet, and in the morning when I left, I kissed him. You remember what that's like?"

Margaret held her lips close. She thought at first Pete meant kissing him, and she knew what that was like. There would be more of it later that night, another embrace, but he meant kissing someone you love or could love. How long had it been?

He went on, still catching her eyes with his. "I called him today. I guess I called at a bad time, or too soon or something. I guess he doesn't really want to date me."

"Oh, Pete." This she knew well enough.

His voice went low. "Nick said it was when I kissed him. That did it. He said he'd been lying there in the morning and it was so nice, and then I spoiled it. If I hadn't kissed him, he would have seen me again."

"What does *that* mean?" she asked.

Pete lowered his head, pulling his body in, the giant who wants to transform into something less noticeable, as if a smaller kind of sadness were acceptable to the world. He said, "If I hadn't cared."

Is it just the young who say these things to one another? They don't know that we are made of words, all other people's. They haven't considered much yet. And these two, our own unlikely lovers, hadn't known it either or they would have stopped their ears more carefully than this. Margaret herself hadn't known her body was a parish bell tolling at every heartbreak she heard of, and that night with Pete calmly sitting on the edge of her favorite chair, invading her private room with words this room was sealed from, she felt it just as a bell would. It struck her right inside, until her bronze skin rang out the news. Not of Pete's story, which had not even made him cry, but some other story she'd been trying not to tell herself. So she sat stiffly there and wept, clanging and clanging like a thing that tested its own breaking.

"What is it?" Pete asked, almost frightened. He'd told too close a thing for their own arrangement. They should have stuck to calling each other lovely. They should have kept silent, closed their eyes, used one another more selfishly.

But Margaret just said angrily, "If you hadn't cared."

She shook her head, the pealing sound of her sobs coming through her gritted teeth. Pete crawled onto the carpet and came toward her on all fours. He held her, tried to still her sound. He kissed her and stroked her cheeks and said he would be fine. It was nothing. It was just a little unkind; forget about it. They had sex there in her room, with her hidden

stashes of memory and unreturned objects looking on, her
piles of useless paper, her radios with broken parts, her unread
books staring with ornate, dusty eyes.

∽

They talked often in the months after that of what he missed.
The odd boniness of men's pelvises. Hair and beards. Sometimes the rude force of hands on his shoulders. He would say
this as they lay in his bed, or more often now in hers, all
white sheets and blankets, as he stared out her window at a
lake. He said it as if he'd never feel any of it again, and almost
the way you describe the house you grew up in, a house you
know would be too dark and small for you now. Margaret
never said a word while he was in these reveries, or when he
made claims about how much better sex with women was, that
at least you always knew what to do and who you were. She
knew neither of them really understood what he was doing
there, lying next to her hot skin.

And Margaret herself had things she missed. The hopeful
look in straight men's eyes when she first took off her clothes.
Their careless bodies. Pete had no impatient lust for her, of
course, and his skin was self-consciously soft and clean. He
used her shampoo, her face cream; he smelled like her now,
and she missed other smells. But neither of them missed the
passion, because replacing it was something just as adolescent
and urgent, as selfish, so that while they tended each other's
broken hearts in bed, they also did not care whom they were
with. It was a blackout, a drunken leap in time. More and
more, they acted like real lovers hungry for each other,
finding each other upstairs at a party, making out in the
closet, clandestinely going to odd gay bars none of their
friends would go to, dancing close to country music, feeling
each other up in the car home. It was as if they grew younger
every week, less able to think clearly on their lives. And they
loved it.

༾

Something changed with winter. They had come one night from the zoo, from a nighttime party for the nocturnal creatures. Margaret had found it a strange place, a zoo that denied itself everything. The old monkey house was boarded over with an informational metal sign denouncing such houses in other zoos, and the elephant cage was just a ruin of bars and chains, a zoo notice proclaiming the freedom of animals. Those animals all lived in zoo habitats now with one another, not caged. They did not know the difference between this habitat and real life—they probably liked it better, said the sign. Margaret kept peeking into those habitats. She couldn't make out anything moving in the frayed darkness.

But they were on their way now to a gay bar to meet his friends, with Pete driving in his nervous way. More than ever before, he smelled of chemicals or of cleaner or of something he could never wash away from his days at the lab. She looked at his hands on the steering wheel, fingers long and smooth and bitten, and thought of the ferryman with the blue rose on his hand, the chapped knuckles and wide, calloused palms. She'd begun to talk to that other man—Todd was his name— in short, embarrassed gaps in their day together as the ferry made its hourly shuttle-throw across the water's wool-blue loom, shouting hellos and "I like your shirt" over the wind's own shouting. The strain in his gray eyes as he tried to hear, the wrinkles around those eyes, made Margaret's body flutter a little. That he would try so hard. So close to each other, working against the wind and engine noise, it had felt like something she should keep secret from Pete. Foolish, she knew. She knew this faggot in her bed was no impediment, but she wanted another secret, one of her own. And Margaret was touched by Todd, by his shy manliness, and her view of him was changing. She had begun to see his gestures before his hands, the smile on his lips before the lips themselves.

Wasn't this a first sign of that great sickness, a relapse of her chronic love?

"Let's go someplace else," she said, staring down the lit streets.

Pete glanced over. "Than the car?"

"Let's skip the bar. Let's go to Al's."

He nodded halfheartedly and went hand over hand on the wheel, crossing his soft giant's hands in the dim light. Al's was a straight bar off near the university, and they had never gone to a true straight bar, the kind with no hip chicks in dark makeup, no bands scheduled to play, no crowds peppered with the odd lesbian or drag queen. Just young men and women off of work, unaware that there were any other kinds of bars. For some reason, Margaret was claiming neutral ground, with her own kind, a place to make him feel foreign. And she was doing this because she wanted it to end. The sinus-pricking chemical smell of him, of his too-soft hands. The way she'd hidden in his body, pulled its harmless cover over her head. The way her heart was silent now.

The bar was lively and quite dark. There were bright tableaux around the well-lit pool tables, but otherwise the place was all wood booths and stools, young professionals and working-class folk sipping their beers from group pitchers, eyeing one another across the darkness. Pete whistled quietly as they entered, began to chuckle.

"You think they'll kill me?" he asked, then grabbed her hand. She felt invaded again. They rarely held hands, but he said, "I'll feel safer. Just keep a hold on my hand and they won't know."

She looked over at him, annoyed. His plain face was sweating from the heat of the room. "They don't care," she said. "You never been in a straight bar? Nobody cares, Pete."

He grinned, a bright thing so high above her head. "Just hold my hand." He wore no glasses that night, and she envied him that he could change so easily.

They sat in their own booth and talked over their own pitcher of thin beer, watching the other couples talk close to each other, holding hands against their chests, earnestly speaking in harsh whispers. The groups of men laughing heartily over some old joke. Margaret searched for another face like hers, another woman here like herself, plain and too smart for boys, but willing to try. Pete was talking on about a fellow at work, but at one point, smiling and blinking his great eyes, he took her arm and said, "Look at this place! Is this how you people act in bars? It's hilarious."

Margaret looked around. "What? This is normal."

"Gay bars are at least for cruising, but this . . . the focus here seems to be *drinking*."

"Well, it is a bar."

He shrugged gaily. "It seems like an awfully unhealthy lifestyle," he said, then laughed at his own joke. She saw his eyes shift over to see her, and she knew this was an act to cheer her. He wasn't as cold to her moods as she thought. Pete touched the place where his glasses should have been and caught himself in the gesture, smiled, returned his hand to his lap. Some loud song began on the jukebox, an old song called "Blame It on My Youth."

Margaret swallowed and said, "I think we really need—"

But all of a sudden he was singing, raising his chin and crooning out the words to her. He sang over her own faltering words, over her doubt. He was louder than doubt, eyes grinning, his singing face half purple in the bar light, half blue, his hands stretched starfishlike out on the table—a mad image for Margaret to see. But her anger passed, and all she could think about was her surprise. Not at what he was singing, or that he was singing to stop her, but that he sang so well. She had never considered that his voice might be this high and clear, trembling heartachingly—who expects these things in friends, in quiet lovers? He was stroking her hand, smiling at her from his pudgy cheeks, letting that voice struggle from him—like the light of a firefly breaking through the cracks of your tight fingers. She saw how beautiful he was. She saw her own beauty.

Pete sang on, pink lips stretched around his voice, and the lyrics, about the painful love young people have, were nonsense. He wasn't saying anything to her but "Let it be for now." It would end so soon, and whom else did they have? That ferryman shouting into the wind? Margaret looked around the bar and saw too clearly how that would go, just as with all her other options here, with all these other men. A prolonged, thrilling seduction. Some weeks of passion. The keen edge of his heart grown dull, his pioneering eyes off again on the horizon. Some soft words, some long lament.

She gripped Pete's hand tight as he sang on. She let the snake within her spine be charmed again, rising from its stiff basket. How could she do better than this? This sweet song, this sad man who was the only one in the whole world who knew that she was beautiful. How could she let this go for a blue rose, for a rough touch? And if you looked at them from across the bar, you would have thought them lovers: a man in his early twenties wooing back the girl of his dreams, a brittle romantic girl in glasses. You would have touched your own lover, pointed, smiled at how that used to feel. You would have been warmed by memory, by the fire crackling in their small booth.

∽

It was in the early spring that, with nothing else changed except the green teeth of buds on February trees, she ran into Pete's old friend Alberto. He was the young man she'd first met at that party long before, the ones whose eyes had told her he'd loved Pete without expectation, without complaint. She ran into him in a neighborhood of used-clothing stores and bookshops, just came up against him on the sidewalk as he steadied her with a hand. He was a short man, Puerto

Rican, with an accent that must have been a put-on, all dressed up in a shiny blue shirt and blazer.

They talked there on the sidewalk for a while, for longer than acquaintances usually talk. He asked her politely if she'd seen Pete lately, and she said not in a week. He said that on a night like this, warm and clear, she should be walking with a beau hand in hand. Where was he? Alberto asked, and she said, "Nowhere. Men don't like smart girls." And Alberto said, "Smart girl, I wish I could tell you what to do, then."

He gave her a look so pitying that she saw he knew. Alberto knew all about her and Pete somehow, and Alberto knew that the one man he loved, rather than use his ready lips, would turn to a woman in glasses. Margaret thought of what a sad thing that was for him to know, and that Alberto's pain was never something she'd considered.

Alberto smiled and looked her up and down. She was in a black wool dress, still ready for a winter that was passing. He said, "Why don't you come with me to a dinner party? Pete's there; it's just a block away. Come on." Alberto cocked his elbow out for her to take—an antique move, and it made Margaret flinch to realize how charming gay men were to women, how effortlessly flirtatious and exciting. It was like a false cognate, like a word too easily misunderstood. She took his arm. They walked up a hill to a house all eaves and withered wisteria coming back alive.

Margaret and Pete's meetings had become more regular in the past months, less a kind of dizzy seizing of whatever moment there was, or a weird solace on nights that felt loneliest, and more a thing to count on. She saw his naked body every Wednesday or Thursday, and if they saw a movie or went to party on the weekend, then that night also. But not necessarily. And other days could be canceled also. Like the love affairs it mimicked, their friendship lost its urgency, but gained in comfort everything it lost, and sex was nicely familiar. If she didn't see him for two weeks, she hardly noticed now because she'd see him soon. Time had caused their rumblings to settle, and she had always wanted this. She had always wanted to know a man would eventually show up again.

So when she appeared at the dinner party, leaned into the doorway with a nervous grin, adjusting her glasses, the look on Pete's face wasn't surprise exactly. It was a little chuckle, an Oh, it's you. And of course, as always, the fidgeting secret.

But he didn't come over and talk with her immediately. She had to make do with Alberto and with a hairless, babylike man named Bob who giggled and giggled. They were all so charming to her, all these kinds of men. But she wouldn't sleep with any of them, really, had they been straight. Only Pete. The unloveliest, there across the room in a wool vest and white shirt, no glasses. So neat tonight, for a party of all young men and this one woman, so swell and unlike himself. Margaret recognized the boy he was talking to, and recognized the look in Pete's eye. The boy was Nick, the one who had been turned off by a kiss, and Pete's eye was all forgetfulness.

When Pete finally walked over to her, just before the roast came out and the host yelled for someone to goddamn help him, he said nothing, but just grinned, holding his wine daintily. So tall, ill-shaped, and awkward. So flushed and full of hope.

"How are you two getting along?" Margaret asked. Alberto was beside her, looking on, and she saw Pete's eyes flicker between the two of them. Wine stained his lips in two thin arcs.

"Great!" Pete said a little drunkenly. He looked down on them, as always, but tonight he wasn't stooping. Pete's chin was up, clean-shaven, and he peered down over it from his great height. Margaret had never really understood how tall he was before.

She snickered, said, "Great? Really, great?"

Pete tottered slightly, stared at Alberto, didn't react. "Are you surprised?" he asked Alberto, but the short man smiled and didn't say a thing.

"Well, it's nice you can be civil," Margaret said, picking up her drink again. For some reason, Pete laughed, and turned boyish and shy again, grinning and whispering how exciting it was to have Nick notice him again. How relieved he was. It had apparently all been a misunderstanding, the whole terrible evening that had made Margaret cry. A thundering piano piece by Mozart began from the speakers and it had to be turned down.

"I think he might . . ." Pete began softly, then stopped. "He said he cares. He said he's sorry. Isn't that the most amazing thing that ever happened? Isn't that silly?"

He was trembling with hope; hope's bird fidgeted helplessly in his breast. He was the one who seemed amazing then; not Nick's fickle loves, but him, Pete. The chemical optimist. Margaret stood there listening to Pete's staccato whisper, watching the curved wine stains of his lips, amazed. She thought about the kiss she'd cried for.

He asked her, "Am I too drunk? Maybe I shouldn't sit next to him."

"No," she said, touching his arm. "Stop worrying." He looked so grateful then.

All during dinner, Pete and Nick sat talking behind their hands, laughing at a joke, pointing at something or someone across the table. There they sat, two men in black and white, their hair shining from the candles, faces pink in the hot air, gesturing gold hands to each other and acting so alive, so taken by this moment. Steam rose from the pink meat on their plates. Margaret could hardly listen to the boy next to her as he explained his line of work, his aspirations, rationalized some clearly foolish choice he'd made. She could just watch the boy she'd known these past months, the laughing boy with a shy finger to his grin, recognizing the gesture before the gesturing hand, the smile on his lips before the lips themselves, gasping quietly with the shock of being in love.

How had it happened? What safer arrangement could she have found, and how had it gone wrong? Had it crept in, tiny as a scorpion in their sheets, growing with each reverie of his, each night awakening with a blot of moonlight on half his face, with each shared bag of popcorn and shared, awkward dance? Or did it wait and pounce this night, full grown? Did it wait for him to shed his glasses, dress in a stiff white collar in gold light? Had it been waiting for that? And what could she have done?

Love works backward in time, like all secrets. It colors memory and first impressions, dull evenings and late sleepless nights. It makes them glow with heat, like coals taken for dead. Margaret thought of the strange events of their first night, the careless evenings after that, the chance kisses, his broken heart, that night he sang so clearly in the bar and she gave up on other possibilities. Another quick draw of breath as she saw how obvious the whole year had been. If she'd told anybody else, they could have warned her. Margaret looked around, scared, but no eyes were on her. She could tell no one, not even now. She had to listen and nod to this dull boy next to her, gasping away at the sight of her lover denying her. As she must have known he would. What did I expect? she asked herself, then caught sight of Alberto quietly eating off the back of his fork. She imagined him lifting his head, greeting her with his bronze eyes, and saying, He'll never love you, either.

Her heart felt like a hot ball of glass, spun by a glassblower, widening its glowing molten form inside her ribs.

Because she knew all too well how it would be from here. Under the table, she crushed her yellow napkin into a ball. Margaret knew how it would be. She knew it from her rapid heartbeat, the panic in her veins. She knew it from the look in Pete's eye when Nick's hand brushed his, from the spot of color in his cheek, from the smile he tried again to hide under a finger. She knew it all. From the fickle blink of Nick's black lashes, from the Mozart playing crazily around them, from the cold air creeping past the window, from the words crawling like smoke from all the chattering men's mouths, from her sudden hungry grief, whose hunger ate up all her memories, ate up her images, her most hidden hope. He was leaving her.

And a leaving without the need for good-byes; that had always been the rule. At the exact moment he had transformed for her eyes, he was gone. The spot of color, that one shy finger. Soon enough, maybe tonight, these two young men would find a room together, and this lovely black-haired Nick would touch the skin she had soothed night after night these months, the body she knew more than anyone did, would smell her skin cream on his skin, her shampoo in his hair— would smell and touch her, in a way, since she felt Pete's body was part of her own now. A sorrowful waxen thing. But Nick would make it vivid again; she never had. That would be soon.

Margaret saw Pete smile at her across the table. She smiled back, thought of his body working furiously against hers in that bed, his face flushed red, and she saw for really the first time how tightly shut his eyes had always been. She'd never thought of what he pictured on those lids, but it was obvious. Never her. Of course not, not ever her. Why would he?

No, no one would ever know. It was impossible to explain, and she was a madwoman recoiling at what she had done to herself. A man not made for loving her, like a merman washed nearby her shore, allowing her to heal him as she stole kisses through the tide. The tide had risen—what could she say? And so she tried to grit her teeth and hold still her wavering eyes. To be in love, and not be loved, that's one thing. But she also had to be silent. She had to quiet her sputtering, broken machine of a life.

So she sat there, hands folded, lips clenched tight as her neighbor talked on. On about his youth, the bad choices of those days, how much wiser he was now. He talked about the caution with which he approached love. He talked about the foolishness of most young people he knew. He laughed at what he'd learned now that he was older. Margaret turned with her stiff face to look at him.

"We aren't old," she said. "We won't be old for a long time. Stop it."

She said it because of Mozart playing. She said it because she pictured a moment far in the future, when this pain would be quite gone and she would remember only gold hands and music, when the clanging beginning in her chest would seem the merest twitter of emotion, when she and Pete would sit together on a bench and laugh. Later, when I'm old, she thought, and heard Mozart's music fiddling gaily in the air. Now she had to grow old. It seemed so far away.

Titipu

⁏⁏

I REMEMBER THE night my mother forgot her lines. No, that's wrong; I don't remember it as my mother at all. I was only a boy of five, and had been caught up in the fiction on the stage, two fingers in my mouth as I leaned back against the window, thinking of her only as Pitti-Sing, a white-faced schoolgirl in Japan. So it's Pitti-Sing I recall, turning to us with such a look of fear. The greasepaint cracking around her eyes, the red pout of her lips during that small-town performance of *The Mikado*. The silence in the room as heavy as her wig. I remember what she said after that, the unlikely words, and all the years that followed them, but I didn't wholly understand she was my mother. Children never grasp great moments when they happen.

Everything beforehand, though, had made it a wonderful night. I wish I knew if it were really memory I was working from, or if I've heard about that night so many times, from so many points of view, that my childish vision has been faceted by others sitting in the crowd. It was never hard, in our town, to hear every detail of an event soon after it had happened, and for years after that. You probably can't imagine so small a town, in fact, planted on a mountain in Canada, a view of a glacial lake and the distant streetlights across the shore. Maybe thirty families, maybe forty, and mail that came only twice a week. I know, because for years I was the postman. Outhouses, chicken coops, wide gardens taking over the meadows, and a dirt road that sometimes fell to avalanche season in February and closed us off for good.

It was the summer that *Skylab* fell, but I don't know if I really saw it. I have a memory of pennies streaking across the sky at night, but that could have been any ordinary meteor shower exciting a five-year-old—the view of the sky was terrific from our mountain.

The summer night of the operetta, though, is clear in my mind. I can see my mother at her amateur theatrical height, red lips on a teacup face. In other performances, as Nora in *A Doll's House* or Helena in *A Midsummer Night's Dream*, she had not pulled off the innocence required, and seemed strained and sunburned from her summer days in the garden with me. But that night, the red grin drew our gaze as if it were a leaping flame or a bright bird caught onstage, not part of the play at all, but something more real, more riveting. When she leaned against her schoolgirl friends, she was the most remarkable of them, trilling in a voice like a startled killdeer: "Three little maids from school are we . . ."

Below, listening attentively despite her old age, sat the piano player, my grandmother, pounding away at her upright all evening before the forgotten speech. You had only to ask her about her daughter up there, and about my home. She had lived in our town for over fifty years by the time I was old enough to remember her. In her youth, she had been a nightclub dancer, but my grandfather found and changed her, bringing her to Canada in 1928 in a passion of Quaker idealism, escaping the port-town squalor of Seattle for a community formed on principles of simplicity, contemplation, and freedom. By the time I came around, she wasn't talking about any of those things anymore. She used to dig in her dahlia

garden with me, telling about the flood of Americans that
came to our town during World War II, fleeing the draft. She
told about the hippies from California building communes of
tepees higher up on the mountain, panicking when the snow
fell deep. She told about the lingering draft dodgers of Viet-
nam, which I probably remembered then but don't now. I do
recall the smile on her face, her white hair tied in braids and
wrapped behind her head, the rusty smell of the earth and the
taste of it.

She laughed at how they came and went, so arrogant with
ideas. The tepees burned to the ground, the American gardens failed, and most went away. But now, of course, they've
all gone, and there is no town or village or anything left.

"For he's going to marry Yum-Yum!" my mother sang
gleefully to us, flapping the arms of her primrose yellow kimono. The chorus bellowed in response, and who didn't feel
a shiver of delight at such foolishness? A small town like ours,
performing for itself? And that Mother would transform so
completely—we laughed freely, all the gentlemen farmers and
dour French Canadians and poor weavers, because we had
fallen too in love with Pitti-Sing to connect her to the tired
woman we'd known. That young woman was gone—the one
whose husband had left from disappointment just that winter.
In her place was this trilling yellow butterfly.

In the second act, she sang along with the Lord High Ex-
ecutioner, a farmer up the road from us named Emery Webb.
He had a thin beard then, but perhaps I'm only remembering
the photographs of his youth, because I think of him now as
a serious man of middle age. I don't mention him because of
his acting, but because he had brought a baby to the theater,
a little girl who sat on a woman's lap and cried periodically.
The baby's name was Solange. Much later, I would learn he'd
fathered Solange with a lesbian, a French Canadian who'd fled
the town in frustrated claustrophobia. He was gay, an acceptable life in our liberal town, and kept the girl for himself

to raise. I would depend on Emery and Solange more and more as I grew older, as people moved away from our town after the mill closed, as I fell in love with Solange. Then, after I married her, I would move up the hill for good.

She was just a baby that night, though, and I was only five, and must have looked on her babbling face with repulsion. I couldn't know how her blue eyes would turn warm and brown, how fickle and lonely she would become, more frightened of life outside this mountain than I would ever be. On her first visit to the closest big town, at four, Solange would watch an old Ford slowly make its way down a street, weaving into the other lane to crash softly into a streetlight. It was a man having a heart attack, but the image would stay with her—this antique car floating helplessly to its doom. She and I would be the last to leave the town.

But there her father was, Emery Webb, shuffling around the stage with his wood ax, too outshone by my mother to do anything but grin meekly under her strident harmony. They knelt beneath a painted cherry tree, pleading for their lives from the Mikado. I clapped and sang along under my breath, somehow knowing it was my mother, but too caught up in her story to understand she wasn't also Pitti-Sing, someone different, happier, more free.

My mother was born in our town, just a meadow away from where I was born. She was used to harsh winters and summers of mosquitoes and splashes in our lake. It never seemed odd to her when a mountain lion ate their only goats, or when the deer nibbled the strawberries to nothing. She could remember when the Quaker schoolhouse my grandfather built burned to the ground, and the first time a yellow bus from the school across the shore came to take them all away. She was a bit too grave a bit too young, and sat by the stove watching for sparks to fly so she could stamp them out. She did well in school, excelled at singing, like my grandmother, and later would sing to me old ballads, the kinds of songs I

would give anything to hear now. She went away to Calgary
to study voice, then came back a year later with a city boy
full of wild ambition about our town. They built the cabin
where I was born—there were bean plants climbing up
wooden poles, a toilet made from a board over a pit, two
goats, angora rabbits in a cage, a high view of the mountains
and the lake. My mother spent her time spinning and milking
and digging, but I don't know where my father was in all of
this. In the five years before he left, I think he just stood
staring glassy-eyed at a world much harder that he'd dreamed
of. The way we all have ideas of how we'd like to be, but must
finally see we're not as brave as we had hoped.

I don't know what my mother thought life was going to
be. I certainly don't long for my father, and I think it's best
he disappeared, but perhaps she stopped being as vigilant as
she had been as a girl, and this once, Mother missed a kind
of spark thrown from the fire. She must have looked around
with new eyes at our tiny cabin, the chores she'd done forever
without minding, the meadow encrusted in snow, the town,
the smallness of solitude among friends.

And then it was time for Ko-Ko to trick the evil Katisha
by singing of a comical dying bird. A little feather floated
down from above, and I laughed with all the other children
in the room, and little Solange cried. Soon, the crowds gathered in bright silk kimonos to celebrate the marriage of
Nanki-Poo and Yum-Yum. Pitti-Sing was a minor character
among them, flinging colored strings into the air—"The
threatened cloud has passed away. . . ." Disaster had been ban-
ished; the town of Titipu had been saved, and Pitti-Sing,
smile bright as a wedding band, walked forward to deliver her
last words. . . .

That was the moment my mother forgot her lines. I'll
never forget how her smile faded, how her eyes under that
wig took on a weird cast, as if she had noticed it was her
crook-backed mother who pounded at the piano, her old

classmates in the audience, thin from winter's hunger, the ones who'd stood beside her as children and watched their schoolhouse burn, never to be rebuilt. My mother opened her mouth, trying for the words. And the wrong ones came out:

"I've waited now so patiently eight long years—for, my Lord, I know miracles don't come every day," she said breathlessly, turning to each of us. "Then this crisis broke over me, and such a certainty filled me: *now* the miraculous event would occur. . . ."

Nora's lines from Ibsen. The amateur actress had reached into the wrong sack of memory and pulled up the Helmer parlor from the fall, its bleak tragedy. The crowd, the town—we didn't titter with embarrassment. I think we understood. We knew that for this one performance in the hundred years of *The Mikado*, Pitti-Sing had broken from her charade of merriment and shown her real face to us—the tense mouth from her lonely schoolgirl's wait for love, the pallor from coming so close to execution, the dead hope for miracles. Even I knew, at five, that Pitti-Sing would never look out from the crowd like this again, crack her white face painfully—"I've waited now so patiently eight long years . . ."—not if I were to see the operetta sung a hundred times, which, despite my constant disappointment, I have.

There is a story I heard from my friend in Calgary who's lived in the South Pacific. He said he knew of a Hindu tribe on a reef-encircled island who watched shadow-puppet plays as their religion. They eagerly laughed and cried at the tales cast by a flaming brazier on the ox-hide screen, tales from the shadow world of a different age, a better age than this, an age when there were still heroes. He said there was one performance when, just as Rama was in the act of defeating the demon-king, something went wrong—the brazier fell and the puppeteer caught on fire. Screams came from behind the screen, shadow Rama began to burn at the moment of his greatness, and the tribe could only watch in horror. Like my town watching Pitti-Sing whisper her sole words of regret, this was the night the tribe witnessed the burning of Rama. And, like my town, no one moved to save the fiery play. It was an ancient tale, you see, of the shadow world, so there was nothing to do. It had all happened so long ago.

When anyone died after the shadow play, each death seemed foretold by that night at the theater. The year felt like a garment with an ever-widening rip. For both the island and my town, some myth about ourselves had come undone.

Somehow, my mother found her way back into the words— "For he's gone and married Yum-Yum!"—and colored strings flew again in the town of Titipu and the marriage went on as it always had. At the curtain call, Pitti-Sing flashed her lacquer smile to the crowd and we applauded, wonderingly, as she gripped hands with Emery Webb and bowed. Within a year, she'd move away and I'd be left with my grandmother, then with Emery Webb and his beautiful daughter, who would see a floating car. My grandmother, she worked away at the chords for all three curtain calls. In a few years, she'd be dead, and I remember a poet's question: If children were to find her bones up there now beside the abandoned meeting house, how could they guess that once they'd danced as quick as foxes?

It's funny how we think the world was born with us, and all the people in it. As that little boy, I believed everyone around me had arrived just as they were, fully formed, and I think they helped me believe that. Grandmother came into life at eighty, stooped over a piano, and Emery Webb appeared for the first time on a walk down my road, holding a baby, and my own mother faded into this world alone with a whole farm and cabin and the knowledge of how to run them. They sometimes mentioned their childhoods, but never once did they reveal what else they could have been if they had chosen differently. They smiled and chucked my chin and acted as if people were inevitably who they were, blooming wherever their seed had fallen. They acted as if I were the only one who could change.

But they betrayed me, all of them, by dying and by losing hope, by falling in love with people I didn't know, by forgetting to plant the spinach in late winter, then carrots the next year, then giving it all up and packing a house to leave.

I can't blame it on that night, or on my mother. But there's nothing else about my youth I recall so clearly as the stage brimming with light, my mother's face as she took a bow. I was standing on my bench toward the rear of the theater, near the window, clapping, grinning at the schoolgirl in the yellow kimono who had broken us for a night.

I heard a tap at the window behind me, and turned, afraid. Nothing but a tree, and above it, full of light in the clear air, I could see a different moon than I'd known: an island circled by a reef of stars.

The Art of Eating

⟡

IT WAS CLEAR to everyone, by that time, that she had stayed
too long. They had all expected, when she moved from Montana, that she would stay with her son only a month or so,
but it was going on three months and she was anxious, worried, and embarrassed at how she couldn't pull the simplest
bits of a life together. At night, before dinner, she would walk
close to the walls so as to take up the smallest-possible amount
of space, crouch over, speak in the tiniest of voices, like a girl
trying to fade into the wallpaper after she has done something
particularly rotten. But she was no good at disappearing. Her
ex-husband (whom she referred to by his surname, Faltenfurst, as if he were a butler) had proclaimed her "as ever-
present as God," which sounded nice unless you had heard it
from his particularly raspy voice box.

Her name was Barbara, but everybody called her Bobbie,
and that was how she was, girlish and informal even at sixty,
even when other sons' mothers were stiffening and turning a
stately grayish pallor, sitting in the corners of their sofas, staring out at dim horizons surely long faded away. That wasn't
Bobbie—you could even say that optimism was her hobby,
her little grand obsession, and I say "hobby" because, al-

though she practiced all its skills, its giggles and maxims and cooings at sunsets, she wasn't very good at it. Her pleasant laugh, her cute hair white as a swimmer's cap, the bounce of her bosom when she ran, all concealed a woman who could never quite believe the things she told other people. Her ex-husband, Faltenfurst, had called her "the Typhoid Mary of joy" because, while Bobbie was able to infect others virulently, she never quite caught it herself.

Which might explain, in some way, how she had come to wake up every morning in a series of cool, bright mornings in Montana and see nothing but the stagnant rhythms of the life she'd always led, the coffee shop whose fresh muffins she depended on, the secondhand bookstore through which she daily searched for (but never found) that childhood version of *I Capture the Castle*, the drear reality of her bank teller's job, which had been covered over by too many cups of coffee, too many office raffles, too many shared secrets with coworkers. It was her hometown, as well, and that meant more than it should have. Her ex-husband, Faltenfurst, had first seen her there, sunbathing on a green summer lawn glittering with sprinkler dew. Her children had been born there. She had been young, beautiful, betrayed, and conquered in that town—she had grown old there—it was impossible to live without it now. But on those three consecutive mornings, those mornings whose sparkling air could not allure her, she had found it possible. She had nothing more to do there, so she called her son in Seattle and said she might need to stay a few days with him and his boyfriend before she found a place. As mentioned before, it was going on three months and everyone silently believed she had stayed too long, even for an aging divorcée recalibrating her life.

Each morning, it was the same conversation in different permutations—her son Alex suggesting one career idea or another from the paper. He was a pleasant young man, thirty by now, all thin arms and blond hair, which was dimming into brown in his adulthood. He called her "Bobbie" and not "Mom," and his main quality was, as her ex-husband, Faltenfurst, had put it, his "unflappability in the face of the flappable," which, again, seemed like a compliment but didn't sound like one.

"Workers needed for delicate city electrical work. Will train," Alex would joke, or "Jazzercise instructor, no experience necessary." He'd turn to her, grinning, as she shook her head. After a while, he came up with only these bizarre jobs, since he'd found she never took the real ones. And then in would come his red-haired boyfriend, Zachary, with some too-elaborate breakfast, something on the theme of "Dawn in Arabia," for example. The job list would be forgotten as Zachary (who, Bobbie remembered, had once called himself "Za-sha-*ray*") went into a telling of some mystical experience.

It was just that, underneath, Bobbie didn't really want a job. She'd thought she did, when she moved here, thought she wanted a new house, a new job, a whole new life, but that wasn't it at all. Didn't they understand? She wasn't young like them. She didn't act sixty, but Bobbie *was* sixty, and that was a time, she thought, to begin to close up parts of your life, like an elaborate resort hotel closing for winter, each room being shuttered one by one, the ballroom locked, the kitchen gas cut off. It wasn't a time for anything new.

And then, one morning during this same frustrating routine, Zachary poked his head through the kitchen door, shaking a whisk, and told a story about a friend of his who shared an old lady's home for free rent, and though Alex quickly dismissed this, Bobbie could not let go of the thought. Sharing a home. She looked at her son, poking at his cumin-scented eggs, saw Zachary humming away in their yellow kitchen. Of course she knew they weren't roommates, her son and Zachary, but only now did she recall what it was like to be in love. No one wanted an old woman with a raw laugh. Time to move on.

✍

The first arrangement was distinctly different from what Bobbie had imagined. The lady at the referral service spoke of the situation as "an incredible find," and she mentioned the "beautiful house" these two old brothers lived in, so Bobbie wasn't entirely surprised to see the columned colonial with its iron lantern hanging above the doorway, the potted dwarf spruces glaring on either side. Bobbie still viewed this whole enterprise with trepidation, although she had presented it to her son and Zachary as a "perfect solution" after touching each man on the arm. She was prone to this arm-touching, was an arm-toucher from way back, and found it a useful accent on phrases like "Why, you devil!" and "I've been meaning to tell you" and "I'm sorry about your loss." One could even say that arm-touching was Bobbie Lake's signature. It would not serve her well that afternoon.

Things went badly from the moment the door creaked open. A prim fortyish woman with a silk bow tie stood there, her hair glistening with hair spray, and she invited Bobbie in with an English accent that sounded posh in America but in Britain would probably come across as common. Her name was Rita and she was the housekeeper, but her duties did not include taking care of the Mercatizer Brothers, so that was why they had called the service. Rita explained why all the doors were closed, all the shades severely drawn, claiming she ran things in a "European manner."

In the study sat the Mercatizer Brothers. If one was older and another younger, Bobbie could not have told you. Both men had the same white fuzz of hair and powdery skin, the same tilt to their heads, the same blue velvet ties against black suits. The only distinguishing feature was that one man (Bernard, it turned out) wore sunglasses. Bernard, Rita explained, was blind.

"So you must remember!" Rita admonished, glancing at Bobbie's hand near a wooden sparrow on a side table. "No object in this house can be moved from its position."

"I understand," Bobbie said merrily, touching Rita's arm. The housekeeper recoiled and looked at Bobbie as if she were insane.

The seeing brother said nothing, but merely stared at Bobbie's chest. Blind Bernard loudly explained that his brother, Frederick, could see but had dementia, so there were rules regarding him as well. Bobbie was seated in a low rocking chair as Rita hovered above her, and Bernard listed the rules on his sensitive fingertips:

"Can't cook certain dishes. Reminds him of terrible parts of his life. So no bouillabaisse. Too resonant of a summer in Nice and a . . . a ravishing beauty . . . plus, no cilantro, due to a famous trip to Bolivia and . . . and no chili peppers," he finished, raising his white chin. "That is for me. I despise anything spicy or"—and he spoke the next word with distaste—"*tangy.*"

Bobbie stayed for the hour or so they wanted for the tour, for more rules, for a confusing moment when Frederick lagged behind them and was lost into an antelibrary. She stayed, thanked them, made vague promises, and then, as the three waved feebly and morbidly from under the hanging lantern, sped off in the car, feeling quite relieved she had never had money like that, had never met people like that, and never would again.

∽

"I felt like that woman in *Rebecca,*" she told her son over bowls of something called cioppino.

"Jane Eyre?" Alex asked. "You mean Jane Eyre?"

"No. That woman in *Rebecca.* The movie, where she's moving into this mansion—"

Zachary chimed in as he brought a bowl of meticulously chopped red pepper: "The second Mrs. de Winter. We never hear her first name. Joan Fontaine, lovely."

Alex leaned in over the seafood broth, oil floating in it like gleaming islands. He put his hand on her arm, that inherited gesture, and said, "Maybe the next one."

Bobbie regarded his smile as the steam clouded over her glasses. Not: You can stay longer. It was: Maybe the next one. Part of her, she realized, had hoped this failure of the home-share would be the end of things. The end of her search. She realized her own sad hope that Alex would arrange things, as he always had. That her life would appear behind a door for her like a surprise party. Of course, of course that wouldn't happen.

Later that afternoon, Bobbie came around a corner, to see her son sitting in the middle of the living room, in a chair, his gold head erect. Around him walked Zachary, spreading his arms in circles. His red-haired lover was "cleaning his aura," he explained, and at that moment, Bobbie felt so touched and sad. The man mystically encircling her boy. Her son didn't believe in this, she knew. It was so moving to see how he allowed his lover to go through all this ritual, eyes closed, a smile on his face, all just to please Zachary. And Bobbie knew he would never have sat so still for her.

◈

Her optimism had certainly died away by the second interview. Bobbie didn't let on, of course, insisting to her son and Zachary that this was "the one," even though she dreaded staring up at another Dickensian situation. But it was all she knew how to do. It seemed ridiculous, she knew, to act so full of hope at her age, to be searching out the quick-money schemes, to be willing to save up money at a bad job for ease in the future. Ridiculous, because, as she knew only too well, there was more past to her than future. But Bobbie never spoke of the past. As with her sniping mother, and her stiff father, she cut out the past like articles from a newspaper, leaving her with palatable bits and squares of nothing. And so that dewy morning decades ago when she had lain sunbathing beside her house, that evening in Philadelphia when she had been drawn to another man, that hour she'd spent in the armchair after her ex-husband, Faltenfurst, left the house for good, they all went untold, and hardened in her mind like crystal things.

She was surprised, therefore, when the house turned out to be a modest yellow place with eaves straining out toward an unkempt garden, a wildly blooming dahlia bed. Autumn had fully settled on Seattle and, unlike Montana, where the trees rusted and dropped their leaves within a week, whole maples and tulip trees were clinging to chemical-colored leaves. Bobbie could see various old iron chairs on the porch beginning to flake their paint, and, around the corner of the building, a small carriage house with a roof patched in different colors.

The man answering the door was no older than Bobbie herself, but formal, dressed in a business suit and wearing a gold wristwatch he checked periodically throughout the interview. The room they talked in was bright from the unusual fall sunlight, and the man kept squinting as he talked, making him seem to smile, although he wasn't. There was something, Bobbie felt, terribly sad going on that he wasn't mentioning. She couldn't find it anywhere yet—not in the colored maps on the walls, the neat bookcases full of books in plastic library sleeves, the porcelain side lamps done as caricatured mandarins, not in the glimpses of other rooms, the dining room table covered with blue felt, the corner of an aged green cupboard with one cracked teacup hanging from a hook; nothing gave away the inhabitant. And that was perhaps because this man was not the inhabitant—he was finding a caretaker for his father.

He explained that his father had lost his wife two years before and since then had been unable to live the way he used to. He needed supervision, a few meals, sometimes attention to his medicines, but little else. She could live here in the house, if she liked, or maybe in the studio out back. The dead wife had made jewelry back there until her hands stopped working properly. Bobbie got the sense, during this exposition, that the wife was not Tom's mother. That she was a woman he hardly knew at all.

But it sounded good to Bobbie. The house, even down to the strange Chinese lamps, had the feeling of something that had been waiting for her, the way a good book waits for you on the shelf of a bookstore, or how a bottle of wine bides in a restaurant's cellar. She believed in little, but she believed in this: that the important objects in her life—not the people, but the objects—were scattered carefully through the world, awaiting her use. Arranged, placed to be tools in her life. She stared in the corner at an upright piano. Who knew? It could be that one particular key was trembling already, waiting for her to touch its dusty ivory.

"So what do you think of her?" It was a raspy voice, coming from an old man standing now beside the sliding door to the dining room. Like his house, his body revealed so little about him. Unlike the testy Mercatizer Brothers, there was nothing extreme in his old age, no palsied hand or crazed wisps of hair. A long rectangular face punctuated by three dark dots: his two eyes, and the tender gape of his mouth, the kind of man her ex-husband, Faltenfurst, would call "too old to live, too rich to die." He wore a black suit and a maroon turtleneck, and when Bobbie saw the look his son gave him, she thought maybe the old man had dressed up just for her, taken out his clothes from when he was sixty-five, when he wore these things to parties. He wanted to impress a woman.

"Are you a terror, Mrs. Lake?" he asked her straight-out, and she laughed. "Are you going to terrorize me? No," he said, leaning his chin into the folds of his neck as she kept laughing. "No, you're too young, aren't you? Maybe better that you watch out for me."

She moved in the next weekend, into the dead wife's jewelry cottage, which was still cluttered with toolboxes of glittering beads, glossy wires, and ceramic moons. Alex and Zachary moved all of it to the basement, according to Tom's instructions, and after it was gone, Bobbie stood in the small room and despised her own selfishness, her inability to live with someone else's things around. And later, when the boys left, when Zachary had tied some kind of shining bauble above her doorway "to keep in golden energy," when her son walked forward, eyes low, and kissed her, whispering that she could call anytime, she knew she couldn't. She knew that when they left, their lives would be a tiny bit happier without her. That much of life, she knew.

And what about her? Was she perhaps an ounce lighter now, standing in a low-ceilinged garage with a cement floor, its casement windows showing a yellow quarter circle of leaves? The boys had left, and Tom had left, and Bobbie felt if she stood very silently, she would hear the old man breathing from across the yard. The tentative heartbeat, the scraping lungs. She held her breath and listened.

✍

"You know, I don't really need you here for anything," James Hilary told her immediately over dinner.

It was the second night, and she'd come into the house to check on him, really unsure of what this job was, how often she could leave, what was expected of her. Was she a surrogate daughter, neurotically attending to a father who ignored her? Or a nurse, coolly confronting all his moods with a condescending stare? What was the role Tom was paying her to play? When she entered the house, she found the old man sitting in the library, wearing earphones. He was in an old

Danish leather chair, and he was dressed as formally as before, in a neat blue shirt his son must have bought him. The family obviously had endless money. James Hilary removed the earphones without moving his head, rotated his eyes to her, and said she should come to dinner. The maid would be cooking chicken in a banana leaf.

And all day, Bobbie had considered that banana leaf and whether she could take it. People eating leaves? Where in the world did people eat leaves—weren't bananas enough?

She'd come to dinner in her Bobbiewear, her tights and a long pink sweatshirt sporting a cat with two rhinestone eyes, only to find James Hilary feebly adjusting a bright bow tie in his seat. The table was small but extendable, and she could see multiple leaves leaning in the corner. What kind of life needed so long a table? What was his life now that the table was shrunk to nothing? The walls of the room were deep green, and from the ceiling hung foreign plants and empty birdcages. And there was James Hilary in the middle, sitting in candlelight, and that seemed the strangest thing of all. A six-armed silver holder flared before him and he stared into the flames, one finger in the air, as if he were trying to touch the wax. The gesture of a little boy alone with fire. But the candles—it made Bobbie want to leave. She was not paid enough for decrepit lechery.

That's when he turned to her, his bronze-lit face loosening like an unclenched hand. That's when he told her he didn't really need her there.

He went on quietly: "I have a doctor who comes. I don't need you to read to me, because . . . I have books on tape. My wife recorded herself reading books. It was charity work, and now I listen to them. I am reading *The Magic Mountain*. Have you read it?" Again, he only moved his eyes. Bobbie suddenly felt very tired of strangers.

"Yes, a long time ago," she said, misremembering a book with a similar title.

James Hilary did not think this unlikely at all. "It seems to go on a bit, don't you think? Or maybe it's just the way my wife reads it. Tom hired you to eat with me. Did he tell you?" "He didn't . . . not specifically. . . . Is that the maid? What's her name?"

An older woman, thin, with a sun-creased face, was walking toward them with a look that indicated she was thinking about something else entirely, something pressing, which she couldn't dash from her mind. She carried two large white bowls high in the air, one on either side of her head.

He said, "Olga made this herself. She was with me on Java, and she learned this. Do you see?"

The bowl that was placed before Bobbie had a slick green leafy bundle in it, and her stomach wadded up like newspaper.

"I think you'll like it," he said, and his face was tense again, eager. Bobbie unfolded one of the leaves with her fork, looking over at James Hilary's plate and noticing he had nothing but soup.

"You're not having leaves, too?" she asked.

He let his spoon rest in his soup, where she watched it slowly sink. "I can't eat it. I can't eat anything but this, this kind of thing. There is . . . maybe you can hear it," he said, putting both hands around his throat like a delicate choke-hold. "Something wrong with my esophagus. Let's not discuss it while you're eating. Try it. Tell me what it's like."

Bobbie smiled and politely took a bite under his watchful eyes.

"Is it sweet?" he asked her. "Does it taste earthy and sweet?"

She said it did. Bobbie said it was all the things he asked of her, and, like the book that she had misremembered, she lied and told him everything he wanted to hear. She watched his eyes close, his hands lift together under his chin, his nostrils flare with memory. Perhaps saliva even ached in his mouth, not tasting, not smelling, but just thinking of what she said. Bobbie praised the banana-leaf chicken because she had been raised this way, and because she realized quickly that this was James Hilary's old vice. Bobbie watched his faltering lower lip, a dark peek at the failed mechanism of his tongue. She knew him, the kind of man she'd never understood: the reckless hedonist, the confident young man with flashing eyes, the kind of boy she'd envied as a shy girl. But those boys always faded away, did themselves in too soon, and here was what they became if they survived: weak. Senses gone, suddenly helpless. Suddenly, finally, dependent on the shy palate of someone like her. Imagine that—someone like *her*.

"It's wonderful," she said between dry mouthfuls, shuddering at the odd bitterness of the leaves. Never had she tasted anything like this.

His fingers shook in the air over his bowl. "It's made—you see, I taught her—it's made by squeezing grapefruit, and marinating the chicken, and not just grapefruit, you see . . ."

It was so dreamlike and dim an evening, and Bobbie, smiling her bright lipstick smile, felt a clouded pleasure as he talked on, wondered how she had come to this, tasting the food of a man without a tongue, lying about her own senses. Had she come so far from Montana for this, given up everything and a hometown to lose herself in the steam of banana leaves, grapefruit, cumin seeds toasted and then ground?

". . . and of course it should be served with salek fruit, but there's none of that here. In Java, we had a grove of salek. They look like snakes, and taste like apples, and in the rainy season . . ."

He talked on about that time, and the salek fruit, and Bobbie closed her eyes to listen, turning the raw flavor of leaves over in her mouth, trying not to guess at what a salek fruit would taste like, part snake and apple, but smiled at the pain of her fading self, growing into a tongue for this old man, and at his story of women in checkered sashes with ornamental fruit piled on their heads, walking slowly toward a temple where smoke rose in a spreading cloud, all while he, a young man, sat in sandals on the dirt, ate a salek fruit, and thought of his recklessly broken heart.

∞

Alex wasn't pleased by this at all.

"You're a food taster?"

"No . . . no, well, it's complicated," Bobbie said. She was over at their house for dinner again, and everything, even in these few days, seemed to have changed without her. The guest room was a library again, full of shelves and comfy chairs with afghans, every trace of her wiped away. She no longer belonged here. Had she given up belonging when she'd moved away? Was that what it meant to have left home so late in life?

On the table was a glass dish of lasagna, geometrically sliced, with three square pieces missing. Bobbie had asked for lasagna before she came; she also asked, "Do it normal, please."

"I think he's lonely and he misses his wife," she said. She wore a turtleneck and a cardigan—it was getting colder—and a gold mouse on a chain around her neck. Her ex-husband, Faltenfurst, always called that mouse "your horrifically gilded rodent," and though she didn't really like it, even now Bobbie wore it to spite him. "I think they used to go out to eat a lot, and I think he used to cook her food all the time."

Zachary licked his lips, holding his fork straight up, his red eyebrows raised. "I like him. A sentimental old fool. Cooking is always for love, you know. Always."

Alex touched his arm. "Cafeterias? Mess halls? And you wouldn't say that if you'd tasted my dad's pancakes. Made with hate."

Bobbie took a bite, smiled at the familiarity. She swallowed and said, "It's all right, except . . . you see . . . he is a little disturbing. It is a little creepy. It's sexual."

"Bobbie!" Alex shouted.

She shrugged, dug herself another piece of lasagna. "That's all I'm saying. Maybe after this month, I'll leave. That's all I'm saying."

∽

Bobbie felt entirely justified in her theories when James Hilary, via a note on her door in womanly script, invited her to eat out. "My one vice," he called it, and this angered her. But how could she not agree? He met her at her cottage in a tuxedo, walked with her to the car. She wore her mouse and a thin cotton dress that made her shiver. Bobbie took the wheel, silently cursing this whole arrangement, wondering what other ridiculous outings he could engineer to take her over, what new ways he could find to buy his faded senses back. It was too much; so many years tied down to people, years in marriages and children, that old dreary town, her teller's window. It would never end. She saw all people as kinds of people, and she was the kind who couldn't drift too freely, and the kind who couldn't change. So her face blushed with petty anger, and she consciously chose a radio station too jangling for his old ears. Bobbie drove him to the restaurant, furiously blinking at mascara flakes falling into her eyes, singing along coarsely to songs she didn't really know.

James Hilary sat stooped beside her in her Honda, dressed in his dusty tuxedo, saying, for once, nothing at all.

Bobbie stayed cool in the restaurant, a place of varnished air, soft, pillowed sound; glinting with clinking glasses, high fiery chandeliers. She tried not to act impressed, and when it came time to order, she valiantly chose something simple, something James Hilary couldn't have her describe too exotically, and although she knew she'd miss the stories this would bring from him, she couldn't bear to taste the things she saw on the menu: fig ravioli, celery root napoleon, coulis and confits and *escabeches*. Never had she felt more illiterate, more like a second grader in a classroom, asked by the waiter to call out the words on her menu and finding them mere blobs of ink. Bobbie imagined the clinking glasses to be the tittering of brighter students. A steak? she asked, shining with worry, turning her face to the waiter. Could she have a steak? To her relief, it was easily arranged.

James Hilary poked one crooked finger into the air. "Do you have preserved lemons?" he asked, leaning sideways toward the waiter in expectation. Much sorrow, there were none of these in the kitchen. James Hilary dropped the finger, *hmm*'d, and raised it again. "You have lamb chops here in peppercorns. . . . Is it possible? I wonder," he said, as if it were a scientific proposition, "I wonder if it's possible to finish them in a different way? You see, it's a favorite of mine. My wife cooked it this way, I think it's called marches style. At the end, you take a beaten mixture of lemon juice and egg yolks. . . ."

Bobbie was amazed to see how easily the old man talked the waiter into this. It was like watching her ex-husband, Faltenfurst, talking a salesman into free delivery; some people could do this. Bobbie would never have imagined such a way of living, asking more than you were offered.

"It's too bad about the preserved lemons," James Hilary commented, hand on chin, gazing around the room after the waiter left. "They're quite extraordinary, and really very simple. Of course, it isn't something you can whip up. It takes about a month," and on he went, telling of how to quarter the lemons, how to salt them and lay them in a bowl, cover them with a heavy plate and stir daily until a month passed by, remove them to a mason jar, but Bobbie was hardly listening. She was watching two young men her son's age, a brunette and a coppery blond on a date, glancing shyly at each other over some shared pot of stew. She would give nothing to have that again. Everything unknown. Everything worth doubting.

She could feel a draft coming around the corner. She wished for someone to touch her shoulder and speak of familiar things.

Bobbie was relieved, when the meal came, that her steak was a mere steak. But James Hilary, presented with his designer lamb chops done in the marches style he had requested, glittering with the layer of raw egg and lemon, stared hopelessly at his plate. Bobbie tore at her filet vehemently, repressing a wish for steak sauce, and watched his nostrils widen as curiously as a rabbit's, anxiously sniffing the air above his food. He closed his eyes and smiled.

"Isn't it okay?" she asked, finding her mouse dangling into her plate like the hungry, "horrifically gilded rodent" that it was.

James Hilary looked up and said nothing.

"Did you want my steak? Oh, I guess you can't have it. But you can eat lamb?"

He shook his head and looked back down at his plate. The clatter of knives and jewelry around them seemed to rise and she saw again his odd mania.

"Why did you order it?" Bobbie asked, adding bravely, "I won't eat it for you. I have my own meal."

But he talked her into a bite of it somehow, a slice of that raw dish she couldn't even bear to look at. He used the same soothing tone as with the waiter, making it seem like she'd be glad if she did. That it wasn't for him at all. And really, in Bobbie's mind, it wasn't; the first bite came only from a sudden curiosity. Why did he love this? What memory was so intensely conjured by this strange dish that he would order it without the possibility of eating it? She watched his eyes blink darkly, flecked with desperation, like a child waiting to hear a beloved story, and she thought of how humiliating it must be. To be thought of as a child. After his life, as she saw it, of risks, and various passions, and many things tasted, to savor now nothing more exotic than water. How humiliating to wait anxiously for the tip of some crass woman's tongue.

Bobbie took the bite he cut for her and tried to ignore the slippery coating of the meat, the lemon pinch inside her cheek, the rush of her saliva. She tried to picture someone making this for her, in a concrete house on Java, the smell of temple smoke coming through the screens and two small glasses of rare port before her.

"It was during World War Two I went there first, I think I told you. Then years later, twenty years later, the company sent me back, and it was such a relief. . . ."

It was a unique taste, the lamb, and all the food he would feed her in their later dinners, each a piece of his memory. At the table that night, Bobbie knew James Hilary wouldn't have eaten the lamb even if he could have. It would have spoiled things. He had a fantasy so pure, it reached even this woman in her black cotton dress, in her careless life.

". . . and my wife—you should have met her—would take a green mango . . ."

His dead wife must have eaten like this for him. Bobbie saw that. She must have eaten the food he loved and told him what it was like, must have sat hour after hour in that library streaked with rainy-day light and read every book into a tape recorder. Hour after hour, with her soft heart failing. She must have known for a long time that she was dying, and she prepared so well for his life after her, like a mother packing food into the fridge before her trip. What a child he was to her. She'd filled his life with so many voices, he might never know he'd lost her.

". . . and jackfruit, you can make it taste almost like meat, in coconut milk, you can trick even the cleverest British palate that way, as my wife did with an ambassador. . . ."

૭∕ળ

Perhaps he really was a bore, but not to Bobbie. Not anymore, not with the days growing noticeably darker in a town
she hardly knew at all, not with her son falling back into his
life without her, quarreling with Zachary in their bed, no
longer worrying about his mother in the other room, not with
rust leaves sparrowing outside her cold carriage house. Here
was a man who depended on her for his very life; the kind of
man who'd always ignored her, asked her to count his change
at the bank, print his account, wait for him at a malt shop
where he'd never arrive. Now Bobbie was essential to living.
So she listened to his stories, ate the food he ordered in restaurants, and told him what it was like, first lying and proclaiming all the intricacies of some flavor she could barely
make out on her tongue, and later revealing what she hated,
what she didn't understand, and in the end, like him, growing
to prefer the simplest foods done perfectly. She even grew to
like the awful marches style.

She drank his brandy. She tried his rare cigars and
coughed, laughing, holding the awful thing from her body as
James Hilary hid a creaking guffaw under his pallid fingertips.
Bobbie was willing, at dinner, to accept three different desserts as long as she only had to take a bite of each—apparently, it didn't matter to him, the cost, which was something
she couldn't understand. She knew her body was being
bought. She knew that all the time. But Bobbie didn't care at
last, because she'd thought her body too old for wanting. And
here some wrecked old fellow had found parts of her still alive
enough, still young enough to please him. She did want to
please him. She couldn't explain him to her son, this man
she'd rejected as a lecher and a rich voyeur of senses. He was
nothing like a lover, but what he gave her was a lover's belated
present.

There was a night, one of their last, when, after a dull
evening at a ballet with far too few intermissions, they were

eating in a French restaurant near closing time, and, in a sleepy way, James Hilary asked her about her ex-husband. "Oh that!" she said. "That that, oh no." She laughed and kept on eating her ruby duck, but he insisted. He spoke these days with a clatter in his throat, like sticks being shaken, and words fell slowly, cracked brown leaves.

Bobbie held her mouse in one hand and touched his arm with the other. In a fast and quiet way, she told him. She talked about that first afternoon when she lay sunbathing in the backyard in the grass, in the sprinkler dew, when he had walked around the corner in his suit and hat, a man come to see her father about a job. She recalled her swimsuit—one-piece, bold red chevrons—and how thin she was. She recalled his long face and dark eyebrows, the confident smirk on his tan face. His outstretched hand to help her to her feet, his eyes on her young body glinting with water. She told him about the small blackened cabin they lived in for so many years, his father with the ancient Model A clattering around the corner, the way she cleaned the house three times a day to convince herself they weren't poor, the importance of having forks that all matched. She told him about Falten-furst's hateful tongue, and of the other women, and all the things Bobbie knew were true but still could not entirely believe. And most of all, most of what she told him about, was the food she made for him.

Meat loaf wrapped in bacon, baked yams and melted butter, peppery instant rice, salmon croquettes she sprinkled with thyme, roasted chicken stuffed with a lemon, spaghetti loaded with ground beef, boxed mac and cheese, boxed flaked potatoes, frozen broccoli, and all the butter she could give him, butter in the frying pans and in the pound cakes, pats and sticks and pounds over all those years. She listed meals she'd made on significant days, nights he hadn't come home, noon lunches when he kissed her recklessly in the doorway, whole menus of holidays and children's birthday parties—beef Burgundy on the night Alex came out to them, chicken piccata on the night her husband left, leftover pasta she ate in that armchair all alone. It was astounding. How had she remembered it all? She hadn't made an effort—how had every dish remained so indelible after all conversations and glances had faded? The heavy iron detail of her memory was too great at last that night for Bobbie. She covered her face with her hands. She must have cried loudly under those palms. Salt was on her tongue.

When she was done, James Hilary had nothing to say. He touched his own lips and was quiet. Bobbie sniffed through his silence, knowing his wife still talked to him in books. And any pain of their life together was too long ago to be remembered now.

Later, as he was paying the bill, his crippled voice talked calmly about itself. His throat cracking like a broken branch, the burnt, useless flap of his epiglottis. He looked much older than she remembered, a pile of leaves heaped across the table, and he talked about his death, which he knew was coming soon, and it was a subject more pertinent to him now than his life, those stories he had told her of green mangoes and lemons preserved in salt. At the word *salt*, he winced. James Hilary said he thought all the time at night about how it would be fine not to wake up, to die alone like that. He said he thought that would be fine. "Enough" is how he put it. He always said that, Bobbie realized now, about a time in his past, or a night they'd had together, as if "enough" were a good thing.

Waiters were putting chairs on tables, turning out the small lamps at the bar. Bobbie looked over and saw James Hilary had already fallen asleep.

It wasn't until she went to her son's house again for dinner that she saw what a comical creature she had become.

Over lentil meat loaf, Zachary shook his head, saying, "Bobbie, you're always so . . . you're always so easily swayed. We've been thinking. Maybe you should move back in with us. Maybe you need to move back in with us."

"Look for a job," Alex said. He touched her arm, and she realized what a false move this always was. "You wanted to be independent . . . is that what this is? Do you feel independent with this guy? I know he's rich, but I want you to have your own life."

She dropped her napkin and their dog skittered across the floor to grab it. No one made a move to stop him, so he curled near Bobbie's feet and licked away. Bobbie said, "I like him, though. He's not terrible. He's very lonely."

Alex said, "Maybe you are, too. We're not trying to be critical of you. We love you."

It was true. She was ridiculous. She knew her son had talked about her to his friends at parties, held his head in his hands and made her situation into a funny story for another dinner table, fancier food than meat loaf, good-looking men in cuff links laughing at this fat old mother and her brandy, her cigars, her preposterously high-tone meals. She, in rhinestones and sneakers, blue eye shadow and a too-harsh permanent, sixty and still giggling like a girl, a kept woman. She closed her eyes and tried to shake the image of those men laughing in the candlelight. Each person broke your heart so uniquely.

"I'll just do it a little longer. I've been looking in the paper," she lied, convinced by them so quickly, the way James Hilary had talked her into a bite of lamb. "I've been seeing some jobs I'd like. Just a little longer," she pleaded, as if those suspicious faces had any say in her life.

༄

But quickly things were solved for everyone. Not much later, as Bobbie lay sleeping in her jeweler's shop, Olga took a late tour around the main house and found James Hilary sitting upright in his bed, hands around his throat, silently choking. A white face beautiful in the dark room, his tongue purple and extended, all of it perfectly quiet and still. Bobbie heard only the shouting, the racing ambulance. By the time she was outside, it was all over, the smell of smoke drifting in the autumn night air, the door open and fiery orange with light, and Olga weeping on the stairs in her thin batik robe.

James Hilary left the hospital to live with Tom in their house, with a nurse keeping a stern, vigilant watch, and a tube put through his neck into his throat, bypassing his rotten mouth and collapsed senses. Nothing would ever touch his tongue again. He was under orders not even to speak.

There was no need for Olga anymore, and less for Bobbie. She had to pack up her bed, her chest of drawers, her few books and clothes again. Alex and Zachary helped her to move back into their guest room, converted once more from a library. Within a month, James Hilary's house was sold. It all happened quickly, quietly, and she and her son decided this was providence after all, that her life had been handed back for her to start again.

∽

There was a day, four months later, when Bobbie stood in the kitchen of her new apartment. It was small, smaller even than anything Alex had lived in during his years of eastern colleges. The kitchen was just six squares of tile in the same room. She had a job as a bank teller again, with the same bank as in Montana. She saw Alex and his lover once a week, usually on Sundays, when Zachary, now out of his elaborate cooking phase, produced something humble and comforting for the winter.

It was a sunny day, a Saturday morning, and the finger-prints on her windows glowed like living things. She was drinking a cup of coffee, and she realized James Hilary must be dead.

It was a mathematical thought, not a revelatory one. She had been told by Tom how long his father had to live, and that allotted time had passed, and so the old man must be dead. She was only a little surprised that nobody had called her. That old James Hilary, propped up in his bed, a tube taped to his throat, had not written on a pad of paper that she be called. But it didn't matter. There probably had been no pad of paper. Just earphones on his tired ears, playing the voice of his wife at seventy, reading *Middlemarch* until he fell asleep. And after everything he told her, Bobbie thought, he probably hadn't died alone. She would never know.

Above the sink, in front of the window, sat a mason jar of murky water catching the light, and in it, bent like quarter-moons, a dozen lemons preserved in the brine. They glowed in the sunlight. Bobbie fished one out and put it on the counter. She cut a piece of glossy rind and put it on her tongue—oh, the pinpricked corners of her mouth, the knife slash of flavor. What could she say? Whom could she tell? Who would listen to a teary old woman's word? That it was sour, so sour. That it cut her like a thing you can't forgive.

The Walker

∽

A SQUARE INCH of her would feed the city for a week. Not
literally feed—he's thinking of the price of food. He's judging
the wealth in that square inch, the subtle, priceless black fabric, the imported underthings, the soft, massaged skin, the
arteries already plump with that expensive meal—she had the
pork and figs; he had the rabbit—add a few drops of the wine
("Let's make tonight a little special," she'd whispered), and
he can almost see her freeze into a block of solid gold. A
square inch of that, and light the city; watch it shine. She's
fifty or so, lovely and thin, smiling nervously over the black
gauze of her wrap because they're late. He's still dreaming,
though, about that square inch—about how she's been
wealthy for so long, she doesn't know what it means; she
thinks she's thrifty, and normal, but look at how even her
eyes are richly cared for, glimmering, searching him for a sign
he's going to hurry.

Furman bustles beside her and holds out his left arm for
her to take. He can feel her getting up the nerve to enjoy
this, how she straightens her back as they approach the
crowds of her acquaintances in their gold-and-white-and-
black, how she starts to la-la a little Puccini to make herself

feel comfortable. It's the first time she's been to the opera since her husband left her. Her hair is white, piled high and sprayed firm, light catching fire on the surface, and her face is long, with small eyes and almost epicanthic folds. This is a hard moment for her. Furman puts his hand over her arm, patting her gently, and Mary Babb looks quickly up at him. She exhales loudly and gives a little laugh. Furman walks her grandly into the opera house of Greenville, South Carolina. He does it perfectly; he has been walking women into rooms for nearly three decades now.

When he first came onto the stage at a debutante cotillion, at fifteen, he stumbled as he stood next to his date, blinked into the spotlights. Later, as he escorted more young women, he learned to stand a little behind them, smile only faintly, let the attention fall on the girls. His mother taught him this; it's how he acts tonight. It's how he brought his wife into this very room six months before she died.

The crowd stirs a little, water lilies floating from the prow of a boat, and faces turn to see Mary Babb and who she's come with. "Furman!" some of the men shout heartily, and he gives sharp waves to them. He tries to remember sport scores and stories of the week, because that will help. If not, he'll simply grin and listen over a cigar. Yes, a cigar will give him something to do. An overly made-up young woman takes his tickets as Mary Babb moves past him into the crowd, laughing as she's carefully hugged and kissed—she's back. The ticket taker stares at Furman and he gives her the flint spark of a grin.

Like Mary Babb, Furman doesn't see himself too clearly, even in his mid-forties. Furman doesn't know that he's more handsome than the other men in the opera house; he has never really known this about himself. As with Mary Babb and her money, it's something he's had for so long that it's invisible to him; he misunderstands why women gather near him, thinks they laugh because he's witty, nod because he's wise. Of course he wouldn't know—how could he have read the dozens of secret letters women, even married women, wrote to him and never mailed? How could he know that it's different with other men, that salesclerks don't blush at them, and women don't smile on the street? He is handsome so effortlessly—you couldn't dress him wrong; you couldn't catch him too early in the morning; you couldn't wreck his looks without a knife.

That's why the ticket taker stares, and why he automatically grins. If you ask him later, he will not remember anything about the girl. This kind of moment happened with his wife and made her fall in love with him.

She saw him at a tea dance at the college. She was nineteen years old; he was eighteen. She was giggling with some friends under the bell tower, the autumn air gray and marked with geese over the lake, and Furman walked by with a girl whose name nobody could tell you now. He looked across the lawn at the young woman in organza who would be his wife; she bravely held his gaze. She loved him first, and they both always felt it through their marriage, that it was she who longed for him when they were young.

Time will desert him, of course. Later than most other men his age, but eventually, his handsome grin will cloud into something merely charming on an old man. The gray eyes will unravel, the straight nose bend. He will lie in a hospital bed, hair white as dandelion fluff, holding his sister's hand. She will be old, too, distracted, tired. Out of nowhere, she will say, "It's a shame about time," and he will think she's talking about him.

But tonight, the women approach as always, even with the bell sounding in the open lobby, coming like church doves falling on scattered seed. He knows them all, of course, and waves and grins his Southern-boy grin but gives his arm to Mary Babb, who's looking overcome now, worried. He takes her upstairs, where they all are headed, up to the second-tier lounge, where she talks quickly with a waiter, then to her box. A goateed man is sitting in the little anteroom, head in hand below the mirror, and Furman parts the red curtain for Mary Babb to find her seats. She has had these seats for thirty years, and for two years they've been empty. Everyone has found this a pity—it takes decades to earn such perfect seats, off center, back from the edge. She kept them; she must have known she would be back.

Past the curtain, all the theater is full and buzzing, the orchestra seating and three tiers of balconies—a great wild reef of plaster and velvet set before the open air, people moving colorfully within, little live corals waving in the wash of tides.

"It's a wonderful production—you've never seen it before?"

He wonders if he should pretend to have seen the opera but not the production, and he begins to say, "I really love . . ." before he realizes he has no idea how to pronounce the title of the opera, whether it is Turan-*doh* or Turan-*dot*. Surely not Turan-*dot*, he thinks, and yet you never can be sure about these things. *Vichyssoise* catches him every time. All this is going through his head in the millisecond after "I really love" and Mary Babb sits, skin moist and aglow as a Southern woman's skin should be, awaiting his commentary. When his tongue finally lands again, he skips the sentence and turns it over to her: "Well, you tell me why you love it."

It is the right thing to say. Mary Babb gasps at how she loves it and those little eyes open prettily, but the lights come down just then, and Furman isn't looking at her, anyway, because a woman halfway around the reef is staring at him. He sees her in the twilight before the air turns utterly black, and she seems all white neck and face, a goblet raised to him.

The curtain rises and the townspeople of Peking begin their bloodthirsty chant.

∽

When Furman's wife died of a heart attack half a year before, falling while jogging alongside the college lake, he had no time to feel alone. Her friends arrived to cloak him in their good intentions. They helped him at the funeral parlor— Juanita Bush suggested she should be laid in the Eastern plot so that when Furman and his wife rose on Judgment Day, they would be standing before God as they stood in the church at their wedding. They helped him at the Southern rite of visitation, when the whole town stopped by, one by one, paying lighthearted respects—Ella Jean Bonight convinced him to wear not black, but khaki. They made a chart of meals to be brought, and at noon and six, a black woman would arrive, one of these women's cooks or maids, with steaming casseroles, banana puddings, pecan pies. This lasted for months, and the ladies stopped by all the time to amuse him, even calling him at the office where he worked as translator. They gave him a sudden sense of a rich social life— parties, fund-raisers, museum openings. He went from event to event over those months, his grief caught like a nut he'd swallowed wrong. He was thankful.

It wasn't seemly for a woman of a certain status to attend events alone, not in South Carolina. If a woman's husband were unable to attend, she might find herself frustratingly kept from the ball, sitting in her own foyer with white gloves folded in fury, except that long ago a solution had been discovered: the walker. A man, not a husband or a lover, who could escort the ladies to museum openings, theater premieres, political dinners, without a whisper of scandal. They weren't gigolos—they were walkers, and they could be the woman's brother, a young relation, or simply a bachelor beyond reproach. This was the place they found for Furman.

He relaxed into the role, weary with grief, relieved to have a woman simply hand him a ticket and tell him where to take her. Evenings moved quickly this way. The balls, the operas— they weren't what he loved, and with so little money left after his wife's death, maybe he even felt more distant from this crowd, different, but he accepted his role. It was this or make some other life from scratch.

He had been born to a different world. His mother was a seamstress near the college, a woman who sewed the debutante gowns in white, red, or black, depending on the girl's place in society. Furman remembers all the yards of red satin hanging over the shower curtain in the bathroom, and the strict instructions not to touch it, or get it wet, and that little terror of so much red. His mother told him, as she cut the shining fabric, about that other world she clothed, about the dances and the way young men acted. It would be wrong to say she made him for that world, like a jacket she could tailor, but perhaps she simply longed too loudly. Children listen, and he was the kind of boy who did what his mother wanted. She must have sensed that nothing was coming for him in their dirt yard and he might disappear in one of many unexpected ways. So she had him meet the girls at the door, and by the time he was fifteen, he had learned how to smile and make them blush, how to stare at them with those beautiful gray eyes, shells under water.

Those eyes, though, were not unique. Every man on his mother's side had them, back a century, always with that tilt, always with that shade of gray. Eyes rolling in the heads of laboring young men, specked and reddened with summer dust. Furman's eyes were special not because they were new with him; they were just the first to be seen by rich girls.

He married in, and now he had to find a place. Early on, while his wife was still alive, he was put on the Carolina Cotillion Floor Committee, and found himself in men's clubs smoking cigars with nervous debutante escorts, military-school boys, and sons of society. He instructed them on what his mother taught him: how to treat the girls, how to lead them in their first waltz, how to break in on dances every few minutes so the girls would feel wanted by every boy in the room. The boys were so wide-eyed and fearful, their hair always slick and rich, and Furman wondered if they could hear it in his voice, his accent, how little he knew of these things. How these things were pieced together from the memory of a seamstress. That sewing room seemed to recede over the years like a shoreline, and Furman's view of his mother's form, hunched in the yards of satin, grew fainter.

When his mother died, they found a pile of trousers in the sewing room, ones she'd been altering for Furman, half-finished. He stared at them, feeling unexplainably ill, until his wife put them in a bag and dragged them away. A few weeks later, he found the trousers hanging in his closet, finished, pressed clean without the smell of his mother's iron. She's so good, he thought. He meant his wife; he meant she was so good at his life. She picked his haircut so he would fit in; she knew he'd learned Russian in school, and she found him a job at a friend's factory doing translations. He copied the correspondence from their Moscow plant into English, the business letters, the manuals and parts lists. At dinner parties, his wife made this work seem interesting and artistic, and he was grateful.

Furman gave up the Floor Committee years before, but now, with his wife's death, he had suddenly blossomed in this new role, and he was perfect. Handsome enough to be fought over as an escort, and yet too handsome to be scandalous— because wasn't he somehow unearthly, beyond them? He knew nothing of literature; he knew nothing of opera; it didn't matter. He walked and smiled, and that was enough, and at night he went back to his weary Russian manuals, working late to earn more money.

∽

A gong onstage is being struck, the curtain falls, and there is sudden and loud applause. Each person turns to the person next to them and smiles. They agree it is beautiful, the costumes and the set, designed by someone Furman has never heard of. Someone that everybody feels no need to explain about.

"The tenor has a lovely voice," Mary Babb says happily. "And it's just wild, it's wild with all the executioners." They were bare-chested muscle men.

"Would you like a break?" he asks her, and she nods, and they head out through the red curtains. The man still sits in the anteroom. Now he is reading a book, looks up and grins. Out in the second-tier lounge, champagne and glasses wait on their table. Mary Babb acts suave and everyday about it, but he can see she's pleased to be back, to have everything just the way it had been, to have people smile and kiss her as if she hasn't been abandoned. She happily waves to a bald fiftyish man coming over: Buzzy Halloway, member of an old family. Like Furman, a walker, but a gossip, a flirt, and a homosexual.

"My, my, it's Mary Babb. Well hello, Dolly!" he says, bowing and kissing her hand. "You were gone so long, and you look beautiful, of course."

"Thank you, Buzzy."

"Divorce becomes you," he whispers, and Mary Babb blinks because she clearly doesn't know how to talk to him, but he's noticed Furman now. "Look, Furman's here!"

Furman grins. He doesn't know how to talk to Buzzy, either, and he's always been jealous of how this man enters and rules a conversation, commands a room with his wit. Furman can be clever, sometimes, after some wine, but no one has ever thought of him as clever. It's hard for Furman to be something that no one sees in him.

Buzzy's face clenches in a wrinkled smile. "Look at you in that tuxedo. Do you love this production?" Furman nods and blinks; so little response is needed for Buzzy. "It's Mary Babb's favorite. Me, I faint at the sight of blood. That poor prince loses his head, I'm sick in the aisles."

Mary Babb mentions the tenor's voice, but Buzzy points across the room where a beautiful woman with enormous blond hair is laughing.

"I'm with Sunshine Chandler," Buzzy confides, resting his hand on Furman's, "and she says you were a perfect gentleman the other night at the mayor's." He turns to Mary Babb, explaining, "I couldn't go, a nasty cold. I was seeing visions of Ariana Huffington everywhere. But apparently—I'm ruining your story here Furman—apparently, Furman was going down the line, shaking the men's hands, kissing the women's, and you know how that is—you get so tired, you just start looking at the hands . . . man, woman, man. . . . Near the end, he grabs a rough hand and starts shaking it firmly, then looks up. . . . It's Mabel. It's the mayor's wife." Buzzy crosses his arms, looks back and forth at them, gives a little hop. "It's all anyone could talk about. Gotta go," he says, touching Furman's arm just as the bell starts ringing.

Buzzy gives him the kind of look Furman never understands—some kind of knowing, pensive stare with the lips drawn tight. Furman is too ignorant of desire.

"He is so funny," Mary Babb says in a voice that rings like the opposite. She sips her champagne, and Furman looks down, to see his glass is already finished. Sometimes his body works without him. Then she declares to no one, "It's a shame."

The bell rings again, but no one is moving. Downstairs in the lobby, just over the edge of their stone balcony, people rush in again from their cigarettes, but up here the folks know exactly how long they have. Long enough for another quick glass, a visit. Furman knows, too, but he holds the seat of his chair and begins to shake one leg impatiently.

"There's Charles Gribble," Mary Babb is saying. The light is harsh here, and he can see her hands are thin and old-looking, though she is hardly older than he is. She moves her fingers as if she used to smoke, and keeps talking. Furman hears his wife telling a story about this man, who was her cousin, one of those stories in a marriage that repeat too often. He can hear her now, telling how she was five or six, playing in the yard, and heard a scream, then saw Charles Gribble running across the lawn toward her, covered in flames. He always pictured his wife so small in that story, not a girl, but his little wife. Face lit by her cousin's burning. How strange that here that cousin is, a grown man, wearing a beard to cover the scars. And she isn't here. You listen to a story being told over and over, you hardly notice the time, and suddenly you're standing at a coffin.

They get to their seats just as the lights are dimming. The couple in front of them is speaking in Russian, and Mary Babb thinks this is wondrous; Furman doesn't tell her they are squabbling, that the man doesn't know "what you want from me." The lights dim; the couple quiets; the room stills—in the curve of boxes, you can see another woman looking over to Furman from across the room, and Furman catching her gaze without expression. They are the only heads not turned toward the orchestra to reapplaud the conductor. Two profiles badly packed within the open crate of faces.

Onstage, three Chinese scholars pine for the country homes they never see, too worn down by the queen's vengeful riddles.

✍

People were surprised to see him frozen at her coffin, unable to leave. It was, for Furman, the hardest part. The rest of it was such a rush, his emotions all anticipated by those who had done this over and over—"Get angry!" one woman had urged him at the visitation. "Get angry and break something!"—and he was so grateful for the help, the hands always on his arm, his shoulder, the flowers arriving from the funeral home and being placed on the table, the mantel, and the creamy food that came to the door unbidden, though he wasn't hungry. So much bustle just to please him. As if her dying released a cage of feathered women.

Furman brought out photo albums at the visitation, but there wasn't anything suitable to place on the mantel in memory of his wife. People flipped the pages of the albums nonetheless—just trees and rivers, but something to point at and sigh over. The room was so clean. Where were the little messes she'd left behind—the magazine inserts she carelessly let fall on the couch? The water ring from her morning coffee? The ladies grieved, and wanted pieces of his wife, pictures—but they'd missed the clear evidence everywhere of how she sped entropy along. A bra on the staircase, panties in a pile in the closet, papers everywhere. His wife had been the great eroding force on their house. The ladies, though, kindly, quickly, had undone her, just as they might turn off a waterfall.

But there's no real way to know what he was feeling. Furman was quiet and unpoetic. He said the sort of things that everybody says, but he meant them, and when he said those phrases—"I'm taking it one day at a time" and "There'll never be anyone like her"—they were still true. They were, also, the right things to say. He couldn't mention how his wife had been one of the few debutantes to go all the way with him, to tear his clothes off until he felt she might break him. How marriage was something he had seen first in his mother's eyes, then in his wife's, then said aloud himself because their wants had been too much to bear. He couldn't tell them how strange it was that when she left the house for groceries, he became bored and restless, and no book could pace her absence. How she often talked of an idea for him, a trip to Russia, alone or with her, so he could see the world, speak his favorite language. How she built for him that single snowy hope out in the future. He couldn't tell them that no one would wish him Russia now.

And at her grave, he couldn't leave. He had arrived by

limousine with her sisters and a cousin (the parents were buried ten feet away), and watched all the people smiling at the
car. Across the whole flat cemetery sat rows of bronze urns
filled with artificial flowers, no stones or tombs. There, flapping in the autumn air, he could see a green tarpaulin canopy
and under it her coffin—closed, because she hadn't believed
that anyone could make her hair look right in death. Furman
sat front and center and didn't listen to the preacher. Instead,
he pictured his wife lying in that box under the pile of roses—
something every mourner secretly sees.

There was a version of "Amazing Grace" sung at too quick
a tempo, and Furman had to hum once they got past the first
verse. There was a prayer from the Bible telling him to worry
not, and to note how the lilies are arrayed. Then they all stood
up and people came and talked, and met the sisters, and
hugged and laughed, then the tall funeral director told Furman it was time to go, and he couldn't. He stood still in
disbelief; he was a stake the sun had pounded into the dirt.
The ladies grinned and showed him where the sisters were
already in the limo, and he did not move. The ladies touched
him, concerned, the lilac rustling in their hats.

∽

The curtain falls on Turandot's icy fury. Everyone agrees,
though, as they rise, that this soprano seems to be pushing it.
All this wait for Turandot, and she's a dud. There's an excitement about it. And about "Nessun Dorma" coming after
the curtain. Furman makes a note there are two *t*'s in Turandot the way they say it.

Back in the lounge, there's more champagne to finish, and
Mary Babb is delighted by the opera; she, too, notes the soprano's failure, and that the orchestra is too loud, but what
an exquisite Luí! "Do you like it?" she keeps asking, and Furman nods, adding he especially likes the three Chinese, and
she seems confused by this. "But honey, they're all . . . they're

all—Gwendolyn!" Someone has arrived again, a couple. He is a stout, cheerful man from an old banking family and she is cheerful only in the way Southern ladies always are. She's new to money, Furman can see. Her hair's done right, but Mary Babb is commenting too much on her dress, and the woman's blushing, clearly happy to be approved of. Something too flashy around her face, like a Miss Carolina contestant. Maybe, in fact, that's what she is. She catches Furman's eye and seems afraid of him.

"Furman, you watch the game?" the man begins. This is a welcoming phrase, a kindness.

"I can't even talk about it," Furman says, a little relieved.

"Your team has sold you down the river."

"He's such a fool."

"Laney? Well, that's typical. You'll have to admit sooner or later you were born in the wrong state." This man is from Georgia. They are talking about college football.

Furman excuses himself in the middle of this conversation and leaves the man blinking, alone among the women. Furman makes his way to the men's room and washes his hands, using the soap over and over and then rinsing. The room is gold, with green marble; framed nineteenth-century music hall posters hang on the walls. Men wander to the urinal and to the sinks, nodding to one another, noticing Furman, adjusting their black cuffs and frowning. Outside, there is a windowless men's lounge and men are smoking there, not talking. From the lighting of the room, in the mirror, Furman's skin looks greenish and drowned. He pulls at the skin under an eye. He is thinking about the woman he just saw—the woman from the boxes, the one gazing across at him as the lights were dimming. He saw her in the second-tier lounge, and here he is, escaping her. He thought she was one of those debutantes from decades ago, a particular one who used to pick up her dresses when Furman's mother was gone, kiss him in the sewing room's soft light. So many girls pushed him against the yards of precious satin. They stroked his forehead and told him he was handsome. He chose one, for reasons buried now. Furman washes his face. She would have asked about his wife. She would have asked what he is doing here. Or maybe it wasn't her. Maybe she wasn't going to ask. It could be, now that he thinks about it, that he is about to walk out of the men's room and run into someone else who will ask him about his wife; maybe there's no escaping it. This stops him, catches him motionless in the gold and marble room. He cannot decide how to live the next few moments.

When he does walk out, he doesn't run into anyone, though as he's passing through the men's lounge, he notices the man from the anteroom, the man with the goatee who had sat head in hand before the opera began. The man is resting in a plush chair, smoking a cigarette, and Furman can see the box sitting on a table. A cheap brand. The man is reading a book again, a mathematics history, and he is making notes with a ballpoint pen. He looks up, glasses shining. He sees Furman and smiles. Furman feels the smile like a burglar breaking in.

Back in the box, Mary Babb is already seated and she seems a little peeved that he left her so abruptly. "Tommy had nothing to do after you left," she says a little tightly. There is a line of sweat below her white hairline.

"Are you having a good time?" he asks.

"It's wonderful you came with me," she says a little dreamily. "Gwendolyn certainly looked jealous, didn't she?" Furman knows she's misunderstood a number of looks tonight. He hears a lady coughing behind him, and he turns his head, to see her date's seat empty. He thinks of the goateed man—he must also be a walker. Cheap cigarettes, bored expression, that smile. What is it like for him? Did he work his way into this role, or was it chosen for him? Has this rich lady taken him on a cruise around the world, and does he take his mathematics with him? Does he see himself as sitting in society's open mouth, waiting to be chewed? What is a square inch of either of them worth?

Mary Babb has moved on to another subject, watching the boxes with her shiny eyes, saying, "I've got to help out. . . . I'll introduce you around."

"Introduce me . . . I don't . . ."

She makes a pshaw gesture, tossing her hand at him coquettishly. "Oh . . . well, you mean ladies. Mercy, I can't help you there. I thought you'd be one of our famous Carolina bachelors. . . ."

"Oh, I guess I'll get married again."

She looks so pleased, with the evening, with Furman beside her. The light is right on her at the moment and she seems to feel it. She asks him, "And whom are you going to marry, Furman?"

He folds his hands on his lap and winks. "I'll marry one of you."

Mary Babb's face stills for a moment, freezing her smile. The bell has stopped ringing behind them, and the lights begin to fade, changing the darkness of her eyes. In the dimness, she simply repeats, "One of us," and by the time the theater turns to black, Furman understands he will never marry one of them again.

"None shall sleep," sings the tenor onstage as red lanterns float through the darkness. "None shall sleep."

His wife hid all sorts of things. Candy bars in the sock drawer, blank inspirational notebooks in her dresser. She even had packets of letters stuffed under the silver drawer—a decades-long correspondence with the senator's office over civil rights, something she never spoke about with anyone. She had a jar of cream hidden in the bathroom, behind the extra toilet paper, a chemical cream she'd clearly bought off the television and was ashamed of. Half of it was used. She had a set of sexy lingerie Furman had never seen her wear, and they lay, with their tags still attached, in a silk bag in her underwear drawer, ready for some special occasion that never came. His wife's name was Judy and she had long brown hair and glasses. Furman has found so many hidden things in the months since she died; each few weeks, he has accidentally discovered some new part of her, too late. He has tried to search the house for all of them, to rid himself of surprises, but it does no good. There is a dark tunnel stretching from this moment into the future, and she hangs there in wasps' nests from the ceiling. He will stumble; she will sting him.

If he wanted, Furman could think of her. He could start weeping, burn her behind his eyes. He could leap within that tunnel, back to before he can remember, and his mother singing to his shell-gray eyes; the moment he manages to turn from his wife's grave; the time in the future when he sits three boxes down with another wealthy lady, firmly in his chosen place; the time his wife gives herself to him outside the cotillion in the blue night air; the time he sits reading in the men's lounge, his hair white at the temples. He chooses not to see any of these.

"None shall sleep," sings the tenor, knowing he has won the queen's hand. This is not the opera where the man looks back on his dead love in Hell. This is a future king exulting. Furman takes Mary Babb's arm and squeezes it, and she gives him a kind smile in the darkness. He turns to the stage and watches the final act in its gilt splendor. Time rolls over him like thunder.

Four Bites

∽

1

THE FIRST TIME I remember is a cantaloupe salad.

I was probably three or four at the time, a period of my life that my father mysteriously refers to as "the Golden Age." He strokes the stubble on his chin and looks toward photographs on the mantel, and I laugh, although I am privately furious. He makes my childhood sound so mythical, as if he and my mother carved me out of ivory, breathed life into me, let me fall under a curse, and watched as I changed from that rare, beautiful boy into this ordinary man before you. The mythical child comes after the story of their early marriage, even more shrouded in legend, the two of them braver and better looking than seems possible, masters of half a dozen languages, travelers of the earth. I am the sequel to their happiness, with blazing white-blond hair and all the dimples. My store of cute phrases and malapropisms had no end—it was as if, my father tells me, I hired a stable of writers and called them up late at night in my wee voice: "Marty . . . I'm meeting relatives tomorrow. I need cute, real cute. Dazzle me." The next day, I'd have Aunt Gloria in stitches. For me, all I remember of the Golden Age was that I was, for a while, the focus of my parents' lives. Every frame of my memory has one of their faces in a corner, watching how I saw the world.

They were both there, of course, the night I couldn't eat the cantaloupe. They were always there, all four times when it would be like this, a meal impossible to eat. Just my fragile tongue, and the two of them reflected in my plate.

This first time was at the house of Rose Chao, a friend of my parents' from graduate school. She was the only living witness of their early life together in Chicago, before marriage, when my mother lived scandalously alone in an efficiency apartment (there are photographs of her in a miniskirt, posed with a cynical expression and a casserole), and my dad lived with Harry Chao. Together, the bachelors played stupid pranks, and destroyed each other's stomachs with octopus pizza and three-beer chili, laughing drunkenly under a huge poster of Einstein, that one with him sticking out his tongue. All three were chemistry grad students, if this explains anything, but Rose was not. She entered the picture, she and her son from a previous marriage, and started feeding "the boys" with good Chinese food, taking my mother to art museums and political marches, changing (so the mythology goes) everybody's life. The two couples married within months of each other in 1965. The Chao marriage was San Francisco Chinese, with Harry looking stunned and Rose in a red dragon dress, touching the flowers in her hair. My parents' was Southern Baptist, with my sullen mother in uncharacteristic white frills, the maids all wearing yellow pillbox hats, and the men beaded with Carolina sweat. My mother was the maid of honor for Rose, and Rose for my mom, and Harry was best man for my dad, and so on.

The night of the cantaloupe was as many years later as I was old. My dad and Harry had both found postdoctorate positions at Michigan, so both couples moved there (my mother, with her impressive publications, got no offers until

later; her first glimpse at a woman's chances in science). Our
house near the university is where I grew up, near other faculty brats, but I don't recall the Chaos coming to see us. I
first remember Rose Chao on that night. I didn't meet Harry,
and it turns out I was never going to meet him—he had left
Rose and her ten-year-old son a few nights before and was
not going to see either of them again, or my parents, or any
part of the life he'd previously led. I've heard he went to live
with a glassblower in Vermont, which, from a distance of
thirty years now, seems hilarious, but of course it wasn't then.
My parents didn't know anything about this when they
brushed the snow from our car, packed me warmly inside,
drove out of town, walked to the snowy porch, and rang the
bell of that dark, sloping modern house. I think Rose couldn't
bear to call them. I picture how she put off canceling the
dinner, staring at the phone and feeling frozen, day after day,
until it was suddenly time to start cooking.

We stood out on the porch, waiting, and my parents
laughed about things far over my head while I stared at a
stone dog sitting next to the door. Oblivious to the rest of
the scene, I remember that Chinese dog most clearly. I think
I must have been wearing my navy officer's uniform, an amazing suit with fake medals sewn in, which shows up in most
Golden Age photos; it was, apparently, a phase of mine. I'm
surprised I remember my parents so clearly—my mom young,
with a flip of brown hair, wearing her new contact lenses, a
knit wool short skirt and sweater, talking in her Carolina
drawl about some jerk at her laboratory; my dad with a flat
plane of thin hair, a dark beard, chuckling as he wiped his
snow-dewed glasses on his blazer. I wish I had watched them
more carefully together. We were only out there for a moment, but—perhaps because of the cold, or the carved dog I
stared at—the scene is long and tender in my mind.

Rose answered the door, and a soft odor of smoke came
curling after her. Apparently, she had wanted to make a fire

in the living room, but she had never done it before, so she used pine needles from the yard as her tinder. Her husband, Harry, would have told her how they'd smoke, but he wasn't there, and she didn't know about flues, so it had been something of a disaster—all the windows had to be opened to the cold, and all the fans turned on. So Rose looked a little shivery and teary-eyed at the door, which was too bad, because all she was trying to prove to herself was that she could go on, and here she was, already, clearly not.

"Oh God, I'm glad to see you," she said, grinning and hugging her thin, cold body. "The most hilarious thing happened. . . ."

She rushed us into the living room, laughing and chattering about the fire, which was cheerfully aglow, still tossing bouquets of smoke from behind its screen like a lady off on a cruise. It was a high-ceilinged modern room with cedar walls and frightening lamps on metal springs, and it was cold because the windows were tilted open. Snow was coming in. Rose had her hair sprayed and high, in cylindrical curls, which had wilted in the smoke disaster, and she was one of those women in the sixties who appeared, even in summer, only in long dresses and long, long strands of necklaces with pendants. Fiddling with these pendants was part of her conversational style. That night, she wore a long red dress patterned like a Persian rug.

She grabbed my mother by the arm, and I remember noting how odd this was—somehow, I knew no one touched my mother like this, that our family was not to be touched. But Rose did. She grabbed my mother and talked laughingly, painting a picture of herself and her son, Wilson, running around the house, opening windows, shrieking at the powdery snow coming in, coughing and giggling together. I imagine her in that Persian dress, her necklace swinging like a brass censer, ordering sullen Wilson around in that panic before old friends arrived. My mother laughed, too. My father leaned over the fire, frustrated, and began to explain about flues. No one was listening to him. At that point, apparently, I said something astonishingly cute, which made everyone feel comfortable. Where has this magic gone?

"Josh, come here and look at this flue," my father said, pointing at the fire while the women began to talk. He began a careful explanation of air currents, turning this into the kind of physics lecture I always got when I asked for some simple answer about, say, which way to turn the wheel in an ice skid. "You won't get the *what* until you get the *why*," he always said. He still says this. I didn't understand at three, and I don't understand now; it's the curse of families that children will never care about their parents' passions. I could see only the amazing fire.

My dad got himself up and put the screen back in front of the fire. I stood there, a little blond admiral, staring at the flames and blinking away the soot. I heard them all whispering, just like the noise of snow falling through the windows now and curling in the air above the fire in little question marks before it disappeared. I reached out to touch it and there was nothing to touch, just an effect.

"Josh, why don't you let Wilson show you his trains?" my mom said, appearing next to me, her head near mine.

Rose held her necklace in one hand and pointed to her son, who stood in the doorway. Half his forehead was covered in a birthmark. "You want to show Josh your trains?"

"You'll like that," my mom said. I watched her face as I started to walk. "Go on."

Wilson Chao walked away with me, and we heard the tinkle of breaking glass and another sound as we made our way downstairs to the basement. It was low-ceilinged, but walled with great windows of snow and pine trees. In the center of the room was a raised island of tracks and mountains, a reproduction of a small Swiss town. I was amazed. We must have stood there for an hour or more watching the two trains braid across the putty landscape. Wilson seemed like a god to me, and his dark birthmark was a sign of this. He was bored with me, though, with even his obsessive train set, but he quietly let me rearrange the people and the trees as he sent the trains puffing their smoke. Ten years later, I would learn that Wilson Chao dropped out of college, followed a girl to the Midwest, ruined his early chances. That's what my parents said, shaking their heads at dinner and glancing at me.

We were called up to dinner and both of us hesitated, waiting for the black train to clear one more bridge, then rushed madly up the stairs. A long teak table had been moved out into the room, too long for just the five of us, but wonderfully laid out with thick white china. The adults had flushed cheeks and were still talking, but in quick bursts of code—"I still don't know how to feel"—so I couldn't understand. I was put between two empty chairs for the women, who were off in the kitchen getting shiny brown bowls of food. My parents seemed distracted; I felt like maybe they were angry at me, so I clowned in my chair. They weren't watching. The windows were closed and the room was warm and bright inside the snow. There was no sign of broken glass.

A bowl of cantaloupe salad was set in front of me. Almost phosphorescent pink, with wisps of coconut. I must have squinted in disgust.

"Eat your fruit, Josh," my mom said, sitting next to me. I could hear the chirping noise of forks in bowls around the table. My dad looked angry again under his beard. "You love fruit."

"He doesn't have to eat it," Rose Chao said to me, touching my hand. She looked flushed and clean, and smelled soapy.

My dad pointed the tines of his fork at me. "He loves fruit. It's like watermelon. Try it, Josh," he said, turning to my mom, "and if he doesn't like it, Deborah, he doesn't have to eat it."

I was only three or four. How could I eat a bowl of cantaloupe?

Rose insisted, patting me annoyingly. "I bet he doesn't like cantaloupe." Wilson was chewing slowly, staring at me.

My mother leaned over now. "But he does." The Southern accent she had taken such pains to hide was coming through strong now.

"Deborah . . ." my dad said to her, his fork down now.

I looked down. That cold, fresh smell of the cantaloupe, that pink flesh in the bowl. I felt like we were all cannibals.

"I don't like strawberries," Rose Chao offered, but no one was listening.

Then I looked up and said something terribly uncute. I don't remember what it was, but I remember Rose's smile after that, strangely limp, a ribbon pinned up at both ends. My parents shifted to look at me—they seemed like two people annoyed by a ringing phone. How dare I act so selfishly at a time like this? They looked away from me, toward each other again.

Later, I would get the usual discipline, the usual disappointed faces, but it would feel so different. They had looked away—something else, however briefly, had been their focus and they hadn't time for my petty tongue. I couldn't have known that the Chaos' life had run so parallel to my parents', making it easy to navigate, like a river beside their road—the river had curved away, so now what? Where were we? I couldn't have known this, or that Rose was unhappy, or that she was the kind of person bad things would always happen to. I had only heard a new tone in my parents' voices, like the ring of struck glass, which they never used with me. I know now it was left over from their young life together— the sound of a conflict that had come before me, would always be older than me, like a brother you can't live up to.

My mother took the bowl into the kitchen, and my father

started talking about me to Rose. She smiled down at me, her hair shiny and beautiful, gold hanging from her throat, surely planning already her time after we'd leave, lying on the bedspread in her long dress, rubbing her eyes in wide circles.

So there's a life I didn't save. And I was only three or four.

2

The next bite came years later, when I was eleven or so. My parents' finances had changed: larger scientific grants, better professorships, lucrative textbook deals. We moved to a larger house, which I think of as leagues away from where we'd lived, but which, if you look at a map, is really less than a mile. It seemed far, and it was meant to seem far; during the move, my parents threw out all the worthless furniture from their grad school days, tossed the inherited family crap, and ended useless old friendships, as well. Everything must go. Rose Chao faded from dinner parties; I never saw Wilson again, or his trains; and Harry never returned under a photograph of Einstein. Something about their marriage shifted, too; during the move, my parents stored their wedding photos in a cardboard box marked MEMORABILIA, and that box lay taped shut in the basement for a decade.

Part of our growing isolation could have been my father's sickness. It was described to me as sickness, and later as "a trouble-breathing disease." It changed him very slowly. He'd been so shy and clever, the funny young professor with a stack of computer cards he carried around like a pet. He stayed late at the university, working on theories at his legal pads, while mom and I ate meals entirely of french fries. At dinner, he sat holding my mother's hand while she talked, ready to say the one phrase that would end an argument. He was careful that way.

But this "trouble-breathing disease" conquered him so slowly, he couldn't be careful. He had to change. He became irritable, and entered heated political arguments with my mother at dinner, where he'd storm out, his meal unfinished. He'd fall asleep at the university and come home at two, furious at his lost time and his jellied brain. I remember, too, the trouble breathing—I saw him once crawling from the bathroom on his hands and knees, gasping for air. He told me the room was too small, that it didn't have enough air. The confused look on his face, the dust on his hands from crawling. Later, he shaved off his beard because it had blocked his breathing.

I think he knew this was foolish, and the arguments he picked nightly with my mother, but he couldn't help himself. I didn't recognize him, or my mother with the pinched face she wore to talk to him. They were so different from the couple at Rose's dinner table. Sometimes, his rage turned on me. I once left half a banana in his bedroom and he found it, days later, blackened and rotten. He called me in and made me eat it. It was confusing and awful for me, but my father, the brilliant man, must have felt more confused. My mom yelled at him while I sat in my room, drinking orange juice she'd given me to cover the taste. They fought like that often while he was bedridden. I don't count this as a bite I couldn't swallow.

By the time I was eleven, in the summer, I was sent away to live with my grandparents in South Carolina. I wasn't told why; it was just the sort of random thing children are always having to do. But I was sent away because there was no "trouble-breathing disease" at all, just my depressed father in a panic of failure. I was sent away, I think, so that my mother could leave him.

South Carolina was muggy and flat, and I spent all my time riding a tricycle around a tree-lined dead end and walking down the prickly road to the local swimming pool. The other kids were nice enough, but were poor, of course, and didn't have very many toys. Nothing electronic. The children were all heavily religious, something my family was not—my parents had a Baptist wedding but were committed atheists who sent me to an Ethical Society Day Camp each summer, where, instead of "Reveille" each morning, we struck an antique Burmese gong. Down South, it was assumed, however, that children would be adorably Christian, and my grandparents were embarrassed when I said Martin Luther was black. This sort of behavior brought on a subtle and carefully orchestrated indoctrination by my grandparents, and when I finally returned home to Michigan, I was telling everyone about my new best friend. "Who's that, Josh?" my mom's Communist friends would ask.

"Jesus," I would answer with my best *Reader's Digest* angelic face. I thought the looks around the table showed how unusually cute I'd been, a return to the Golden Age. Then would come my mother's voice in her deepest Southern accent:

"WHAT?"

But I came home because she didn't leave my dad. Somehow, he began to recover. Maybe she'd found a drug he was willing to take, or maybe he just grew frustrated with himself and walked into the enclosed darkness of the bathroom, forcing himself to inhale and not to tremble. This is not a story I've been told. I wish I had watched them more carefully years before, out on Rose Chao's doorstep in the cold, because I might have seen them young and amused with each other. I might have caught a look in his eye, the one that might appear in his sickness when he grabbed her arm and pleaded, the one that might make her stay.

So I was called home, and my mother met me at the airport, clutching me to her, which was uncharacteristic. I had no idea what had happened; I was just glad to be back on familiar ground. What I remember most is that she had a dramatic new haircut, which I found shocking and saddening and told her so. Her long hair was part of the comfort I found in her, but any change in anyone then seemed like a betrayal to me. She solemnly told me my father was feeling better, and I don't think I understood this, either. I hadn't ever accepted that he was ill. It's so hard, when you're a child, to contemplate great changes; time itself hardly seems to pass.

I wonder why she was so silent when she drove me home. Our neighborhood was brilliantly green, even in the wilting afternoon heat, and pollen hung in the air like static electricity. Maybe she had expected me to be more loving and happy than I was.

She sat me down at the kitchen table when we got home. Something was different, but nothing I could notice, no new furniture or paintings, nothing as terrible as my mom's new hair. I must have sensed the thick air, air captured for weeks with closed windows and drawn curtains, captured like an escaped bird, with the thought that somehow if it got free, the walls might fall inward. My dad was upstairs in the bedroom, asleep or tired, and she told me to be quiet and eat my supper; I was eating alone.

It was brought to me on a heavy yellow plate. A dozen green peas, a square of corn bread slathered with butter and honey—my favorite—and a slick oval of meat, which I knew, without tasting it, was inedible beyond any hope.

"What's this, Mom?"

She looked over at me from the refrigerator. That new haircut made her face seem emptier, filled only with her thick glasses. Again, that quiet look of astonishment I couldn't place. "Oh, it's something special just for you," she said, grinning a little. "I hope you like it."

I was left alone with the meat. Say what you will about hunger, but guilt is a better sauce. So I took a bite.

It was, of course, terrible, thick and chewy, and it seemed impossible that it could taste like an eraser, but it did (what child hasn't tasted an eraser?), and it sat in my mouth, unswallowed, therefore making me taste it all the more. Had she fried up a pot holder by mistake? My mother was nowhere to be seen, and it occurred to me (for the first time ever!) that maybe I *didn't have to eat it*. Maybe I could *lie*.

What would my friend Jesus think?

I heard my father coughing above me. It sounded like my mom began to run upstairs, then stopped and ceased making noise. I looked around for some place to put my half-chewed meat. A spider plant hung above me, dangling its pale legs into my hair.

"So how's that dinner coming?" my mom said, suddenly returning to the room. She had removed her bra and held it in one hand. She looked expectant.

"What is it again?" I asked. Above me, the spider plant swung suspiciously.

"Oh, something very special I made for you," she said, turning away.

"When can I see Dad?"

My mother touched the doorway with one hand and looked back at me. The gaze of a woman thinking, the look I'd seen often when I visited her lab, when she'd lean over her gold-foil-coated device as it hissed cold vapors, studying the results. The look said nothing, but I felt it touching me; perhaps I sensed what I know now, that my parents weren't together in the way they had been. Their early love—the love that had grown always taller than me, that invisible mark above mine in the doorway—it was too old now.

I did eat my dinner that night, or at least half of it. Slowly, over the course of an hour, and with a few bits in the spider plant and more than I could handle in my stomach, I managed to down it. There were noises all over the house, of my father trying to move around, of my mom in other rooms, clearing the messes, throwing things away, standing in the middle of a rug and staring at a scrap of paper. Who knows what was going on in that house? There is the bustle after death, but this was something else, of course. My father had grown sad and they had hated each other in this house, and how could that be swept away? There was an unquiet now in the dustless room, because a dark panic had blown by, and silent choices had been made, and now there was a life to come up with again. A marriage—that second patient suddenly restless in its bed.

She came back into the kitchen, and with the way her glasses caught the light, and her missing hair, there was almost nothing I could see of her face. I, of course, was obliviously eating and hiding the terrible food. I sat up, blushing and alive. She looked pale. Sometimes I wonder if his recovery was really why she didn't leave him; I wonder if she simply lost her nerve.

"You done, honey?" my mother asked, glasses flaring. "You finished?"

"Yep. It was great, Mom."

Her whole body seemed to come apart just then, because she burst out in laughter. The glasses came off with a wipe of her hand, her shoulders convulsed, and she had to lean into the wall to keep herself erect. When she calmed down a little, she looked at me, her face glowing, and announced she'd given me liver.

"You poor boy!" Then she fell into the stove, cracking herself up.

I stared, confused and betrayed. It was unthinkable she'd be so cruel. I hated liver, but no one hated it more than she did. Was this some health kick?

But Mom just kept trying to pull herself together, then bursting out into unholy noises and a wide, plain, guffawing face. I'd never seen her like this—my mother, the chemist with Communist friends. This woman who flinched at a touch was bent hysterically over the stove. I couldn't see her as a prankster, like Dad and Harry Chao in their bachelor pad— was that part of her, too? And that loud laugh! In it, you could hear the frantic genius she hid so carefully beneath her Carolina voice—how it was a kind of madness to think like she did, to see patterns in crystals, to understand formulas in terms of color. To laugh like a drunk woman when her life had nearly burned down.

I imagine my dad up there in the bedroom where he lay blinking at the noises coming from downstairs, hearing his wife this way. She must have seemed as foreign as she did to me. Still in a haze, still wrestling to breathe, perhaps he knew life wasn't going to change and this made things harder somehow. He was going to get better; he was never going to die the way I'd secretly feared. That would be life's trick on me—my mother was the one who would die there, twenty years later of cancer, on the same green bedspread.

But it was awful and amazing to see her that night when I ate liver—doubled over in her kitchen, eyes closed, shaking in a private rhapsody.

3

It was ten years before I couldn't eat again. My father seemed better, even forgetful of that period when I was sent away; he was like those people at Lourdes whose scars heal without a mark. By the time of the next dinner, he had grown a long gray-striped beard and two enormous eyebrows; Rose Chao was there, as well, with a dyed streak of white in her hair; and my mother, too, sat by us, wistful and fat. We were in an apartment in San Francisco, summer sun coming through a potted palm, and my father and I both glanced at each other, unable to swallow the cobbler.

It was my summer vacation from college, and I worked (typically) in a bad bookstore in the city, sleeping in a small room in the Mission I rented from a bickering couple. Their Siamese cat kept me up all hours screaming, but it supposedly had a tumor and was allowed all kinds of wild excesses; if I didn't let it on my lap, for instance, I got animal-cruelty stares.

My parents came to visit that summer, and the three of us spent months planning over the phone, shouting above the cat's screaming. My parents talked on a speakerphone, which made them both sound trapped down a well, bickering. In this planning, there was no free hour left to chance, and since my parents had long ago perfected their traveling style together, this meant an even split between marathon walking tours for my father and uninterrupted blocks of reading time for my mother. I admired the compromise but disliked how they had separated their lives like the parts of an egg. Both, at least, insisted on eating out every meal—except, they informed me, for Thursday, which we would spend with Rose Chao.

I had last seen Rose Chao at my mother's fiftieth birthday party, where she trapped me near the refrigerator and gave me a thrilling testimonial about the benefits of Prozac. She wasn't tipsy; she was happy, still in a long dress, still playing with her necklace as she talked. My parents had run into her after her son dropped out, and they had started up a friendship again. I think it was curiosity. I think they wanted to see what this woman, whose life had started out so similar to theirs, would have become. It turned out she was moving to San Francisco, and that she was going to get married. My parents had come to see me, but they couldn't resist the chance to meet this fiancé.

The afternoon of the visit belonged to my mother, and we spent it eating chocolate in an outdoor café. Overhead, a flock of pigeons spun around and around a tower, pointlessly, and my mother kept commenting on how beautiful it was. We watched them circling in and out of the sunlight. Eventually, my father mumbled, "What the hell is wrong with those birds?" and this irritated my mother, who drank the rest of her coffee in silence. My dad didn't seem to notice. Her mood changed, however, when we arrived at Rose's building, and Mom told us that she recognized the place. We got out of the cab in front of the ornately decorated white building and my mother put a finger on her chin and started to tap. She ran in front of us, staring up, peering into the entrance hall through the iron and glass gates.

"I've been here," she announced, as thoroughly surprised as anyone. Apparently, she'd been sent to San Francisco when she won the South Carolina Science Fair at sixteen. This was news to me and my father. "It was a hotel. I stayed with four other girls, on cots. . . . There was—oh, we ordered room service!" We were inside, walking through the halls, and my father and I stayed behind her as she gazed around, grasping the glass dish that held the dessert she was bringing—she had clearly forgotten that whole summer of her life, when she was skinny and frightened, a mousy Southern girl unchaperoned in the city. "They took us on a tour in a bus—it's hard to remember. It was hot, I wore little white gloves and no one else did."

She touched the walls, her mouth wide open. She was heavy now, and wore an elastic-waist skirt to hide it. It wasn't her bookish life—it was her cancer treatments, which enlarged her cells, so that she grew like a sponge no matter what she ate. It had maddened her at first—she turned out to be vain after all, wearing girdles and weird striped dresses—but she had resigned herself in the end. Signs were hopeful, though, and we all felt a reserved joy that afternoon.

It was the fiancé, not Rose, who met us at the door with a loud "Hello there!" that sent my mother stepping back into the hall. The first thing you noticed about him was that he was young, and then that he was short, and then that he looked like he might eat you. Rose Chao's face was visible behind his shoulder, pink and gold under her streaked black cap of hair, and the contrast in their ages showed clearly in that moment—was he thirty-five, forty? Was he—unthinkably—as young as her son, Wilson? He showed us in boisterously, hugging my father strongly, which looked bizarre because of my father's great height. The hug was over in an instant, and he turned to me. There was so much energy in him; it was exciting, and his muscles jerked and tensed as if he might pounce anywhere. He pounced on me—a brief strangling hug—and then my weak mother. She cleverly put him off by kissing his cheeks, at which he laughed.

"There is so much life in this room!" he yelled, throwing up his arms. He was stocky, strong, and larger than his height because of his presence. He had a giant head of hair, which rose half a foot over his face. His name was Alex, but Rose (we soon discovered) lovingly called him "Zorba."

My parents' faces were pursed already in disapproval. Alex ran to make drinks for us all, and they arrived quickly, snapping into our hands and spilling down our wrists. I felt rebellious toward my parents, that old couple shaking their drinks in the corner, acting startled whenever Alex turned and asked a question. I was afraid they'd start fighting, and Rose would be embarrassed in front of her fiancé. I liked Alex's enthusiasm, and felt this was what Rose had always needed, what any of us might need after an unhappy life. My mother whispered something to my dad and he nodded. I shook my head and watched Rose and her young man. She sat there, eyes closed, as he leaned over to kiss her on the cheek.

We learned that Alex was a high school history teacher, then that he was a substitute in the Bay Area, and that was why they had moved here. We learned he was half Greek and that the only place for spanikopita in San Francisco was at such and such, nowhere else. Then, suddenly, he was up and off into another room.

"He has to start making dinner," Rose explained, staring at the clinking ice in her drink. She looked so different from the Persian-dress days, shorter and thinner and less energetic.

This was because she'd fallen two years before, as she told us, slipped on magazines in her front hall and "bruised the sac around my heart." She wore a cotton T-shirt covered with a rosebud pattern, and, except for the white streak in her hair, looked consciously youthful. Or was it that my mother looked old?

I saw Mom's chubby face. It's as if she said aloud to me, Starting dinner now? When are we going to eat, ten? Eleven?

Rose must have seen this also, because she leaned forward, touching my mother's knee. "Oh, we eat like this every night," she said. I saw my mother flinch visibly at the touch, but Rose didn't notice. I was angry to see her flinch, although I always did it, too. Rose went on: "No planning, no worrying. He just looks around and sees what we have, then improvises. He's wonderful, he's a wonderful cook."

"It sounds wonderful," my mother said quietly, which hardly veiled her real comment: You look so foolish, Rose, you look so foolish like this.

My father was silent throughout the whole conversation, thumbing through a secular inspirational book he'd found on the coffee table. He studied it with a frown on his face, as if it were a sticky translation from a German science journal. I love that face on him, even in deception.

Dinner came sooner than we'd expected, although there was a lot of sitting around the dinner table waiting. The tablecloth, Rose told us, was a sarong from Alex's travels in Asia, and you could make out saltwater stains in the corner. Guatemalan candles matched the plates. Soon, Alex appeared with a steaming bowl of pasta.

"This is bucatini. Have you had it?"

"Yes, I've had it," my mother told him.

He grinned wildly and put it down before us, using a metal claw to scoop the pasta for us. "It's bucatini with mussels, which I bought today because they looked so good. That's how I like to do things, you know."

We toasted to their marriage. All of us had glasses of white wine except my mother, who held club soda in a glass, although Alex said this was bad luck. The food was good, and even my mom's face calmed to see that he'd been right, that maybe it was best this way, with mussels bought at the market in the morning, and yellow peppers haggled over with the Chinese lady on the corner. My father ate silently, but my mother looked for once a little happy. With her, it was always food that did this. Or maybe, it occurs to me now, some memory the food evoked.

I noticed my dad's usual deductive gaze had focused on Rose and Alex in the corner. They were eating their pasta out of one bowl. Two forks, one bowl. I finally kicked him to wake him from his own fascination, and he smiled at me.

"I have to say this about chemistry," Alex was saying. He'd been talking about cooking, and Greece, and how things were done there. My parents both raised eyebrows at the topic, curious. "I see it every day in schools, in science classes. This Anglo science, you're all so rigid! There's no life in it! The kids, they have to experiment the way the *teacher* says to experiment, and plan it, and plot charts. . . . I wanted to ask . . ."

My mother sat in expectation, looking as if she had swallowed the bay leaf. Alex leaned forward to her: "Do you Anglos, in your science, is there ever any joy?"

No, sorry—*that* was the moment she swallowed the bay leaf.

Alex went on, gesturing brusquely into the air, saying, "It should be like this. Life should always be like this, like it is in Greece. You have an imagination and you act on it. You have a question, you look around and see how to answer it. I want to know how this plant gets water to its flowers." He leaned back and pulled a flower stem from a lively geranium, peered at it, then presented it to Rose. "There, I see the little vesicles. Now I know. Isn't that what science should be? You tell me."

My mother smiled and used my grandmother's tactics. "Well bless your heart," she said, which my family knew was a curse. "Now what do you mean by 'Anglo'?"

He laughed. "You're offended! No, I just meant all of you, the Puritan white America. And England, too, Newton and other rigid thinkers."

"So, sugar," she said, another cruel word, "it's the scientific method you're against here." My father watched her; I was surprised how closely he studied her, as if for a sign from her that he should move in.

Alex seemed enlivened by this discussion. "That's it! Like anything old, it loses its original life and spirit. Like old men, in England, you see them puttering around the park feeding the pigeons." He made universal feeding-pigeon gestures. "But in Greece . . . the men drink, and walk around in the sun, and don't stop living. There is a saying we have. I'll show you." He took a pack of cigarettes out of his pocket, put one in his mouth, and lit it with a candle. "Someone here won't like me smoking. It's like that here, with Anglos. But in Greece we say you seize life. You have to do what you feel." He puffed and the smoke was carried out the window.

Even Rose looked astonished. I saw my mother put down her fork and smile, and somehow this was a sign for my father to cease his quiet. I knew this because my mom got up and walked into the kitchen, and my father shifted his whole body to focus on Alex.

My dad told him softly, "You're an interesting young man. I can give you the names of some books, and after you've read them, maybe we can talk about this again."

"But life! We may never meet like this again!" Alex pointed out.

"You know," my dad said, smiling, "you know, I bet you're right."

"I've brought dessert!" my mother announced.

I hadn't noticed it at all over the decades. I'd seen my parents, usually, as two forces in collision, two stars battling out their gravities, but it was clear I'd missed something along the way. They weren't in conflict at all—they were together—they were a frightening creature, of two long arms, one holding off Alex while the other brought in a distraction. How had this come about? Did my mother still stand alone in rooms, letting an old memory descend like a spider on its silk? Did he still crouch in small places, frightened in ways he couldn't explain to her? Were these privacies gone, or were they allowed by treaty? Or else—it could be that they came together in this cancer. That this cancer was a partner, too.

I only recognized that they'd done all this without me, without worrying or consulting me, that something enormous had happened in their lives outside this disease, or attached to it, and it was settled without a word. They would remain in love. They would be silent about it.

"It's peach cobbler," my mother said as Rose cleared all the pasta away. Mom put her glass dish on a trivet. "I made it from peaches I got just last week."

She did this every year, made my father drive her to a farm in Virginia to buy crates of peaches. She'd skin them, boil them in syrup, and freeze them for a winter's worth of desserts. It was almost, strangely, an argument against Alex. A call to baking, chemistry, measuring, and planning. The top glistened with sugar, and my mother slipped a spoon into the side, bringing out a heavy scent of peaches.

It took eight years for my mother to succumb to her disease, after having grown weak and then strong again over the years, gained and lost dozens of pounds, grown thick white hair, only to lose it over and over. After her funeral, I opened the basement freezer and saw the twenty or so bags of frozen peaches she had made so routinely, so optimistically that summer. I took one with me on the plane back to San Francisco and made a cobbler out of it that very night. I used my mother's precise, laboratory recipe, and ate it watching a rented movie with a woman I was dating. It was our second date, and I didn't tell her that my mother made the peaches, and that she had been alive just a week before, just last week on our first date. You can't tell that to strangers. She was a thin, beautiful redhead, and I watched her gingerly eat half her portion, put the rest aside, and I knew she wouldn't work out, either. I felt angry that I'd wasted such a treasure.

That night at Rose's, the cobbler wasn't good. Terribly, unfairly, it was the bite I couldn't swallow. I saw it on my plate, soft and doughy inside, uncooked, but my mom didn't seem to notice. She ate hers happily, and the rest of us tried, but my dad and I finally looked at each other with a panic. The treatment had dulled her tongue; she was growing prematurely old; we were losing her. Our faces showed these thoughts to each other, two cracked reflections of the same man.

Yet there my mother sat, fat and happy in the last sunlight coming through a potted palm. Later, in the elevator, she would turn to us and laugh all the way to the car, but here she was, chatting away with Rose, old friends, remembering the time she'd lived in this building when it was a hotel, the time she'd sat up late with two other girl scientists, whispering into flashlights, giggling about the handsome boys down the hall who came from Texas.

4

Some memories are briefer, like the last unswallowable bite. It is a meal my father made, just a few months ago, in his apartment, where he lives alone. My mother has been dead for years now, but his place still seems inert—paintings he bought with my mother lean against the walls, three or four of them together, and books still sit in piles on cardboard boxes. The sheets are mismatched, the towels, too, and I wonder how he has managed to take my mother's carefully organized belongings and thrust them into chaos so quickly. Are they never going to be right again? The place is like a drunk asleep in a bed, unwakeable, bedclothes strewn everywhere. His old beard is gone, but now he shaves intermittently, leaving gray stubble. He has taken up a pipe. Is this a sign of some decline? Or is it, in the end, how he always wanted things?

There are two photographs set neatly on the mantle, though. One of me from the Golden Age, holding a daisy, and one of my mother backlit by the sun. She would have hated having that picture out.

I know his place because I live nearby, having moved back to Michigan to follow my wife's career. My father and I are still getting used to having each other close, I the married one and he the untidy bachelor. It's hard, and may always feel this strange.

Last April, he had me over for dinner. He was in the kitchen, telling me a story about how he took my mother to a dirty movie when they were in Chicago. He was spooning something into wooden bowls, saying, "It made her very nervous, so we walked out and found Rose and got Chinese food. This was in Chicago. Your mother was giggling the whole night. You'd be surprised," he said, pointing at me. "We were young once, too."

He brought the bowls and set them down. I looked in and saw something pink and inedible. "It's cantaloupe salad," he said, grunting as he sat down.

Life sometimes clasps together like a locket.

He added, "I had it in a restaurant."

"You should've married Rose Chao," I said, chuckling.

He grunted, straightening his napkin. His thoughts seemed

far away, like boats out in the fog of a lake. I tried to see and failed. I ate the cantaloupe, forcing it down so he'd know he was doing fine alone.

But I'm sitting here, a mile from him, and I think maybe thirty years ago it seemed less sure who would be in love with whom, and how they would manage it. They couldn't have known, in that apartment under the sign of Einstein, that it would take so long to conquer marriage. And then lose it, like the only draft of your great genius novel left on a train.

He lifted the salad bowl and nodded at me, asking, "You want more of this? I'm just going to throw it out."

You want to go back in time and swallow every bite you missed, to please him. The cantaloupe, the liver, the cobbler, the ones you've forgotten. You want to go back to that night, take your father by the shoulders and shake him. He should have married Rose Chao and eaten demonic bowls of cantaloupe with her into old age. In retrospect, it might have made more people happy.

I said, "Don't throw it out, save it."

He grimaced, looking into the bowl. "I'll never eat this stuff."

You want to protect him and to change him. You want to burrow inside his dried life and crack it open to the sun, but this can't happen. He sits and rubs his stubble in a tired apartment. You drink beer and wonder if you married right. So you can't say a word as he stares blankly at his food, for you will never see for sure the owl inside him, swooping down upon some scuttling memory to feast on.

The Future of the Flynns

✐

THIS IS CHRISTMASTIME. The restaurant's air is polished with reflections from bright Italian ornaments—red spindles, wide-mouthed angels, a donkey stamped from tin—but otherwise sits unchanged. To the Amalfi's waiters, the odor of this air is ordinary, sharp with tomato and full of steam. Sometimes when the kitchen door opens, a foul waft comes through onto table twelve: the scent of old mussel shells rotting in their juice. Paulo, the maître d', always puts old people at table twelve, because they cannot smell anything, and cannot taste anything. This evening at twelve, an old man sits folding white napkins into rabbits. Paulo keeps supplying him with the napkins. The ice coating the old man's shoulders is melting into the tweed, and he orders minestrone to warm himself. Table seven is open for a party of five. A family.

That is the table for the Flynns. How many? Six—they have miscounted somehow. Ella Flynn has counted her twin sons as one child. So soon another chair will have to be hunted up for the extra four-year-old. His name is Danny and he will order, at the climax of the evening, a plate of "calimari cooked in its own ink." When the boy orders this simple squid, Paulo will notice a strange horror from the adults at the table. Paulo will wonder about these looks all night, wonder what could be so terrible about a little boy's whim.

The Flynns are getting in the car. The car is still outside their house, surrounded by puffs of snow on either side, the thriftiest kind of snow. In Washington, the mayor has not allotted money for snowplows, so its fallen shapes will remain. The Flynns are all in snow jackets of artificial fibers, clutching themselves and thinking how clear and deadly the night air is—that if it drops one more degree, the Flynns will freeze up like eels in a pond, caught in just these self-hugging positions of fear.

But in fact, they aren't all Flynns; two are Hagertons. Ella's parents visiting from Georgia. Ed Hagerton is talking to Alan Flynn about the car itself, a deep blue Dodge Dart, a used car. They are discussing the advantages of a new car, and Alan Flynn is thinking he and his wife cannot afford it, a new car, that his whole life his family has never had a new car. Ed Hagerton drives a new Cadillac. He and his wife also cannot afford it on his butcher's salary, but they are getting old, and when Ed went to war, he promised Leona a new Cadillac one day if he lived, and he lived, and so he drives a new Cadillac.

Where is Leona? Still in the house. A small house, a first house. Mostly living room. A high coffee table sits in the middle, tiled with burnt yellow squares, and around it pieces of wooden furniture: a long-legged rocking chair from when the twins were babies, a dining room chair set out for company, the lusterless leather couch with wings of teak (the great luxury of the room, the new Cadillac of the Flynns). A spider plant hangs above in a beaded macramé cradle. The walls of the room are thin and white. Paintings of abstract orange flowers cheer feebly above the couch.

Leona Hagerton, Ella's mother, is bent over the coffee table. Her thin hair, dyed a believable red and teased into a dull hot-air balloon of lacquer, catches the fluorescent light. It becomes a glowing nest. She leans over her purse and inserts a letter. It is a letter from the soon-to-be president, Jimmy Carter, her boy from Georgia. It is an invitation to his ball in Atlanta. She is taking it to the restaurant as evidence. It is to be used in her story of why she loves Jimmy Carter so. He invites her, little Leona Hagerton, who dresses so poorly that she shivers in her long coat even in the house, Jimmy Carter invites her to parties. Of course, everybody in Georgia gets these invitations.

But that's wrong. Jimmy Carter's election is in November of 1976, so the twins would be six years old at dinner, but that makes no sense. Danny cannot order the squid at six and still seem to auger an unexpected, harder life. No, the story is wrong. The twins are four. But let it go. Let her be inserting a letter from Jimmy Carter nonetheless. It doesn't matter.

Outside, the Flynns are in the car, closed tight against the black air, with the heater rattling away like a katydid. The twins are quiet and wide-eyed. They don't know, sometimes, what's going on. They are in red corduroy jackets with ski masks rolled up on their copper hair. Their mittens dangle from their sleeves. Both of their noses are red and snotty, and each breathes an identical quiet cloud. Sometimes they speak their secret language to each other. But not tonight.

Leona makes her way across the ice. Her shoes are impractical for this, and she looks worriedly at the Dodge Dart to see how late she has made them for the letter. Ed is not watching her. He, like his twin grandsons, is breathing a quiet cloud. Leona puts her arms out like a bird to balance on the ice, to balance in the air, which is one degree from ice and thick with that possibility. All around her, snow is blunt and plain under the streetlights. She makes it to the car. She sits in back with her daughter and the twins. They are late, the Hagertons and the Flynns, for dinner at the Amalfi.

The reservation is just for Flynn, though. So while there are two Hagertons, for your purposes, they are all Flynns. Maybe make them Alan's parents. It doesn't matter.

In the Amalfi, the old man is still eating his soup; he has put off folding rabbits for a while. He is warmed at last. The waiter, Paulo, is comforted by this man. He asks so little. For dessert, the old man wants half a pear, cored with a spoon so a soft depression will form. Paulo will drip port wine into a pool there. It is all already planned.

Behind the door by table twelve, where rich and slightly foul odors fan out, the sous-chef is angrily popping mussels with a blunt knife. The dinner special involves mussels, and everybody wants the dinner special, though all the seafood is surely frozen, even on the Potomac. No one has ordered calimari, however. The squid sits in a metal bowl, wide-eyed and quiet.

The Dodge Dart is performing well and all of those Flynns crammed inside have made it hot as a brothel. They are dressed up. There is no occasion except the gathering of the Flynns, which will never happen again here in suburban Maryland, they all know, because Ed and Leona hate flying, will claim to be too sick to fly. So this is their only trip to the Amalfi.

Ella is in a gray dress to please her mother, Leona. Leona has always forbidden her girls to wear red. It draws attention; it is the color of a whore. Ella wears thick glasses and pats the heads of her twin sons. Her hair is barretted above her ears, and she is afraid it makes her nose larger. Her father, Ed, once told her she had a Roman nose: "It roams all over your face!" He always made her sing for guests. I remember that, she thinks to herself. That was how he used to be: lively and brutal.

So Ed and Leona have to be her parents after all. They could never be Flynns.

Leona wears a pale green pantsuit she bought at Sears. She is thin as a blade of grass. Her face is made up in pinks from Avon; she sells Avon back in Augusta, Georgia. For Christmas, she will give her daughter Avon perfume and the twins Batman

Avon hairbrushes. She is worried, talking furiously about her neighbors to her daughter, although Ella does not know her neighbors. This loud worrying comforts Leona. She would never talk of this comfort. Sometimes she asks Ed a question—"Isn't that right, Ed?" or "What was her name, Ed?"—but he doesn't reply and she doesn't expect him to.

Ed doesn't talk, doesn't tell stories anymore, or make his daughters sing, or bring home funny strangers to dinner. In 1960, a man came to the door holding his hat over his chest, asking to talk to Ed. Ella overheard the news: Two women had died in a car crash in Kentucky. She learned this was her father's first family, a wife and daughter he left for Leona twenty years before. Ella shouted her rage at him for keeping it a secret, this whole other family he abandoned as a young man. Leona left the room, but Ed took his daughter's fury. He stared at her red face and flying ponytail and began to shake. Perhaps he moved, in that moment, from the half of life when you build things to the half when they fall apart. Afterward, people would say he seemed "touched," perhaps had come undone. Ed hushed, and became this man, this kind, silent, dopey man in the front seat, just smiling without a word.

Fifteen years from now, Ella will leave her own family, Alan and the grown-up twins. Her father, Ed, will mail her all his butcher knives, dull and half-rusted swords. It will be her old father, the defiant one who died in that car crash, who sends them. Ella will open the tissue paper, kneeling, put a hand to her mouth, and swallow wordless grief.

But they are all dressed up tonight!

The twins are finally speaking in their secret language because no one else is talking to them. You would never be able to tell, but they are making up a story. It's about a green boy lost in a house, and all the ghosts around him, but there's another little boy there, also green, so it's not so bad, it's never so bad then. Here's what they sound like:

"Babba bitty boy gitta ghosty house, gitta ghosty babba round. . . ."

They sound like babies.

They haven't thought yet about the restaurant, or being hungry, or being cold, or the snot drying on their noses. Danny hasn't planned that he will order the fateful squid.

But wait—why Danny? If they are twins, why wouldn't Marky order the squid? They dress alike, talk the same languages, tell the same stories. They are the focus of each other's worlds at four years old, so why wouldn't they both order the squid?

They are becoming different already. Marky, for instance, is very shy. He hides his red nose deep inside the fake-fleece hood of his coat. He lets Danny tell the frame of the ghost story. Marky knows the details, and adds them only when necessary: a *green* boy. He likes to run very fast. He despises mushrooms—his father jokes that this is because he dropped Marky on his head as a baby.

Danny is louder, standing in the middle of the room and yelling, "*la! la! la!*" until a parent notices him or Marky joins in. When he was three, he drew a picture of himself as a girl. Ella found it. Danny got to see a psychoanalyst at only three. The man said not to worry, that Danny must have looked around him and seen only male-female couples—his parents, partners at day care, his grandparents, Donny and Marie Osmond—and thought since Marky was obviously male, he must be female. This explanation did not dispel Ella and Alan's worries. So the psychoanalyst gave them a book called *Growing Up Straight*.

Leona knows about the drawing and the psychoanalyst. Ella regrets telling her about it in her own, inherited fit of worrying. And Leona is weird about it. She's told Alan that when she was a little girl, all boys of three wore frilly dresses and curled their hair. That is to say, all children did. Boys grew out of it, and girls never did, and the time to worry was later.

Alan glared at Ella during this speech. And Leona has begun on this trip to pay a lot of attention to Danny, which is exactly what *Growing Up Straight* says not to do. Ella is going to talk to her about it.

So there is already a subtlety to the twins. There is something quiet about Marky, and something dangerous about Danny. The twins are quite unaware of all this. Marky does not remember being dropped on his head, and Danny already doesn't remember the psychoanalyst or the drawing, which has been thrown away. Here's all they say: "Babba bother bitty boy bidda ghosty house. . . ."

And Leona is still talking. She is telling of her neighbor who puts up green tomatoes so that this time of year all of the cul-de-sac can eat relishes for Christmas. She tells of an Indian family who moved in down the street, who gave Leona a bottle of chutney. Leona did not know what to do with it; it was not relish. She had no interest in it. But her sewing partner, Wilma, got all excited just to see it. So Leona gave it to her because she seemed to want it, but she feels sorry for Wilma. Wilma gets excitement only out of new and different things. But Wilma is very sad. Leona says she thinks it's fine to be brave, but it's another thing entirely to be brave and never satisfied.

Ed nods and smiles at this story. He's heard it before, and likes it this time, too.

And the car turns the corner and stops. The Flynns have arrived at the Amalfi!

Now they have to go out in the cold again. There is a moment of hesitation when Leona has to choose between the cramped backseat of the Dodge Dart or the frozen air outside. But everyone else is already outside. The twins are dancing around near the bumper, their mittens twirling from their wrists, and they have to be rounded up. Outside, the Amalfi is dark brick with an archway entrance. Dirty yellow lanterns light the side, and the windows are diamond-paned and multicolored. This, Leona thinks, is what a real Italian restaurant should look like.

The boys throw off their coats inside. They, too, are dressed up: both in ruffled shirts. Marky and Danny have wanted ruffled shirts for a whole year now, and Alan had to search all of Washington to find some. Neither parent has any idea where the boys saw them. Marky's shirt is pink; Danny's is light blue. The boys are always color-coded this way: Marky red, Danny blue. Their whole lives, they will claim each, in all honesty, as their favorite color.

Paulo guesses that these are the Flynns. The old man is eating his pear now after letting the port seep in. Paulo admires the man for his imagination. Paulo walks up, smiling fiercely, with five menus. Coats are being flung onto hooks and all of the Flynns are red-cheeked, eyebrows high, as if surprised by the cold. Ella explains they are six. She must have counted the twins as one. Leona pinches Danny's cheek and jokes that they almost forgot him. Danny stares at his bee-hived grandmother. Another waiter is sent to get the extra chair for this dangerous twin.

Again, all is Christmas inside the Amalfi. A Christmas tree studded with electric candles, the dented Italian ornaments speckling the walls with light, wicker-bottom bottles of Chianti strung everywhere. The tables spiral out from the tree: two white tablecloths draped at diagonals to each other. Paulo insists on the two cloths when he is maître d'. He saw it once in a magazine.

Leona is mildly flirtatious with Paulo. He smells her Avon perfume and can tell she has dressed up for the Amalfi. She tells him how handsome he is, even touches his cheek with a pink fingernail. And he is handsome; he has a Roman nose. Leona clicks her tongue when she notices he wears no wedding ring. "Don't Italian boys get married young?" she asks. Paulo blushes, but under his dark skin, no one can tell. The Anglo Flynns are blushing openly, though, blushing from the cold as if afire. Paulo doesn't answer her question, just smiles and gracefully passes out the menus.

Danny and Marky are speaking in their secret language. Alan makes them stop.

Paulo has left to help the old man at table twelve get up to leave. The man says, "Back out into the cold!" and chuckles. Paulo nods.

At table seven, Ed has begun to talk. Everyone else is quiet, watching, their faces pinched in curiosity that he would speak. Even Leona is silent. He is talking about how all his family were musicians. This has come out of nowhere. He is motioning slowly with his red butcher's hands, rowing through the tin-lit air, telling of the ragged South Carolina porch of his old house, and how all of his brothers and sisters would wake up Sunday mornings, polish their instruments, and sit in a row to play for the people going to church. He must have been three or four, and Ed describes himself as "no bigger than a cricket." He remembers most clearly the cedar crate of instruments, and his siblings reaching in for—not any particular one—whatever first touched skin. They worked with whatever they picked up—trombones and little Jew's harps, a concertina and a limberjack. They could play anything in their hands. People always came by to hear them, and Ed remembers how one day a Negro family walked up early on a Sunday morning with a viola in a case. Even Ed could tell that they were poor, poorer even than the Hagertons on their leaning waterlogged porch. They had been left this viola by a grandfather, and not one of them had ever heard it played. And how his tall brother Furman lifted it from their hands, carefully undid the case, brought out that shining thing, and played it all morning.

Ed fingers the table when he talks. He pushes the words through his sullen lips with concentration—this is not babbling. This is the storytelling of a man who knows his quiet's coming on again. He goes on, though, tells how he was so young then, dizzy on those raucous Sundays, and by the time he was ten, all his brothers and sisters had grown up, with porches and dull children of their own, had sold the instruments for flour and sugar and beer. When he tried to speak of that time on the porch with them, that happiest time, they all denied it. They said he'd made it up, made up the whole story. Their frivolous musical youth was an embarrassment, you see, a workingman's embarrassment.

Certainly no one knows what to say to this. The tin ornaments clink in the silence. Ella will remember this speech when the butcher knives come in the mail. It will be a time to regret things.

Luckily, Paulo comes back with a little white pad and chattering indecision commences. Leona finally chooses the spaghetti. Her daughter has the veal scallopini, and so does Alan. Marky gets lots of meatballs, and one can see in his quiet face a joy at the thought of them. Ed is looking down at his empty plate. Leona orders spaghetti for him, too. He doesn't like any other Italian food, she explains to Paulo. Ed says nothing to protest.

And Danny, Danny has the menu propped up in his chubby fingers. He tilts his head right and left, with just the pink tip of his tongue peeking out between his lips. He is concentrating. He sees a line that says "calimari cooked in its own ink," and he cannot imagine what it could be. Certainly nothing his grandmother has ever cooked for him, or his mother. Maybe he imagines a fiddler simmering in the broth of his own song. He puts the menu down on the white double cloth.

New silver is sparkling in Paulo's hand. Danny opens his mouth, and Paulo can see there on that pink tongue, rolling like a beveled ruby bead, a prophecy.

Come Live with Me and
Be My Love

∽

TODAY IS MY fortieth birthday. I don't feel old at all. I've been sitting here for a while, on this courtyard bench, and if she's coming, then she's late. Married couples walk around, trying to interest each other, pointing to the faded pink walls and to the iron balustrades. The men tell the women facts from guidebooks, pretending these are things they know. Wind fans the blond hair of one young man as he takes a surreptitious photo of his bride. Photos aren't allowed here. She grins pinkly, arranges her white hat over an ear. I can see how happy this makes her—not the photo, but the consciously illegal pose. They'll look at the picture years from now and remember most of all the camera's secret whir.

I don't see anyone who looks like my wife, but then I'm not sure what she looks like these days. In college, where I first met her in the mid-sixties, she always showed up at places women never went—club theater, professorial bars, psychology debates—and always entered late. It was her rule to be obvious. She'd show up in a brown plaid dress and blond hair curled in a neat cyclone on her head, and everyone would watch. They all would notice the strange thing—her eyebrows were painted on, and one was drawn in a hysterical, curious arch. That was what I first noticed about her: this painted expression.

We never talked until the day she grabbed me outside the refectory and insisted I go with her to audition for a movie filming in Providence. I refused until she intimated that my overbreeding showed in my lack of adventure. So I went, and I remember they wrote down on my card "handsome college type" and on Britta's "wild-girl type" and we both got parts somehow. It was a terrible Rock Hudson movie, *Halls of Ivy*, and if you ever catch it late at night on television, you will see Britta's gigantic hat and laughing face emerge from Rock's shoulder. And even in that one second, the frame of action slows, drawn curling and enamored into the bewildering dream of her life.

So we dated for a while, the kind of formal dating set up back then. At least that was how it began, but Britta wasn't interested in wearing a sweater across her shoulders and having me serenade her. I think she saw in me just enough reticence to be a challenge, just enough self-control, but also the kind of curiosity that, in spite of myself, made me smile and shake my head and follow her. The Rock Hudson movie, the greyhound races, the shop of occult necklaces and masks. She would try on a headdress of silver coins and turn to me, that eyebrow leering under the mail, and I thought here was a girl who could never come home to Kentucky.

Once in a while she went to my parties. There was one in 1964, a New Year's party in Boston held by a fellow I knew from the Jabberwocks, my singing group at Brown. It was a beautiful apartment, with an iron spiral staircase and brass Indian poppies littering the railing. It was Beacon Hill, and everybody there was Harvard or Yale or Brown; the rule was always no Princeton ever, because they stole the girls. The Jabberwocks loved Britta, but you could see the other Pembroke girls in their navy woolen kneesocks and yellow oxford button-downs cringing, shocked sometimes at Britta's loud banging walk or clumsy maneuver with the matron's teapot. Britta embarrassed me, too, getting "clobbered," as the Jabberwocks liked to say, at cocktail parties and relating filthy stories to amazed young men, keeping us waiting forever while she searched a gutter for a Celtic necklace she had lost there—a hollow silver band that rattled at a touch, for inside were Druidic talismans of hope. I bought her that necklace. She played an awful doubles tennis, but our opponents always asked for more matches because Britta's constant deep laughter was entrancing.

She and I walked into the upper room, and they had already run out of olives, so we had to drink Gibsons, which Britta pretended she preferred. A few men were in the corner singing a drunken "Aura Lee."

"You know where I'd rather be?" Britta whispered to me.

"Do tell, darling," I replied, looking around at all the school ties.

"On an island."

"Any island, darling?"

She stared at me and clicked her tongue. "No no no. I'm very specific, and very serious. Saint Eustatius. It's Dutch, with a rain forest and a volcano and very mystical crabs. . . ."

"Those islands are colder than you think. I've been there with my mother."

"But it'd be great. I wouldn't ever drink Gibsons, or listen to 'Aura Lee.' I'd be a pirate, a gilded white scorpion. Wouldn't it be wonderful?"

I didn't say anything, because I couldn't possibly imagine such a thing.

Out on the balcony, I caught my friend Randall all alone, smoking a long cigarette and staring at a view he must have found tiresome.

"What kind of host are you?" I asked.

"It isn't my party, really. Sally wanted it." A Radcliffe girl he'd been seeing, and seemed bored with. He waved his hand girlishly. "You and Britta are my only friends here."

He must have said this for Britta's sake, for she was just then arriving through the glass door, saying something to a group inside who laughed suddenly and loudly. She turned to us, closed the door, and rolled her eyes.

Randall blew smoke out and asked her, "How can you do it? Why does everybody love you, Britta?"

"Are you saying nobody loves *you*?" I broke in.

"Oh, that's no trick at all," Britta answered him, shaking her head seriously and pushing her dark lips into a casual kiss. "You ask people about themselves. They go on and on and then turn and tell their girlfriends what a marvelous conversationalist you are."

I remember she smiled and turned away from him to go back inside, breaking her own rule to make Randall think he had been let into some secret life of hers, a crueler one.

Randall was new to the Jabberwocks, still a sophomore, like me, and slightly in awe of the secret ceremonies and histories of the group, though things like school and girls seemed not to interest him. He was tall, with curly red hair and nearly invisible eyebrows, but handsome and resolutely Irish in his chin and small pink lips.

We had become friends only that Thanksgiving, when we were both invited to be on the Floor Committee of the National Debutante Cotillion in Washington. We took the train together, drinking Scotch the whole way, and met our stiff and beautiful debutante dates quite drunk, our hair messed up and our red sashes disarrayed. Presented on their fathers' arms on that giant stage, their escorts two steps behind, the girls were quite serious, but Randall and I had a blast despite them. We had been to enough cotillions to be bored of the rituals. When the waltz came and all the escorts were to tap the father's shoulder and release the girl into the world of men, we both took the girls into foolish jitterbugs, then waltzed off with each other to the bar. No one said a word, because Randall's family was powerful—wealthy Washingtonian Democrats who had been invited to the front row of the Kennedy funeral. That night at the New Year's Eve party, I remember he wore a tie clip with a small photograph of Jack Kennedy under gold mesh. The tie was Andover. Mine was Kent School for Boys. Those things mattered to us then.

"Hey, Paul," he said to me. "Did Barick say you were moving up to tenor?"

"He's making me. He's crazy."

We were outside on a balcony, and it was cold. Yet we were drunk enough not to mind being alone out there. The only light came through the eyelet curtains, and it beaded on our backs like luminous rain we could not shake. The air was deep blue and all in front of us Boston spread out in a sagging post-Christmas carnival.

Randall went on: "Oh, he likes the idea of a black-haired tenor. He's tired of us redheaded Irish stealing the show every time."

"But I'm Irish. I'm black Irish."

He seemed determined on this point, shaking his empty glass, which glowed in the dim light like a deep-sea creature: "No no. You, my friend, are Scots-Irish. You can tell from that nose you're a rogue clan. You have to have dominion over everything, especially women and horses. That's the South. That's your dear old Kentucky—every one of them rogue Scots-Irish."

"I've never thought of my dad as a rogue."

He turned away from me and lit a cigarette. "What does he do again?"

"He's on the radio."

"Runs the station?"

"No," I said, laughing a little and letting him pour me more gin from a bottle at his side. "He has a show. He's Mr. Social

Security for western Kentucky. They ask him questions and
he answers them. He's kind of famous."

"Wow. That's strange, Paul."

I pictured my family sitting in our living room in the summer, the electric fans blowing and my mother sorting her
Butterick patterns while we heard my father over the radio.
He advised old, frightened Kentuckians in that countrified
way of his about how the government would provide, always
and forever. It was a government-sponsored show. "This is
the Age of America," he always said to those folks, and they
were grateful to hear it. He told me not long before he died
that he was proud to have comforted them, people who had
lived through so much, their children always hungry, going
to bed cold. My father knew all of that—his family lost a
logging mill in the Depression. All of our money came from
my mother.

I am proud of him now, but back then it was an embarrassment. I did not know why I was so eager to impress Randall, but there he sat, his hair gleaming from the apartment
lights, that school tie, the beautiful way his white hand rose
above his head to touch the brick.

"I have to go and host," he said, looking up at his own
hand. His neck was thin and half-shadowed as it stretched.

I leaned to let the light catch my watch. "But it's almost
midnight. You have to stay just a few minutes."

Randall brought his face down, but his hand played with
the brick. I remember he smiled drunkenly. "I should be inside," he said. "Sally will want to be near me when it comes
time to kiss." I chuckled, sounding like my father in my false
comfort.

"All right, you bastard." I stood up and felt the chill of the
air. I turned toward him and the light from the apartment's
curtains dotted me. I must have seemed mystical in that poin-
tillism, seen through a filigree. He sat for a moment, then
needed a hand getting out of the chair, so I pulled on his

wrist. He was very light and his wrist was adolescently bony, and cool. Randall was only nineteen. So was I. That was a long time ago.

Noises came from the apartment, foolish clacking noise-makers and bells and those shrill plastic horns. All of the cabs on the street began to honk merrily, and a whistling fire-cracker went off somewhere below.

"So I have to go," he said. But now there was something fierce in the air: He looked panicked, as if having to go were a frightening thing. His pale face became ruddy, fiery at the cheeks. He jammed his lips together.

I said the sort of thing we always said: "Well, give Sally a kiss for me, too."

But it wasn't the right thing to say. Randall still stared around him, searching all the tiles of the balcony. He said only, "I will. Tell Britta I'll marry her."

Laughter came loudly from some men inside, and our singing group began to sing "Auld Lang Syne" in Scottish accents.

"I guess we should be inside," I said.

"No," Randall said, giving a sudden look, bright and insistent. We stood there for a moment. As he stared, his cheeks burned away in the cold air. I know what the look was now. I suppose I must have appeared the same way. It was: This is the word I've been searching for all day.

"What is it?" I asked.

"Nothing, just let's not go in just now."

"All right." I put out my right arm to settle him, touch his sleeve, but it felt ghostly, as if it floated out by itself in the dark light. Randall must have seen my hand palm out to him. He grimaced at me and crossed his arms, and I put my hand back in my pocket. Or rather, the hand floated back to my pocket. We were both shaking with an uncertain shame, and shame was such an important part of our upbringings. It must have been that recognition that made me smile, despite all my discomfort.

It was the most frightening moment of my life up until then, because somehow I knew neither of us wanted to be in there with our girls. We waited because it seemed someone had something honest and painful to say, but it was not said, so we stood half-shivering, amazed and innocent on that balcony, only nineteen and wearing the foolish ties of our boys schools. Certainly in that moment, I was loved by someone.

And then Britta walked onto the balcony. I turned my whole body away from Randall to face her.

"It's 1965," she said, then waved her hand. "So are you guys going to kiss or what?"

Randall looked at me and laughed, then nodded and put out his palm. We shook hands—ridiculous—then he left through the glass door. Britta watched his progress through the room, the various stolen kisses I could hear but not see, then she folded her arms and looked at me, shivering. She looked radiantly happy.

"What?" I asked. She shrugged her shoulders. "What?"

I walked forward and kissed her for the first time. We had been dating for a while, but never had I kissed her, because Pembroke girls were notorious for anger at such points. And Britta always laughed and turned away whenever we were close enough. She let me kiss her for a moment on that Beacon Hill balcony, then pulled away, and her face was as angry as I'd imagined. I thought to myself, You did it wrong again. But she patted my shoulder, as if the anger were about something else entirely.

"You're a puzzle, Mr. Robinson," she said.

"Not really."

"No," she said, smiling. "Not really."

Britta walked over to the balcony and leaned over the rail, thrusting her head up to catch the new wind. I stood behind her and watched her gold hairdo unravel.

I finally pulled out a cigarette and offered one to her. When Britta turned around, I tried to read her mind, but as usual, it was impossible. I had dated many girls with wide expressions, but Britta was unreadable. She took the cigarette and let me light it in her hand. She looked up into my eyes when she was done with the flame. She would always do that.

✑

Near the end of sophomore year, I caught mono, which was a bad thing for the Jabberwocks, because Randall was sick, too, and we were the only tenors who could hit "How High the Moon." Also, Providence was warm and plush with magnolia at that time of year and all the Pembroke girls would waltz down Thayer arm in arm, their Bermudas flapping and their capped teeth dazzling each bitter young man they teased. So I lay in my dorm room, my roommate having dropped out a month before and gone back to New York City. I watched the fraternity men throwing footballs and shouting names of girls they loved too much.

Britta pounded the door in that way of hers, to find me dressing for a Jabberwock cocktail party with the university's president. I remember she was all in green lace, a dress and a vest, with a worn brown leather bag thrown over her shoulder. She kept yelling at me to get back into bed, and when I wouldn't and stood delirious in front of the mirror fixing my Windsor knot, she offered me at least a cup of tea. I drank it all down, and within minutes I was dead asleep on my bed.

I woke up hours later to find Britta smearing cold cream on my face and humming faintly. She had tied her hair up and had taken off her vest, so she was only in that green lace dress.

"Ah," she said. "You're alive again."

"God, what happened?"

"Oh, I drugged your tea."

I couldn't move, just sat there, feeling her rub the cream into my skin.

"What?" I complained faintly.

"Don't move. I'm cleaning your face. Being sick makes you greasy."

"You mickeyed my tea? Are you a Communist or something?"

Britta wiped her hands off on a towel and knitted her brow. "I wasn't going to let you meet President Keeney feverish and strange, was I?"

"That's illegal, Britta."

She snickered at that and brought over a box of Kleenex to wipe off the cold cream. My view of her face was blocked by those tissues passing over me like clouds.

"How do you know," I began again, "that I'm not on some drug that would react strongly to sleeping pills?"

"Don't be a child, Paul," she said. "Sit back. I'm going to give you a dry shampoo now, so don't move."

"A dry shampoo?"

"You look awful." Britta brought out a bottle of baby powder and began sprinkling it in her palms. "Besides," she said, "I want to talk to you about something."

She dangled her fingers above my face and some powder snowed down on me. Then she slid her hands into my hair, rubbing at my sick scalp and cleaning me all over. I felt utterly helpless and ill, and she was cleaning me.

"What . . ." I said, "what do we have to talk about that you must drug me?"

"I'm tired of living in the dorms, Paul."

"Yeah, really."

"You are, too, right?"

"Those frat guys drive me crazy with their boozing."

"So we're both tired of living in the dorms."

"I applied for off-campus permission," I said, closing my eyes as she stroked my head with powder. It was a lovely feeling.

I heard Britta say, "You know that won't work. No one

gets off-campus permission except married couples. You have to be married."

"Right," I said. I sat there for a moment, eyes closed, until I realized she was staring at me. I looked up and she took her hands out of my hair and put them on her lap. She sat very ladylike on my bed, the dainty dress, the neat green ribbon around her throat, her wide, pretty face, the hair slightly wild, piled on her head. She was expecting me to be wise at that moment.

"Oh Britta," I said, "we've only been dating for a little while."

Then her composure dropped and she laughed. She got up off my bed and walked to my door.

"We haven't been dating, Paul. You kissed me once, half a year ago." Britta closed the door and locked it. She leaned against it and widened her eyes at me. It almost looked like pity.

"What is it, then?" I demanded. "I spend every waking hour with a girl and we're not dating? And now you want marriage?"

"Paul," she said, her chin to her chest, "we're not lovers. We're beards."

The men playing football began to sing the Brown fight song. It had a "Ki yi yi" in the chorus. "What does that mean?" I asked. The moment was entirely frightening to me. Britta seemed a nightmare creature of my delirium at that second, instead of my best friend.

"We're covers. We're false lovers, because we can't tell anyone who we really love, can we?"

"Who is it?" I asked, sarcastic and fearful. "Who is that I *really* love?"

"Paul, I've met your father," she said, walking toward me. "He would disown you. I know my father would disown me. They love us, but they'd kill us before they knew. And then what kind of life would we have? Not this one. I like this one."

"Who is this secret lover of mine?"

"What a relief just to be married like they want."

"You've got mono," I said confidently. "You're the sick one now."

"No," she said, sitting on the bed and putting her hand over mine. "Randall is. You and he have mono together."

I threw her hand from me. I felt nauseated. "What are you saying?" I said. I raged my fingers through my hair to get the filthy powder out of it. A cloud surrounded me, but Britta didn't laugh this time. She put her finger to her lips and whispered harshly, "I don't want to talk about it. I have women lovers whom you need never meet nor mention. I'm not asking to discuss your love life. I'd rather we never discussed it. I'm asking for you to listen this once, Paul." She put her hands on either side of my chest and a worried look came over her face. "We're unlucky. People are talking, Paul. Saying I'm a man and you're a pansy. If we make a mistake, we could be ugly to the world, but we're smart. And we're creative."

I said nothing. Powder settled on her dress.

I will never understand how Britta knew everything I did or felt. It had been only a few months before, over spring break, that I had gone to Randall's house on Long Island. I always did this—there was no special occasion. His parents were gone, as they usually were when he asked them, and we spent a few days getting cold in walks along the gray beaches. We became more and more silent with each other, and yet I was insistent that we take these walks. There was some kind of tea dance going on at Shelter Island, and that afternoon I suggested we go. I wanted to distract him from whatever was worrying him—I'm sure I needed distraction, too. There was a faint flurry falling outside, unseasonal, and Randall had lit a fire. He was proud of the fire. There was something in his father that always made Randall pointedly manly. So he stoked the fire in his thick gray sweater and, not looking at me, agreed. Then he suggested we arrive roaring drunk. Of course this idea came like a relief.

His father had a habit of storing half-drunk martinis in the freezer and forgetting them, so we started with those—there was no other gin in the house. Then we mixed drinks for each other. Not cruelly, though it began that way, but exotically. We made drinks like vodka and crème de menthe, which Randall held up to his red hair. He knew doing that would make him beautiful. He made me drinks of blue-eyed curaçao. Soon it was dark and we forgot all about the tea dance, perhaps had never really meant to go.

I remember watching him talk. I thought it was a trick of my heart. But there, just for a moment in his eyes, his parted lips, I could tell his mind was whirring. I saw the muscles twitch. But really, in the Yankee conversation and polite eyes, it was only a passing, deep, unordinary instant, and I thought it must have been the colored drinks he kept handing me.

Randall played records for me, songs I didn't quite like then—modern jazz and odd, foreign classical—but we danced with invisible debutantes. We made false conversation to them, ridiculed them. We practiced shaming them with cool WASP weapons. Then we danced with each other, silent, not touching, and then, of course, wrapped warmly like an old couple near the end of the night. Then our heads tilted back, and I looked at him. Randall's face was in a shadow, his stare at me the only bright thing there, but I could hear a tiny noise come from him, a kind of realization—*huh*—before he smiled. And then, to make him close his eyes, I kissed him.

The bed we awoke in was two hundred years old, and it surprised me that nothing was different in the snowless morning. I began the lover's doubts: Why is he not holding me? And there, now he's turned over as he wakes and he's looking at me. There, now he's holding my hand. What does he mean? I caught his eye as seldom as I could, out of simple fear. And I almost bolted—only because I knew he was not going to leave.

"Think about it, Paul," Britta said to me that day of her proposal. "You're in trouble now, but this could make things very easy."

I turned away from her, looking out the window, to where the other men beat one another on the backs out of laughing brotherhood, which was also a kind of loneliness.

"I'm asking now because I'm getting scared for us," she said, getting up and pulling her brown bag off the floor. "And because that yellow house on the hill is for sale. Remember we walked by that house with the white columns and the widow's walk?"

There was a knock on the door and a look came over her face, like a child caught burying her allowance. It was a lovely face, serious and innocent. Britta glanced at me and unlocked the door. Two boys from my singing group came in with a mason jar of chicken soup and a folder of dirty pictures. They were quiet around Britta, but after she left, they told me about the Jabberwock party the night before and produced a note from Randall, sick a floor below me, a note sealed in an envelope. They showed a boyish awe when I told them I was engaged.

∞

Britta and I were married in October, in a small ceremony in Maine. She wore a band of daisies in her hair, and a white ribbon trailed down her back onto the ground. Randall was my best man. I did not know the woman Britta chose as maid of honor, but she was beautiful and brunette and nice enough. The Jabberwocks sang at the reception, and Britta and I danced to "How High the Moon." Randall sang the solo, looking at me the whole while I spun that grinning, ribboned young woman around the floor.

My mother bought us the yellow house on Meeting Street, and when Britta came wide-eyed into my bedroom with a photograph of a divan she'd cut out of *The New Yorker*, my mother helped us buy that, too. I still have that divan. The wood is deep yellow, and a sea of striped white silk covers it. We had an upright piano, a Baldwin, and acres of bookcases were built into the walls to house Britta's collection of foreign books and fairy tales. My bedroom was the master bedroom, and my wife slept in the guest bed, which was draped in a ridiculous fall of mosquito netting, which she said made her feel exotic and safe. We were twenty, the same age as my parents when they were married.

The arrangements were unspoken but clear. Randall came over "for dinner" as often as I liked, but he never interfered in the time Britta and I had together. Sometimes I would get out five ingredients and dare her to make a dinner from them, and she always took the dare. And her meals were always abysmal. Her frequent lovers came through back stairs and parked in the church lot. I rarely met them except late at night when I crept downstairs for a book and found Britta and a woman, beautiful and sweet or harsh or distantly intelligent, whispering sincerely over sherry. Britta was never angry to see me. She always pulled her peacocked kimono close around her breast and smiled.

Britta often saw ghosts and haunts around this old merchant town, and sometimes she sat in her guest bed throwing coins to tell the future of all her friends. She would yell out the fortunes to me, things that never made any sense: "A woman," I would hear through the wall at night, "crosses from a wide lake to a river," as if that explained it all.

We didn't live through the sixties, not the sixties everyone else seems to remember. I had Communist friends, but no one who would blow up the Supreme Court for a cause. They were Brown men who despised their parents' fortunes, wore only Salvation Army brown cotton jackets, but always gold watches and rings gave them away. We listened to Dave Brubeck and not Charlie Parker, Tom Lehrer instead of Woody Guthrie, because what we sought was cleverness and not sincerity. None of our crowd stormed University Hall, and we watched with only mild interest as more and more black boys entered our classes. It neither upset nor thrilled us. The change was utterly separate from the lives we had always led.

⁂

Randall threw a party in my honor at our graduation in the spring of 1967. It was in the mansion of an old faggot professor we knew, a mansion down on Benefit Street, with its cobblestones and brass horse rails. A young Portuguese boy had been hired to ensure no champagne glass ever got below halfway full—he crept around handsomely, insistent with his bottle. Soon couples were dancing on the furniture, the Pembroke girls laughing in that silly way and loosening the tuxedo ties of my Jabberwock brothers. Randall poured half a glass into my hair and messed it around with his hand. His own hair, I remember, was copper and curled from the heat of dancing, smoothed back with sweat, as if he were from the thirties. He laughed and looked around for someone else to torment. It pained me that even at my party I couldn't simply reach over to this man I loved so achingly and brush an eyelash stuck to his cheek. Too intimate, too kind. He faded off into a crowd.

"I saw a ghost in our apartment," said my wife, who was standing beside me.

I looked at her, and sadness must have been on my face, because Britta's smile fell for a moment and she lowered her shining glass. She wore blue-black velvet and luminous false pearl earrings in gold.

"You what?" I asked, breathless.

"Are you all right, Paul?"

"You saw a ghost? Tonight?"

"No," she said, then took a sip of champagne as a 45 of the Kingston Trio came on to boos and hisses. "In our house. It was a man."

"Were you scared?"

"Would you ask that if it were a woman? No. It was a very old man, very tired, I think."

"Did he say anything? Where was this?"

"In the kitchen. Just before we came. He didn't say anything," Britta said, putting her hand to her chest. "He stood there confused, as if it were an accident, the wrong house, maybe the wrong life to interrupt, and he stared at me, not knowing what he was supposed to be doing."

"What did you do?"

"I stared at him the same way . . . I think . . . and then he was gone."

Britta looked at me, thinking to herself. One of the baritones asked her to dance and she smiled back at me regretfully, flashing her marriage band, then giving a vampire face, meant, I suppose, to scare me back into the party. I was thinking about other things, too drunk to separate the petty from the profound.

Randall was caught up in this graduation. I think he was obsessively worried about his life after this, giving up all this to work for his father, or, perhaps worse, to go to law school. And maybe he was afraid I'd move away—I still don't know. But something made him shake me away when I grabbed his arm and whispered for him to be quiet—he was saying uncharacteristic things to young men. His glare wasn't just anger—he was sad, maybe disappointed in something, maybe me.

The party went on all night in that old merchant house. I remember that the walls were striped with gold paper and that iron sconces lit up faces with flattering candlelight and shadow. Otherwise the evening passed as many other evenings had in Providence, and even graduation did not frighten those of us secure in futures there and in wives. I passed out in a dining room chair, and awoke to someone telling me the baritone had kindly driven my wife home to bed. Britta was famous for never saying good-bye. I fell back to sleep with those walls of gold stripes papering my dreams.

In the morning I was on the Oriental rug. I got up to go to the bathroom, and felt the left side of my face was ragged and burned from the carpet I'd slept on. I saw others asleep and drugged on couches, their jackets or wraps thrown over them by someone kind and sober, the sun reaching over them, lighting the paintings framed on the walls, all of willow trees. Outside, a radio was playing "Aura Lee." I climbed up the spiral stairs to the bathroom, but there was someone inside coughing. I thought maybe I'd try one in the master suite— the professor had already left and the door was half-open. So I crept inside.

There on the green silk covers lay my lover, Randall, and the Portuguese boy, drunk and dead asleep, shirtless and embracing with a harem of embroidered pillows fallen around them. I remember them well. I remember most of all how sweet they looked, how honest really. Though he was a liar to me, my lover seemed so poignant with that dark boy clutched to him, as if they comforted each other the way young boys do when they have lost a thing together. I leaned heavily against the door and watched the room for a while. The light came in through sheer white curtains, slow as a tide. All around the ceiling, urns with wreaths were stenciled, and above the bed a blue cherub holding a bird. A common bird: a sparrow.

I remember the only thought that went through my head as I walked home in my rumpled evening clothes: I have no claim on him. No one knew I loved him. I assumed no one ever would, not even Randall now.

When I came back to our house that morning, I called out Britta's name and no one answered. The wooden floors glowed yellow with the May sun and all the glass door handles sparked with light, as if electric or releasing secrets. Perfume from some early-morning bath still hung in the air—eucalyptus, I remember—and it scented the cold white walls, the framed maps of Maine and Rhode Island, made them intriguing, as if they trapped inside their surfaces unimaginable gardens. I remember it, of course, as beautiful and strange, and yet I am sure it is only memory, because I know I slumped into an armchair and began to cry.

I don't know when I had ever cried before that, not since grade school certainly, rarely in front of anyone and never in front of my father, but all alone in that warm wooden room I wept, and because I was so out of practice, I wept loudly and badly. I panted and held my face to stop the pain there, speaking half words to convince myself of a grief that needed no convincing, spitting long jeweled strands of saliva onto my lap as I bent over. My jaw shook, humiliated. The sounds I made were ghastly, but this was too much pain. I could not bear it. So I sat there childishly blubbering into the fabric, lost and generous at last with my pain, shipwrecking myself over and over against my old memory of love.

I felt my wife's hand against my shoulder. I was not alone at all. I could not look up, so ashamed with this fit, coughing up the tears. I was so ashamed Britta should see me prone over a red-haired dilettante. I leaned more into the nubbed pink fabric. I turned away. She should never see me like this, never, not this friend. But I felt her other hand against my arm, and then her cold face beside mine. She did not hold me, but floated next to me, silent. We said nothing, and never spoke of it again, but with her gold hair stuck to my wet face and that smell of eucalyptus strong again, I knew there was a part of me, the greater part, that would endure.

༄

We lived on Meeting Street long after graduation. In 1972, I was still working at the Brown Alumni Center. It was good enough, and Britta went back to school so she could open up a psychology practice. I heard Randall went to Boston to work for his father for a while, but after a year he came back to Providence, bought a house near ours. A pink house—it showed how much he needed to be near, that he would buy a pink house. I know now he planned his day to run into me, just catch my eye outside the Alumni Center, and after a while I spoke cordially to him. In those conversations, he was confident, talking about law school at what we considered a lesser college in the area, applying to a better school, by which he meant a better name. And one day I took him back, and it was because the sky was bright around his face. I remember it made Randall the focus of the air, with sky bent to his eyes like that eerie crème de menthe the night I kissed him.

And Britta had taken a more steady lover, a French woman named Nathalie, who worked as a designer. I will admit I never liked her much. She was very quiet. She had a habit of sitting and listening to Britta and me jabber away, just sitting there with the pink tip of her tongue sticking out between her lips, the way you see older cats do. But Britta loved something about her. I heard my wife laughing in her bedroom when Nathalie came over, but I never saw this part of her lover myself. When Nathalie cooked her sacred cassoulets, Britta watched her from the kitchen doorway with a rapt, patient gaze, as if her lover were a book she read for pleasure. We never know what friends see in their lovers. We always expect they will see what they see in us, but it isn't true. What we hate in friends' lovers is a hoard of private moments we thought we would inherit.

She left Britta after some years. I forgot to say she was a married woman, and she decided it was her husband she really loved. Britta and I never spoke of it, but about a week afterward, I took her to Boston to see her favorite place: the Isabella Stewart Gardner Museum. The idea of visiting an old dead woman's house just to see her paintings and her giant pink courtyard made me queasy, but I went for Britta. Randall, visiting Harvard Law, joined us at the blunt medieval entrance. Britta said she wanted to see one particular painting, *The Birth of Athena*, and we toured the balconied, decorated corridors until we came into a red silk room, silver chalices against the window catching sun, paintings all around us in leafy gilt frames, hung with wires from the molding, every one on them entitled *The Birth of Athena*. Britta let out one throaty laugh, bending over with her hands clasped. Then she pinched her lips together and looked at me and Randall wideeyed. I think her loudness made me furious. That must have amused her even more, because she walked up to one of the paintings, dark foliage, with a gleaming white god clutching his head.

"Now here," she said seriously, "here we have a Grecian forest, and what's happening is there's this crack in Zeus's skull, and who pops out of it is Athena." Britta walked to a painting next to it, bright green.

"This one's a little different," she said, considering it. "This one's about Athena popping out of Zeus's skull."

Then Randall burst out in high laughter. I turned, surprised. Randall was not one to laugh in public places, and I saw for really the first time that Britta and Randall knew something I didn't. My lover pointed to a drawing below the painting. "You should look at this," he said, "because it's very unique. It's about this skull, you see. . . ."

"Is it Zeus's?" she asked.

"And Athena pops out."

They snickered together and a gold-buttoned guard came over. I turned away, delighted but ashamed to cause a scene in such a sacred place: a home, and a museum. The guard made us move along into the courtyard, my wife and lover arm in arm, unable to stop laughing at a joke I didn't quite understand. Britta wore a black jumpsuit and a wide black straw hat, which she held to her head as they strode past the yellow roses. There was a blueberry bush, and Randall stood still as Britta moved slowly toward it. I don't know why he stopped—maybe he knew to let her walk on.

He did not look back at me. It was not our moment together watching her. It was his moment, seeing in her some loss he recognized. Something I'd never noticed, never thought of after years seeing her with her occult necklaces, batting at the mosquito netting of her bed and giggling as if love could not be squandered.

So we watched her walk into the blueberries. A tulip tree shaded her there and she stood inside that shadow, turning slowly and taking in the peeling pink on the museum's walls. I admired her, absorbed in the circle she was creating as slowly as a black-eyed Susan might spread its petals. The crowd around us was giddy with noise, but the main sound I remember was the clicking of her shoes and the buzzing of the heat that day.

I walked over to her. Randall finally looked at me. I caught his eye and he seemed to be examining me, the red-haired man, and not critically. As if I'd shown him some new talent in marrying such a woman.

"You all right?" I asked my wife when I reached her.

She stopped at once and looked at me. She smiled—her wide smile with teeth, which I knew was her fake one, though it was beautiful.

"Why? Yes."

"You want to leave?"

She sounded oddly relieved. She took off her hat and looked up into that one tulip tree in this city museum. "No, this is nice. I was just thinking." Britta picked a berry off the bush and put it in her mouth. She quickly removed it and made a face. "These blueberries are terrible!"

"They're still green, darling."

She glared at the tiny fruit in her hand, then threw it away and blinked at me. "So they are, darling."

Randall came up behind me. He put his hand in my coat pocket. It was one of our secret signs of intimacy, as if he were searching my coat, when really it meant, Here I am.

"She loved you, Britta" was what he said, and I still am surprised he said it. I didn't know he saw those things in people.

"No," she said. "You can only love one at a time. Apparently, it's a rule. Like in chess."

"Britta," I tried, "Nathalie wasn't really right, and you know—"

She put her hat back on and interrupted: "No, it's fine. It's not a big deal, really. Let's go back and see the dungeon." She flicked a smile and walked past me and my lover into the sunlight.

"Britta . . ."

She turned around and faced us, faced me, both hands holding her hat against the wind. Her mouth broke down right then, just snapped in two like a twig. We all simply stood there and she shuddered. I watched her pain pooling out into her face, her shaking hand moving to wipe her cheek, and she stared at me with the fear we had never spoken of except in that one silent moment when she held me, smelling of eucalyptus, on another bright, sad day.

"Here's something I want," she said, moving her head from Randall to me. "If we never see one another again, we should still all meet every year right here," she said, tapping the table, "in the courtyard."

"No," Randall said, glancing at me, "in the *Birth of Athena* room."

Britta laughed and said, "Oh, yes yes. But they only hang the paintings on off years, so every other year, then."

"When?" I asked at last.

"Today," Britta said, raising her eyebrows, "on your birthday, darling."

"But we're not going anywhere, Britta. We see one another every day."

She put her hands out in honesty and the hat got away from her. I ran out after it as it rolled around the hot air and into the yellow roses. I pulled it from the thorns and Britta was laughing to Randall again, arms tight around herself, eyes closed, face sideways to the light, which made her golden, valuable, alone.

⟡

Every two years we still met at the Isabella Stewart Gardner Museum. We did not go all together, of course. We pretended for that day (my birthday) we had lost one another in the span of years, the three of us who knew one another so well that we could imitate any of our laughs, and each loitered in the *Birth of Athena* room, staring benignly at a painting until someone finally recognized another and screamed that person's name aloud in delight (Britta recognizing Randall the first time, Randall seeing me the next). Then there would be more screams as I joined in the reunion, and for all the guards knew, it was really the most astounding coincidence.

And so it went for years. Those ridiculous meetings in the museum marked the time for me, much more so than the Alumni Center, which brought more and more of the same well-bred men and, in 1975, women through my doors. I barely noticed the changes at Brown, either, except the one time a rally walked by my window. In that old brownstone building, the windows were drooping glass, so at first I couldn't make out the words on their signs. Then I saw one in pink: GAY IS GOOD. I sat immediately back at my desk, looking to make sure my door was closed. I felt I had witnessed an obscene act, a prurient display shown to me without my wish or consent. I felt breathless and ill, and I put my head on the desk. They were chanting something, too, which, luckily, the paneled walls muffled into a harmless rhythm. I concentrated then on that rhythm and tried to breathe along with it, get myself back to the man I had been five minutes before, and not until the sounds passed down the street could I bear to look up again. And I regained myself.

That was 1977. It was the year Randall moved to Boston. He was finishing Harvard now, and he had no time for Providence commutes. Instead, he or I drove to the other city on weekends, or met together on Cape Cod or in Mystic. These visits also meant my time with Britta was separate from my time with Randall. My lover and I took more cold, stony walks on beaches. He was growing more serious as years went on. His father was already dead, and I saw something tempting him. It was not another man—that was past—but the temptation to tell his mother about me, his male lover, and let all this fall to rest. We never spoke of it, but I tried with every clench of his hand not to change things. I liked things as they were. I still like most things as they are—my father taught me this immutability, this cowardice.

A hurricane came that year to the East Coast. They named storms after women then, so a female hurricane. Britta and I were bored with it at first. It distressed the routines we had developed, and I see we were turning slowly into those practical adults who hated the snow because of driving, hated staying out at night because it was hard to see in the dim light, hated most disturbances that were no longer new. So we hated taping up all the windows and pulling the shutters. She was particularly grouchy in the matronly quilted robe my mother had bought her. But then, when Britta found a hurricane lamp and lit it and the soot blew out and blackened her face, we laughed as we had as college kids.

I asked, "What is this, minstrel hour suddenly?"

"You are a racist, darling."

The lights flickered. "Clean yourself up. We have to get a fire going, or do you just want to go to sleep?"

Her eyes widened in shock. "Oh no! Are you crazy? It's a hurricane night! We're going to stay up all night tonight, on a hurricane night."

I said we should read to each other. Usually she liked that. She shook her head.

"No. We're going to do what I want to do. This isn't Randall you're with tonight. We don't have to arm wrestle to have a good time. You're a gay man, after all, no matter what you think."

She took me upstairs to her room and gave me her peacock kimono. She told me to strip down and put it on while she washed off the soot. She walked out of the room with the lantern, and I was left with just my dim candle there, in her room with Chinese coins strung along the mirror, striped masks on the walls. I stripped naked and put on her girlish robe. Randall hated robes and girlish things on me. Shame, again, always that.

Britta came back wearing a white nightgown. It was small and thin on her, and then I realized it wasn't a nightgown. It was her wedding dress. She put her hand to her mouth, then held it out as if to stop me. "Perfect," she said. "You look perfect. Now, just follow me." She grabbed a bag and a book from her dresser and blinked her glassy eyes for me to come.

Down at the fire, she made me rub sage oil in my hair and tie it up with a towel—I must have looked like a faggot then, but I was letting her control me that night. I made her wear her blue clay mask, and so we were both ridiculous. She was letting me see at last the kind of life we would have led if our hearts had been otherwise.

We read messages from a plastic Ouija board she had, and she swore she wasn't cheating when it spelled out names of men I'd had crushes on long, long before. Men who now were long married and buried in their children. These messages professed undying passion. They told of my innocence. Britta, or I could believe some ghost she found, told me stories I needed about myself.

She threw my I Ching. She told me a narrow river opened onto a lake, that I would cross the dam onto an open space. Her own fortune involved a girl with a package, and she read its meaning secretly to herself. She sat cross-legged before the fire. I could see more of her body than I ever had. She was gaining weight. But there was something newly compassionate in her larger body, the way her breasts now rested on her skin—I could see them beneath the thin fabric, and when she threw the fiery copper coins. I wonder what my older body looked like to her. Sometimes I wonder if she was in love with me.

She slept in my bed that night. It was in the corner of the house, safe from the hurricane. The lamp was on all night, but the glass blackened from the soot and it might as well have been off for all the darkness in the room. Once I woke up and the kimono had come undone—I lay naked on my half of the bed, and she was turned toward the wall, so I let the green night glow over me and imagined this was marriage, this was love, and the person asleep, smelling of sage oil, was a lipsticked man in silk. A man who knew me naked, green in the night, listening. And that all this was perfect.

In 1981, a friend got me a job offer in the Alumni Center at Harvard. I hadn't even told Britta that I was looking around, and at the time I told myself I wasn't serious anyway, so I needn't get her involved. But I told Randall. Randall knew about every step, every college I talked to in Boston. I think he knew what would happen, even then. Living in a larger city, a liberal one, he saw the changes going on in the world, changes that freed him after his mother died and he could live without pretense. And he changed. People at his law firm knew about our relationship, relatives, old friends. It was the eighties, a unique time in America. During those years in the late seventies when I was searching, he must have smiled to himself, thinking of my old-fashioned, ridiculous situation.

I finally talked to Britta in the fall, a rainy late afternoon. She was home from her practice and lay on the white divan, reading *Harper's* and eating potato chips from a garish bag. A white candle lay flickering next to her. Her hair was still feathered blond, but lighter at the temples, as if faded from so many years in sun. We were thirty-six.

"Honey," I said, sitting down in the armchair, "I have a great job offer."

She looked up, her face wide open. "Really? Oh, that's fantastic! Oh, Paul, that's great!" She threw a chip in her mouth and it crackled.

"It's in Boston."

Her face considered this. She ate more chips. "That's fine. I'm bored of this place, really. We should have packed our bags years ago, and . . ." she said, pointing her finger, "you'll be closer to Randall. This is perfect."

"Randall wants me to live with him."

She closed her eyes and rubbed a finger over the lids, perhaps to be more awake. "Oh," she said as she did this. "So that's what this is about."

"I was shocked," I said. "I didn't want to, I don't want to, but there's this part of me—"

"That really does. I know, Paul."

"And it's bigger than I thought." I leaned over and held my hands loosely together. "And maybe . . ." I said, wanting to skip past the next impossible sentence: "Maybe it's time."

She put her hand to her mouth, which was a movement I could not read. She wiped the crumbs from her navy skirt.

"It is time," she said.

I waited, saying nothing.

"We both knew this was to make life easier. And now it's silly, isn't it?" She nodded, agreeing with herself. "Being married? Isn't it?"

I couldn't nod, but I did smile.

She kept talking. These were not the exact words we said to each other that afternoon—my memory is never perfect. I don't usually remember her in quotations, anyway. What I remember is how we talked in this way, all that afternoon, as if it were a cocktail party we were canceling and not a life.

So she said, "Now I have to come up with something else to want. But that's okay; that's a good thing. We've been stuck."

"We have been," I said.

"Being stuck is comforting, isn't it?"

And I know I didn't feel that way at all. I was forcing myself to be sad and serious, but inside me I was thrilled to live with Randall and change my life. I am ashamed to say I wanted Britta to smile and pack her things, to come up with something that would make this dull conversation end, so I said a common thing: "It's been wonderful."

She sat with her hand on her chin, looking up at the ceiling. She had long ago grown her real eyebrows in, and they were dark and thin. Her neck was half-shadowed, just like Randall's on that night on Beacon Hill when none of us knew what our playful facades would make of our lives.

"It is time," she repeated, as if trying it on. "It's time I did something, too."

"What are you going to do?"

"Well," she said quietly. "I think once I wanted to live on an island. Didn't I? Wasn't there an island? What was that?"

Now she did make me laugh—it could have been relief. "You said you wanted to be a gilded white scorpion."

"Really?" she asked, grinning at me. "A scorpion? Right, be a wicked woman on a Caribbean island. Wouldn't that be something?" My wife looked at me and I could almost imagine it.

Later she told me firmly, "But this is lucky. This is very lucky."

These were the kinds of things we said. But I can't picture us saying them. All I see is my wife talking in that dim, streaked light, leaning into the cushions, and—I'm sure she didn't know she did this—drawing on her forehead with her thumb. Telling me stories of how she always knew this wasn't what I wanted, but sketching those invisible pictures on her skin. What I remember best is that. Not much, just that.

✐

It took Britta only a month to pack what she wanted, which wasn't much. She quickly closed her practice and sent her clients to a friend, wrapped up the paintings she loved, only three, her clothes, some jewelry. I walked behind her, begging her to take things, but she told me, "Anyone who can't fit their life into two suitcases is stuck forever."

The day she left, I remember she took a long shower and I tried to shove things into the crevices of her bags: my grandfather's pocket watch, my mother's diamond ring, a first edition of a Dorothy Parker book. I wanted to give it all to her because I felt she was hiding behind this adventure, escaping the grief at my selfish act. I was so guilty at the thought of being happy up in Boston, living with my handsome lawyer, arguing playfully over whose china got put in the cabinet. But she must have known—there isn't much to do with friends who leave. Just these rituals of packing, but you can't say anything to keep him there. You can only repeat that once you drugged his tea.

My wife Britta came out of her room in her traveling clothes: black dress, red jacket, and, over her arm, the trench coat she claimed had always saved her. The hollow Celtic necklace lay around her throat, jingling hope, and she walked to me as she pulled on a silver bracelet.

"I'll send you a card from the island when I get there," she said confidently. "I think the phone's too expensive. Then you'll write to me."

"Of course I will," I said. "Are you crazy? Of course."

"And," she said, then let out a sharp laugh, "will you and Randall still be in the museum two years from now?"

"You still want to do that?"

She pouted and shook her wrist to let the bracelet settle. "Anyway, I'll be there."

"Then I'll be there."

Britta started to put the trench coat on. Frost was on the windows that morning, and the last leaves on the maple tree looked frozen, thick as wax.

"I saw a ghost last night," she told me, one arm in the coat. "I think it must have been the maid or the governess. She was in the attic—what was I doing in the attic at that hour, even I don't know—and all green. A green ghost, can you imagine? I watched her for a little while, picking up invisible things and putting them back down, things that must have been here a long time ago. It was fun figuring out what they were—like I think one was a humidor." She looked down to pull her jacket sleeves through, and there they came, red and alive. "She was afraid she'd forgotten something. Afraid she'd left something important behind." I caught her calm look in the mirror.

I heard a horn outside and the cab was there.

"Oh!" she said, frantically picking up leather bags with too many straps. "Case in point! I left my lipstick in the upstairs bathroom! I need it; I can't live without it. Put me on a desert island and I'd trade the two books I brought for lipstick."

I put up one finger, then ran out and up the staircase, which creaked at each pounding step. On the sink was a gold tube of that garish red that had embarrassed me for years, the red of dirty stories and her Dutch island and of the silk-lined museum room. I ran downstairs with it and saw the bags were gone.

I glimpsed out the window just a tumble of trench coat into the cab, and then it sped off up the hill and over. With Britta, once again, no good-bye.

∽

Today in the courtyard, as I wish myself a happy fortieth birthday, as I stare at the green blueberries, I know Britta might not be coming. It's been hard to contact her for two years now. She did go to Saint Eustatius, and she bought land there from an old dying man. She wrote lots of letters then, all about the insane things she saw there, the governor who was a tyrant, the rich white people on the hill hoarding a pile of wood, which on the island was like gold, her travails building a house of gingerbread and jalousies.

Randall and I didn't show up here in 1983. There was so much going on at the time: living together became sometimes more unspoken hostility than love, and I changed jobs to MIT and had to go home to my father's funeral. That birthday passed unnoticed. Randall still lives on Beacon Hill, and I now live south of there. Sometimes we meet and hold hands—you can do that now on the street—but I know his fright at middle age has brought other men into our old apartment. And the notes from Britta have been brief, businesslike.

That morning when she left our yellow house on Meeting Street, I walked outside in the October cold and saw the cab drive off, watched long after as the sun began to rise and make the brittle ice on the lilac bush glitter and break off. I sat down on that square wood porch, beneath the peeling columns, and could not think of anything to think. I'd given everything away and not even seen it. All the week before, I had been eager as a boy, excited to move up to Boston, experience the warm change my life would make, and never realized what I thought had weighed me down was simply love. I had sent away the one person I really loved, and made myself think it was a kind of freedom, and now I saw the empty space this freedom revealed.

I leaned against our house and cried, ugly as before, and there was no excuse this time for ugliness. I didn't coax the tears with self-pity or remembrance; they just filled me. A little boy wearing a birthday hat walked by, and he stared at me weeping with no consolation now. I thought he might give me the shining present he held, but he gripped it tighter and moved on. All my muscles gnawed at me and shook. I became angry with my body for betraying me, and I gritted my teeth as I trembled with more tears.

It did no good. So I let go. My hands fell to the cold white wood and I let go, and the pain of losing all those years moved over me like a warm sun.

The courtyard here is sky-lit and warm, because it is spring, and damask roses, century plants, and palm trees grow here in their careful rows. All the rooms look onto this courtyard, and I'm searching one Moroccan window for a woman, middle-aged by now, pounding rudely past the guards in perhaps white island-cotton robes, or a gold-threaded turban. She wears a hollow silver necklace and a kind of brave compassion. You'll recognize her laugh.

There's a red jacket leaning to the window. It begins a loud, annoying tapping noise against the ancient glass, until a gold-buttoned man takes her arm and mouths irritation. A flash goes off nearby—someone taking a picture—and the guard leaves her again. The red jacket returns, slides open the lock, and swings out the window with a snow of black paint. I jump up at my wife's laughing face and thank God, thank God.